The Detective Wins The Witch
Nocturne Falls, Book Ten

Kristen Painter

THE DETECTIVE WINS THE WITCH:
Nocturne Falls, Book Ten

Copyright © 2018 Kristen Painter

All rights reserved. No part of this book may be reproduced in any form or by any electronic or mechanical means, including information storage and retrieval systems—except in the case of brief quotations embodied in critical articles or reviews—without permission in writing from the author.

This book is a work of fiction. The characters, events, and places portrayed in this book are products of the author's imagination and are either fictitious or are used fictitiously. Any similarity to real person, living or dead, is purely coincidental and not intended by the author.

ISBN: 978-1-941695-39-5
Published in the United States of America.

Welcome to Nocturne Falls, the town that celebrates Halloween 365 days a year. The tourists think it's all a show: the vampires, the werewolves, the witches, the occasional gargoyle flying through the sky. But the supernaturals populating the town know better.

Living in Nocturne Falls means being yourself. Fangs, fur, and all.

Private investigator Wyatt West finds his job a little tedious most days, but that changes when he meets a bewitching blonde florist who needs a favor in the way of a wedding date. There's definitely something magical about her, but little does he know just how correct that first impression is.

Single mom Marigold Williams finds herself instantly attracted to Wyatt, but doesn't dare tell this handsome human that she's a witch and things in Nocturne Falls are a little spookier than he suspects. He's just a nice guy who's offered to be her plus one. She doesn't need to turn his world upside down with the truth over one date.

Despite that agreement, their feelings deepen and both agree to try a relationship beyond their current temporary arrangement. Now Marigold *must* tell him about her witchy side. After all, he has a right to know who he's dating.

But when Wyatt unwittingly frees some dangerous magic, Marigold knows a life changing sacrifice is the only way to set things right. Will her magic save him? And will he be able to handle the truth that comes with it?

*In loving memory of Scooter,
our real life Frank the Tank*

One more sunflower.

Marigold Williams finished the arrangement she was creating by adding the last bloom, then stood back to admire her work. The happy bouquet sported a mix of hot pinks, bright yellows, and vivid oranges.

Hmm. One of the roses wasn't quite as open as the others.

She cupped the flower in her hand and pushed a little magic into it. The petals opened wider, matching the rest in the bouquet. "Better."

She twisted the vase the arrangement was in to see all sides of it. "What do you think, Frank the Tank?"

Frank, Marigold's newly adopted shop cat, didn't react from his perch on the counter. He just sat there, sleepily blinking his wise, gold eyes.

Marigold didn't take the lack of comment personally. Frank's job had more to do with keeping the shop rodent-free than it did critiquing her arrangements. So far, the burly black feline was doing a good job of it, too.

Also, Marigold already knew that Birdie Caruthers, the recipient, was going to love the bouquet.

The man paying for the flowers, Jack Van Zant, was sure to enjoy Birdie's appreciation, as well. He'd been sending her flowers once or twice a month now. Mostly with little notes on the cards that said things like, "No reason is reason enough" and "Thought of you, hope these make you smile."

Theirs was an adorable courtship that had the whole town of Nocturne Falls smiling.

Marigold sighed and scratched Frank's head. "Maybe not the whole town, huh, Frank?" Because while she was truly happy for Birdie, she was also, down deep in her heart of hearts, a little sad that Birdie had found happiness while she had not. Marigold felt utterly ridiculous about it, and a little embarrassed, but the truth was what it was.

She rolled her eyes at herself. "I'm clearly a horrible person. I love Birdie. It's not her fault I'm single. Right?"

Frank lay down on the counter, curled himself into a loaf, and drifted off.

"Thanks for your input." She frowned at him. "Also, I'm not sure sleeping is much of a mouse-deterrent there, buddy."

He answered with a sound that was half grunt, half snore.

With a little laugh, she added the card to the clear plastic pick and fixed it in the middle of the flowers. But her mind returned to matters of the heart. Hers, and everyone else's.

Nocturne Falls was chock full of people in love or falling in love. And people getting married. She knew that part *very* well, because she was usually the florist who provided the flowers. Which was great. She loved the business, loved the enthusiasm of the brides, and really enjoyed helping turn their dreams into reality.

But it was hard to do sometimes, because it made her that much more aware of how stuck she was in Singletown.

Being single kind of sucked. But being a single mom wasn't anything Marigold would change for the world—she loved her daughter, Saffron, with the ferocity of a thousand shining suns. And the fact that her ex had walked away from Marigold when she'd told him she was pregnant only meant he was never the right man for Saffie to call Father.

But would a date now and then—especially one for Pandora's wedding—be so much to ask?

Apparently.

She put Birdie's bouquet in the fridge. She'd probably have Leah, her one employee besides Joe, her delivery guy, take it down to the station when

Leah came in at ten. It was a quick trip, and Leah liked doing the occasional small delivery.

Marigold checked her to-do list. She had her sister Pandora Williams and their mutual good friend Willa Iscove both coming in today to finalize their wedding flowers.

Marigold smiled, although she didn't feel it as much as she wanted to. She really loved doing weddings and loved the business they generated, not to mention these ladies were both very important to her, but at the moment it just seemed to underline the melancholy she was feeling.

Or were their impending weddings why she was feeling this way?

Or maybe her melancholy was because she'd had a look at her bank account this morning. Had anyone ever gotten rich being a florist? She doubted it.

Of course, she wasn't in this for the money. She loved flowers and plants, and loved being able to bring happiness into other people's lives with her creations. And this really was the best job for her. One where she could use her magic to make her work stand out.

Still, it was a good thing the orthodontist took payments. Saffie's braces were not going to be cheap. Then there were her soccer fees (and the upcoming soccer camp) and the cost of her school uniforms, plus the screen porch really needed rescreening, and Marigold's car was making a funny sound.

She could probably get Cole, Pandora's very handy fiancé and Marigold's soon-to-be brother-in-law, to handle the porch, but she didn't know any mechanics.

She paused and inhaled all the green life around her, finding her center. Then she reminded herself that being around all the flowers and plants wasn't just the perfect job for a green witch like herself, it was the only job. At least, the only one she'd ever wanted.

"I've got to snap out of this, Frank." Maybe she needed a little more of the ginger-carrot-kale juice she'd whipped up for breakfast to really shake this funk and focus on the work at hand. She had some left in the fridge in her office, which wasn't an office so much as it was the back half of the store. It served as their work space, flower storage area, and Frank's multipurpose room.

His litter box was tucked in the corner on the wall where the big coolers were, but his food and water bowls were beside one of the workbenches on the opposite wall.

The center of the room held two large workbenches where the general construction of arrangements was done, then there was a small desk on the wall opposite the coolers that usually had her laptop on it. The workbenches were usually where she and Leah ate their lunch. Joe joined them sometimes, if he was in between deliveries.

When she was alone in the shop, however, she usually did her arranging on the front counter, where she could keep an eye on the store until Leah came in. The wall behind the counter held a smaller, glass-front cooler with ready-made arrangements and a few buckets of the cheap and cheerful stuff people expected to see when they came into a flower shop.

The bell over the front door jangled, so she turned her head to greet the customer. Her mouth bent in an easy smile when she saw who it was. "Good morning, Mr. Mathers."

The old man shuffled in. "Now, Marigold, I told you to call me Newt. All my friends do, and I'd like to think at my age I could consider a pretty young girl like you a friend."

She laughed. "I'm not that young or pretty, but I'll take the compliment. *Newt.*"

Newton Mathers was a frequent visitor to Nocturne Falls, and a minor wizard, which meant he wasn't all that naturally gifted but more a student of the arts. He had some inborn talent, but much of it was learned. No harm in that. Some witches were the same way.

"You are both, my dear." He shook a gnarled finger at her. "Never argue with your elders."

When Newt was in town, he stopped by every morning to buy a flower for his lapel. It was such an old-fashioned but charming thing to do. But then, he was a rather charming gentleman.

"Well, thank you very much." She wasn't a complete hosebeast in the looks department, but Pandora and their other sister, Charisma, had gotten the lion's share of beauty. Pandora had gotten the extrovert vibe, too, while Charisma was loaded with ambition.

Marigold had gotten the...okay, she wasn't entirely sure what she'd gotten. She was a single mother, for crying out loud. Who could think about their best qualities when they were trying to raise a child who was only two years away from coming into her witchy powers, run a business, and keep their house from looking like they'd been fighting off poltergeists?

Motherhood was not for the fainthearted.

"You're very welcome." He peered at the cold case behind her. "I believe I'll have a carnation today. A red one."

"How very jaunty. I'll get that made right up for you." She selected the prettiest red carnation, trimmed it, and handed it over. "There you go."

He admired the flower, then tucked it into the button hole on his lapel. "Just lovely. How much do I owe you?"

"Two dollars."

He shook his head. "My dear, you are never going to make a living selling things so inexpensively."

"It's not like I had to do anything to it but cut it down to size." She grinned. He always complained her prices were too low. But today she could kind of see his point. "Would you like a Casablanca lily for eight bucks instead?"

"That might be rather ostentatious with my linen suit, don't you think? It's not as though I'm summering in Singapore."

He sometimes said things she didn't always get, but she nodded anyway. "I agree. Best stick with the carnation for today."

He handed her two crisp one-dollar bills. "Thank you very much. I shall see you tomorrow. Have a lovely day, Marigold."

"You too, Newt."

As he left, she went back to work organizing the wedding look books she'd put together for Pandora and Willa. The books started out as mostly pictures of flowers, ideas for how those flowers could be displayed, some color swatches, and rough estimates based on certain flower types.

At this stage, with both weddings only weeks away, the books were blueprints for the floral builds. Inventory sheets, sketches, numbers of bridesmaid bouquets, boutonnieres, centerpieces, estimated times, placement of swags, any large builds that needed to be done...the books had it all. She lived and died by the books when it came to wedding prep.

Which was why she did them for every bride, but with Pandora's and Willa's books, she definitely put in some extra time and effort.

And why wouldn't she? Willa was a good friend and basically fae royalty, even if she had abdicated the throne. And beloved Pandora was Marigold's sister. She wasn't about to scrimp on either one.

Right now, she was glad she'd made the books so detailed. That meant nothing would be missed. Everything would be perfect for these two very special women.

Just like it would be for Marigold's own wedding. Someday.

Maybe.

Wyatt West slumped down in the seat of his rented SUV and held his phone in front of his face like he was engaged in something very important. Which he was. Surveillance on the auction house across the street. He just hadn't seen anything worthwhile, yet.

Suzanne Anderson, his client, had hired him to track down and recover a very valuable pair of candlesticks. She'd said they'd been in her family for nearly a century until they'd been accidentally sold in her late aunt's estate sale.

Now it was his job to get them back before another family member did, something Suzanne had warned him was a very real possibility.

Granted, hunting down family heirlooms wasn't the most exciting work he'd done since becoming a private detective, but it paid the bills. And it wasn't another cheating-spouse case that had him peeping through the windows of some No Tell Motel at all hours of the night.

He sighed. He'd done enough cheating spouses and divorce cases to turn him off marriage for good. Not that he didn't love women. He did. Women were fantastic.

Marriage, on the other hand, seemed to be a losing proposition. Not just because of what he'd seen from this job, but his history as a foster kid had shown him a lot of fighting couples too.

A car pulled into the auction house parking lot. He scrunched down a little farther in the seat. Not that anyone was going to pay attention to a person in a car parked across the street in the chiropractor's lot in little old Millersville, Georgia. The town defined *sleepy*.

But old instincts, the kind he'd picked up on the police force, died hard.

Another car pulled in, then another. The auction house would open in ten minutes for the preview of that evening's items.

He let a few more minutes go by, let the place get open and the first onslaught of lookers go in, then he started up the SUV and drove across the street to join them.

There was a good handful of people in the business now, but he still kept his hat on and changed out his sunglasses for a pair of clear, non-prescription lenses to give himself a little bit of a disguise. It wasn't much, but no one was there to see him.

They were there to peruse the goods that would soon be up for bid. Including Mrs. Anderson's candlesticks, which were, frankly, some of the ugliest, clunkiest candlesticks he'd ever laid eyes on. Maybe one of her ancestors had made them in third-grade pottery class and then become famous. She hadn't really mentioned the story behind them or why they were valuable, just that they were.

She was paying, and paying well, so he wasn't going to nitpick.

He pretended to inspect the merchandise like everyone else, all the while side-eyeing those around him to see who else was checking out the candlesticks.

No one, really. Most seemed to be focused on the paintings, some furniture, and a glass statue of a semi-naked fairy. He was a little bummed there were no dogs-playing-poker paintings. His place could use one of those.

With a little laugh at how bad his taste was, he made a slow loop through the goods, working his way back around toward the candlesticks.

Even if Mrs. Anderson could afford for him to bid as high as five grand on the pair, he was hoping to get them for a lot less. Because he was also hoping she might see fit to float him the leftover as a bonus.

He finished his loop at the table full of pottery where the candlesticks were, but no one was paying much attention to them except for an older man with a red carnation in his lapel. Who wore a flower like that? It seemed like such a funny thing to do. Unless you were going to prom or meeting a blind date, and neither event seemed next on the old guy's agenda.

The man lingered by the candlesticks, glancing once around the room to see who else might be looking at them.

Wyatt bent to intently examine a footstool.

Mr. Carnation started walking again.

Wyatt followed.

Mr. Carnation paused in front of a painting of a half-naked woman draped across a velvet couch eating an apple. The painting was yellowed with age and looked like something out of a museum.

Not at all Wyatt's taste, which probably meant it was expensive.

The auction house manager, a thin man with round glasses and a fiddly mustache, approached Mr. Carnation. "It's a lovely piece, isn't it? Seventeenth century. From the studio of Pierre Gobert."

Mr. Carnation nodded like he was giving the painting great consideration. "I thought it was Gobert. Is there a reserve on this piece?"

"Yes, but I don't think we'll have any trouble reaching it. Especially if someone of your stature is interested in it." The manager leaned in with a knowing smile and said something Wyatt couldn't hear.

He frowned and turned so his good ear was closer to the conversation. He wasn't sure what was worse: the accident that had caused the hearing loss in his left ear, being forced to take early retirement from the force because of the hearing loss, or the constant nuisance of missing a lot of what was said on his left side.

Mr. Carnation laughed awkwardly. "Yes, well, you've found me out. I was hoping I could attend anonymously, but I see that's not a possibility now."

The auction manager cleared his throat and leaned back with a sly smile. "I promise, I won't say a word."

So Mr. Carnation was somebody. Probably in the art world, guessing by what had just happened. If so, and he was interested in the candlesticks too, Wyatt could very well end up spending all of the money Mrs. Anderson had allotted for them.

In fact, he should probably call her and make sure that five grand was her cap. Before he did that, however, he was going to do one more thing.

Get a picture of Mr. Carnation.

He took his phone out and pretended to call someone. Instead, he pulled up his camera. Then he positioned his thumb over the button to capture images and put the phone to his deaf ear. He started snapping pics as soon as the angle felt right. "Hi, Mom. Just wanted to tell you they have some nice pieces."

The auction house manager gave him a stern look. Apparently, phone calls weren't cool inside the auction house.

Wyatt ignored him to take a few more pictures. "Sure, I'll see what I can do. Okay. Love you, too. Bye."

The manager was at Wyatt's side. "Sir, we ask that all calls be taken outside."

"Oh, right, sorry." Wyatt gave the man a big, innocent grin. "I was just leaving anyway."

Marigold hung up the phone and smiled. The flowers for Pandora's wedding were scheduled to arrive tomorrow, but the supplier had assured Marigold that the extra five dozen ivory roses wouldn't be a problem, although they probably would take an extra day.

That was fine, because those roses wouldn't be necessary until the day before the wedding.

The archway under which Pandora and Cole took their vows was going to be spectacular. Those ivory roses would look lovely mixed with the fairy lights woven throughout the swags on the arch and with the extra glow from the Edison bulbs that would be strung in the trees. The backyard of their home, a beautiful Victorian that they'd worked as a couple to fully restore, would hold the hundred or so guests with plenty of space.

The whole evening would be stunning. But not as stunning as Pandora.

Marigold brushed her hand over the photo of Pandora's wedding dress. The custom-made embroidered and beaded lace gown had elbow-length sleeves, a scoop neckline, and a simple pearl belt at the waist. A short, sweeping train added a little drama to the rear view. The whole thing was in ivory, just like the flowers (with accents of blush and peach and lilac), which perfectly complemented Pandora's red hair and fair, freckled skin.

Cole was wearing an ivory linen suit, just the thing for a backyard summer wedding. He'd look good, too, but not so good that he'd distract from his stunning bride and her gorgeous dress.

Of course, it was easy to have a beautiful dress when your mother owned the bridal boutique in town. Ever After was *the* place to get wedding attire and formal wear in Nocturne Falls.

Marigold glanced up at the photo that hung on the wall by the register. The picture had captured a moment with her mother, Corette, and her sisters at the Black and Orange Ball that happened every Halloween. The picture was nearly thirteen years old now, older than Saffron, but the sight of her family always brought Marigold happiness.

Funny that she'd been thinking this morning how hard it was being a single mother, and yet, her mother had raised three girls practically on her own after their father had left.

"Like mother like daughter, huh, Frank?" She gave the cat a scratch. "Maybe I'm not supposed to have a man in my life until later. Like my mom."

Frank stretched, offering his belly for more rubs.

"And you know what? I'm okay with that. Well, maybe not completely just yet. But I will be. She did a great job with us and now look at her, happily engaged to a great guy. So if my mom can do it, so can I."

She carried the wedding books back to her desk for safe keeping. Joe should be back any time for this afternoon's deliveries. Occasionally, she did a few herself, but with the weddings to prepare for, she couldn't spare the time unless it was something she could do on her way home.

And once the flowers for Pandora's wedding came in, Marigold would be in production mode. She'd have help from Leah, of course, but it was still a tremendous amount of work.

The bell over the door jangled.

"Joe?"

A wheezy laugh answered her. "No, not Joe."

Marigold tucked the wedding book away, then leaned to see through the workroom door. "Hi, Mr. Mathers. I mean, Newt. I didn't expect to see you again today. Everything all right with your carnation?" It still looked fresh, so if there was an issue, she couldn't imagine what it was.

He came up to the counter, smiling tentatively. "My carnation is still lovely and bright, thank you. I've come to see you about a more personal matter."

"Oh?" Now that was interesting. She met him on the other side of the counter. "What can I do for you?"

He sighed as though the world was crashing down around him. "I'm in a bind. There's an auction this evening at Oswald's Auction House, the one over in Millersville?"

"I know it." She'd been there once with her mother and her mother's fiancé, Stanhill. He'd been after an antique gold pocket watch. He'd won it too, but not without spending a considerable amount.

"Good. Very good. There's an item going up for auction tonight that I had dearly hoped to win. Unfortunately, Glen Oswald, the manager, recognized me when I went in to have a look at the items today."

"And that's not good?"

"No, it's not. You see, I'm rather well known in the antiques business and I'm afraid now that Glen knows I'm interested, he'll do everything in his power to drive up the bidding. Based on my interest, he'll assume this item is worth more. He'll push the crowd." Newt sighed. "I was hoping not to spend too extravagantly."

She nodded. "Sure, I understand. But how can I help you?"

His face brightened. "Go to the auction in my stead. Be my proxy. I'll pay you a hundred dollars for your time. Even if you don't win the item." He grinned. "But I think you will. And for a very good price."

"I..." A hundred bucks would help a lot with Saffron's soccer fees. But it meant giving up her evening. Or part of her evening. Time that she could be working on wedding stuff. She sighed and weighed the options. Wedding stuff? Or chipping away at some bills? "How long would I have to be there?"

"Just until the item is procured."

"How do you know I'll win it?"

"Because I'll be bankrolling you. Up to ten thousand dollars if need-be."

Her brows went up as her eyes widened. She had no idea Newt was so flush. And if he was willing to go that high, how much more would his presence raise the price? This was all so curious. "I don't know..." That was a lot of money to be responsible for. "What if something happens and I don't win it? I would hate to disappoint you."

Or lose him as a customer. Not that his two-dollar-a-day carnation habit was paying her light bill or anything. Still, he was such a nice old man.

He patted her hand. "You could never disappoint me. You're helping me out. Tell you what, I'll make it two hundred. And I will consider it a personal favor and be in your debt." He looked longingly at her.

Passing up that much money would be foolish. "Okay, I'll do it. What time do I need to be there, and what am I buying?"

He clapped his hands. "Brilliant, thank you. You need to be at the auction house by six thirty so you can register for a paddle and get a good seat. And I must ask that you tell no one you're there as my proxy. That would defeat the point of using a proxy, after all."

"Makes sense. I won't say a word."

"Excellent." He took out his phone and pulled up a picture. "And this is what you're after."

She studied the photo. "Those are…interesting."

"They're hideous." He laughed. "But worth a fortune to the right buyer, whom I happen to know."

"If you say so." But it seemed to Marigold that the right buyer would also have to be someone with absolutely zero taste in candlesticks.

Mr. Carnation hadn't shown up yet, which struck Wyatt as odd because he'd assumed the man would arrive early. Mr. Carnation was actually Mr. Newt Mathers, something Wyatt knew because Suzanne Anderson had identified the man from one of Wyatt's slyly snapped photos. Newt was Suzanne's uncle once removed or something.

Whoever he was, the man's presence proved that her suspicions about another family member trying to buy the candlesticks had been on point. She'd gone so far as to say that if Newt was wise to the auction, other family members might be too.

She'd upped her highest bid, giving Wyatt some more room to make the purchase.

He checked his watch. Fifteen minutes to go. The place was filling up. Fortunately, he'd already registered and gotten his paddle. He was ready to go. He'd even found himself a spot at the end of one of the rows of folding chairs that put his deaf ear to the wall.

He was okay with that. The wall wasn't going to say anything.

The spot also gave him a nice vantage point to see the rest of the crowd. Only the door wasn't in his immediate field of vision, but that required just a little turn of his head.

He turned now, to see if Newt had shown up.

Newt hadn't, but Wyatt momentarily forgot about Mr. Carnation thanks to the shapely blonde at the registration desk.

She must have just come in, because he would have noticed her already. He had a weakness for blondes, he knew that about himself. But this one was above average. She wasn't a twentysomething, either, which he immediately loved.

No, this woman had an air about her that said she understood how the world worked. She had kind eyes, but there was something about her that said she wasn't going to put up with a lot of nonsense. He appreciated that. He felt that way himself a lot lately.

Her attitude did nothing to affect her beauty. If anything, it made her more beautiful. Maybe not to a lot of other eyes, but it did for him.

He should probably stop staring, but she hadn't noticed, so he indulged himself a little longer.

She was curvy in the way of old-fashioned pin-up girls, and that appealed to him. Other men could have the supermodel waifs, he liked something to hold on to. Her blonde curls were a little wild, in a sort of earth mother kind of way that made him suddenly picture her in a sunny field full of wild flowers.

He blinked. Where on earth had that come from? That seemed like an awfully romantic image.

He turned back to face the front of the auction house and opened his program. He had work to do. Work that did not include weird, Hallmark-esque fantasies about some random blonde. Who was, granted, incredibly attractive.

He glanced over his shoulder for one more quick look, but she'd moved on. Good. He didn't need the distraction. Until maybe the auction was over.

"Is that seat taken?"

He twisted to see if the question was for him. And looked straight up into the face of the woman he'd just been thinking about. He swallowed, trying to loosen his tongue. Up close, she was impossibly beautiful. "What?"

She used her bidding paddle to point at the chair beside him. "I asked if that seat was taken."

She wanted to sit next to him? A quick scan of the crowd told him she didn't have a lot of other options and that he should stop thinking this was in any way related to him and not just all about the seat. "Sure. I mean, no."

"Thanks." She gave him a quick, polite smile and started past him.

At the same time, he stood up with the goal of letting her by.

They collided in a tangle, and he ended up falling back into his seat. Quick action made him spin her in his arms. She came down on his lap. Without thinking, he leaned in and sniffed her hair. *Lilacs.*

Her eyes flashed with…anger? "Do you mind?"

He jerked back. What on earth had he done that for? He held his hands up, having suddenly realized they were gripping her upper arms. Which were tight and toned and very nice. "Sorry. I was just trying to keep you from falling."

He hoped she bought that and didn't think he was some hair-sniffing creep. His time on the force had certainly taught him better than that. "I swear."

With a frown, she pushed to her feet. Her expression softened. "Thank you. I just…overreacted."

Hands still up, he widened his fingers and shrugged. "Hey, I would have too if a strange guy grabbed me. But I promise I didn't mean anything by it."

She sidled past his knees and sat. "I know you didn't. I didn't mean to snap. It's not your fault we ran into each other."

"I'm still sorry I upset you. Are you okay?"

She laughed. "I'm not that delicate. I'm fine. A little embarrassed maybe." She shook her head. "Don't worry about me."

"No problem." But having seen her up close, having touched her, and having inhaled the summery, flowery fragrance that surrounded her, he was the one with a problem.

And he didn't even know her name.

Marigold liked to think she was smarter than the average bear. And plenty smart enough to know what her conniving sisters were up to. Especially because for months Pandora and Charisma had been doing everything in their non-witchy power to get her hooked up with a guy, including bugging her to try online dating.

Her sisters were sure that was the answer to her relationship woes. Everyone was doing it, they'd told her.

Worn down, Marigold had relented and set up an account. But after swiping through some of the options and getting some less-than-polite messages from men, she had quickly deleted her account.

A dating app was not for her. It seemed more like a place to meet a hookup as opposed to a life partner. Which was great if a hookup was all she was looking for, but she wasn't even remotely ready for...*that*.

Now, however, as she sat in the folding chair on the auction floor, she was keenly aware of her current situation and taking stock of all that had happened.

Because through some seemingly random circumstances (some might even say magical), she'd ended up at this auction next to the hottest guy she'd seen near Nocturne Falls since...well, she didn't get out much, so she wasn't sure since when.

But holy blazing sunflowers, the man was causing butterflies in her stomach. Butterflies. In her stomach. Up until now, she'd been pretty sure the only thing down there were cobwebs. She snorted.

"What?" he asked, suddenly looking at her.

She couldn't help but look back. In fact, she took the opportunity to stare just a little bit. His eyes were the deep green of the water under the falls that gave her hometown its name. Not the spot where the water was churned up, but farther out. Toward the center of the pool, where the depth of the pool showed itself in the deepening color of the water.

In other words, the green had a hint of blue in it, and it was mesmerizing.

She slowly shook her head. "I didn't say anything."

He gave a little jerk of his head, acknowledging her answer, then went back to scanning the crowd. No more conversation.

She was fine with that, because while she excelled at small talk, she didn't know if she really wanted to talk to this guy or not.

On one hand, she totally did. He was gorgeous and giving off a little bad-boy vibe that was appealing in a way she probably wouldn't admit to if pressed. On the other hand…

Her sisters had set this up. She was sure of that. They'd probably paid Newt to send her on this bidding mission just to get her to the auction house. The ugliness of those candlesticks made that seem fairly plausible. Those were grade A hideous, and she had no doubt she'd be the only one bidding on them.

As if he was really willing to spend ten grand on them. She almost laughed out loud.

But how had her sisters managed for the seat next to this guy to be one of the few free? And for her to end up in it? Magic? Some kind of directional spell maybe? Normally, she would have guessed that in a heartbeat, but she couldn't sense any magic at play here.

Of course, they would have been extra careful, because they knew she'd be able to sense a heavy magical presence.

She closed her eyes for a moment, putting out her witchy feelers for just that sort of thing.

Okay, there was some magic present here, but it was muted. So basically, that meant nothing. She opened her eyes. In a town like Nocturne Falls, magic lurked around every corner. And Nocturne Falls was right next door to Millersville and in the same county. Lots of people came over here for the auction. She could be picking up on just about anything or anyone.

She glanced around the crowd. No sign of Pandora or Charisma. Unless they were in disguise. But Charisma was supposed to be away at a one-day seminar about reaching your inner child's potential, and Pandora was far too busy with wedding prep to have time for this.

Or at least, she'd better be. She'd seemed a little flustered by how much she had left to do this afternoon when she'd come into the shop. That hadn't stopped her from asking Marigold if she'd found a date yet.

Hmm. Pandora had smiled in a strange way when she'd brought up Marigold's potential plus-one. Had that weird smile been because of stress, or had it been because of whatever this setup was right now?

Then a new thought occurred to Marigold. Could her mother be in on this? Corette Williams wanted her daughters to be happy. In all aspects of life. She was thrilled that Pandora and Cole had found each other, but then, Cole was a human familiar and was the reason that Pandora's magic was finally functional after years of it not working.

Charisma dated her share of men, but she was basically married to her job. Corette occasionally mentioned that there was more to life than work, but she had never pushed any of them to be involved.

Granted, their mother had always told them that being alone was better than being with Mr. Wrong.

Marigold leaned back to study the guy next to her. What would Mom think of him?

A little gray showed at his temples, breaking up the nearly black and proving he wasn't a kid. Marigold liked that. She wasn't a kid either. And her mother would definitely like it. Corette absolutely thought Marigold needed a man who knew who he was. Someone who wasn't still trying to figure out his life. Or what he was going to do with the rest of it.

Marigold continued her inventory. No wedding ring. Good watch. Nothing flashy, but it looked very functional. And rugged. Like him. Plain, faded red T-shirt with a black cotton jacket. Probably would have been leather if it wasn't summer. Jeans that fit nicely. Some kind of black leather boots. Not exactly hiking. Not exactly military. Or maybe they were. She wasn't an expert in men's boots.

The way he dressed reminded her of some of the sheriff's deputies when they were off duty. His hands rested lightly on his thighs, and he was scanning the crowd. He looked like he was ready for something. Maybe just for the auction to begin.

She narrowed her eyes. Could he be a cop? Maybe. His hair was almost military short.

The sharp crack of the gavel made her jump. "Oh!"

He glanced at her, his brows raised, but that was all. Just a glance. Then he looked back at the auctioneer.

Okay, if he was in on the setup, he wasn't acting like it. She would have expected him to start up a conversation.

She rolled her eyes at her own nonsense. Going dateless for so long had clearly started messing with her mind. Maybe she should try the dating app again.

He leaned back and absently tapped his bidding paddle against his knee.

The auctioneer welcomed the crowd, thanked everyone for coming, and got things underway with the first item up for bid.

It was a cuckoo clock.

That gave Marigold time to check her phone to see if there were any messages from Ivy Merrow.

Saffie was at the Merrows' house. The Merrows were all wolf shifters, and all wonderful people. Sheriff Hank Merrow and his wife, Ivy, had two children. A new baby daughter, Hannah Rose, who was a few months shy of her first birthday, and a son, Charlie, who was almost Saffie's age of eleven. Charlie was Ivy's son, but the sheriff had adopted the little boy when he and Ivy had gotten married.

The way the pair got on, however, it was hard to tell Charlie wasn't Hank's biological son. The boy clearly worshipped Hank. And his baby sister. He liked Saffie a lot too.

Saffie, on the other hand, *adored* Charlie.

She didn't mind Hannah either, especially since the baby fit right into Saffie's favorite pastime with Charlie. Playing house. The baby fit slightly less into Saffie's second-favorite pastime with Charlie. Wedding planning.

Mostly, Marigold just shook her head and let her daughter be. If Charlie wasn't bothered by playing house with Saffron and listening to her plan their wedding, then more power to him.

No messages. Marigold put her phone back in her purse. All must be well at the Merrow house. No doubt Saffie was walking down an imaginary aisle, headed for her werewolf groom.

Marigold snorted again at the thought. A wolf shifter and a witch. There was a pair. Still, there were some far curiouser in this town.

Next item up for bid was a floor lamp. The base was a tree trunk and a little bird sat on one of the branches. It was all metal, but looked pretty realistic. Marigold sat up straighter. She could use a new lamp in the living room. And the tree appealed to her green-witch side.

Maybe it wouldn't go for too much money.

But five minutes later, it was already over a hundred dollars. She sighed and sat back. Spending all the money Newt was paying her to be here on something she didn't really need wasn't going to help with bills.

Being an adult sucked sometimes.

"Bummer," she muttered.

That earned her another questioning glance from her seatmate.

A little miffed at losing out on the cool lamp, she gave him the same look right back. So His Hotness didn't approve of her taste in lamps, so what? He could suck it. She was a green witch and proud of it. Also, trees were very cool.

"Next up, we have this very interesting pair of candlesticks."

Every fiber of Marigold's being went on alert. She forgot about Hot and Cranky and arrowed in on the auctioneer. Sure enough, the world's most hideous candleholders were up for bid.

She clenched her numbered paddle tighter, her fingers wrapped around the balsa wood handle with enormous sincerity. She was going to win these ugly things for Newt if it was the last thing she did.

That would fix them all for trying to set her up with someone. If that's what this was all about. If not, and Newt really did want those candlesticks, then he'd end up happy.

Could this really be about those ugly things on the auction stand? Maybe.

The thought caused her heart to start thumping in her chest like she was about to stroke out. This was an auction. Nothing that serious. And yet the excitement of it all, the uncertainty of what was about to happen next, was an unmistakable force.

"Let's open the bidding at fifty dollars."

Fifty? That was a steal. Her hand shot up, waving the paddle.

The auctioneer gave her a nod and kept on going with his speedy cadence, the words coming out of his mouth almost like a song.

No one bid anything else until the auctioneer started talking the candlesticks up, mentioning that they were antiques. In what felt like half a second, they rocketed to two thousand dollars.

Marigold was so stunned she just sat there as more bids flew by.

"Do I hear twenty-two fifty?"

She needed to bid. After all, what was the point of being able to go as high as ten thousand if she didn't at least attempt to win the candlesticks? But before she could get her paddle up, someone else jumped in.

Her seatmate.

Wyatt smiled a little, thankful that the pretty blonde's interest in the candlesticks had just been a whim. After she'd missed out on the funky tree lamp, she'd probably hoped not to go home empty-handed, then realized how ugly the candlesticks were.

And maybe she'd still win something else, but she wasn't going home with these.

He stuck his paddle into the air, catching the auctioneer's gaze and buying in at a fraction of what he was ready to spend. He might yet need that excess, however, with the way the bidding was going.

Made no sense. The candlesticks looked worthless to him, but he knew his taste in art wasn't exactly top shelf.

The bidding climbed.

At thirty-five hundred, one of the other bidders dropped out. Then the hot blonde next to him jumped back in.

He stared at her, openmouthed and disbelieving before he caught himself and focused on the battle that he'd yet to win. It cost him four grand to regain his lead. "You've got to be kidding me," he muttered.

She moved to the edge of her seat as if being a few inches closer to the auctioneer might help her win. "You're not getting them."

Her hand shot up again. Forty-five hundred.

"You wanna bet?" He put his paddle in the air and kept it there. Forty-seven fifty instantly became five grand.

She wiggled her paddle back and forth, sending the bid up another two hundred and fifty. "No bets. Just me winning. And you losing."

Her sassy response almost made him laugh, but he wasn't about to let his emotions get the best of him while she was the temporary enemy. When this was all said and done, maybe they'd discuss his victory over coffee.

He thrust his hand up higher and took the lead with a solid six grand. That was his max, but he was confident she'd back down. Six thousand dollars was a lot of cheddar for a lousy pair of candlesticks, and nothing about her said she was rolling in disposable income. Not that she looked destitute. Just not like Mrs. Gotrocks, either.

Speaking of…he checked her hand. No ring. Not that he cared if she was married or not. Just his general sense of observation kicking in.

Somehow, her other hand remained raised—and stayed there until the bid hit sixty-five hundred.

His paddle was the one that came down.

There were no other bidders at that outrageous price, and after a quick countdown, the auctioneer banged the gavel and finalized the sale. "Paddle 1541 has the winning bid."

She gasped and grinned. "Holy holly, I won. I *won*."

He frowned. Suzanne was not going to be happy. But she'd capped his bidding at six thousand, so the loss wasn't his fault. He pulled out his phone to text his client and give her the bad news, but the blonde next to him got up.

She gave him a little smile. Clearly, she wanted out now that she'd gotten what she'd come for. "Sorry."

He stood as well and moved into the aisle. "No problem. I was about to leave too."

She joined him in the aisle. "I meant about you not winning."

He shrugged. "No big deal. I wasn't bidding on them for myself. I was here as a proxy."

"Huh. Me, too. I guess those ugly things are really worth something after all." Her smile broadened.

"Well, I should go pay and collect the candlesticks. Have a nice night."

"You, too." He watched her go to the auction house desk and get in line to pay. One person ahead of her. Interesting that she hadn't been buying those for herself. Could she be the reason Newt hadn't shown up? If she was his agent, that was a pretty sly move on the old man's part.

Pretty being the key word.

He'd never anticipated his competition adding another player to the game, which bothered him. A year off the force and he was already losing his touch? That wasn't good. That wasn't good at all.

Had a shapely figure and a stunning face distracted him that much?

With a grunt of disgust, he went back to his phone. He shot the text to Suzanne, then started to put the phone away, but she sent a response right back. She must have been waiting.

He read it. As he'd suspected, she wasn't happy, but it was game over now.

Another text came in from her, threatening not to pay him. Fortunately, he had their agreement in writing. An old private detective friend of Wyatt's had suggested he use a simple contract with clients. Now he was glad he had followed the man's advice. Still, Wyatt frowned as he answered. *I did what you asked. You capped the spend, not me.*

You should have bid higher.

He rolled his eyes. *Not without authorization. Did Newton buy them?*

No.

A brief pause. *Ask the buyer if they'll sell to you. I'll go as high as 10K.*

He let out another sigh. If she'd have gone that high to begin with, this probably wouldn't be an issue. *Will do.*

He put the phone away and looked up to see where the blonde was. She was heading through the door with a box in her arms. The candlesticks, no doubt.

He went after her, pushing through the crowd that was milling about, nearly getting swatted with a bidding paddle on his way.

The parking lot was packed with cars, but no people. They were all inside. And her blonde head of curls wasn't hard to see. She disappeared around the corner of the building, juggling the box on one hand and using the other to pull out a key fob.

He followed, and when he came around the building, he spotted her. She was opening the back of a black SUV, much like the one he'd rented, but she was still a few yards away from the vehicle. She must have done it with the remote.

He was about to call out to her when two men came out of nowhere and rushed her. He reached for the gun that was no longer there, a habit that refused to die when his adrenaline kicked in. One man grabbed her while the other wrestled the box out of her grasp.

Wyatt charged. "Hey, get away from her."

Startled, the men shoved Marigold down and bolted. The candlesticks fell out of the box, smashing to the ground. The man who'd been holding the box glanced at the shattered pieces, then tossed the box and took off after his friend.

Wyatt let them go and helped her up. "Are you okay?"

"I don't know. I guess so."

He gave her a quick once-over. Her elbow and forearm were scratched and bleeding from where she'd hit the pavement. He gently took hold of her hand, turning her arm so she could see the damage. "You're not okay. You're hurt."

She swallowed. "I-I didn't even feel that. Until now. Ow."

"Adrenaline," he said. "Dulls the pain receptors so you can keep fighting."

"But I didn't fight. I didn't do anything." She was trembling.

"That's okay. Sometimes fighting back can get you hurt worse." He helped her over to the back of the open SUV. "Why don't you sit here for a second? Catch your breath."

She nodded and sat. Definitely in a little bit of shock.

"Did you know those men?"

"Not at all." She squinted a little. "I'm not sure I even got a good look at them."

"Then you probably don't recognize them from anywhere, huh?"

"No."

She wasn't crying. Yet. "I guess they were after the candlesticks."

"I guess. Oh!" She sucked in a breath. "They're completely ruined, aren't they?"

"Don't worry about that. Listen, I'm going to call the cops."

"I don't think they can fix them."

His brows went up. "This has nothing to do with fixing the candlesticks. You were just assaulted and the victim of an attempted robbery."

She nodded. "Right. Of course. I'm just a little shaken up."

"Completely natural. Don't worry, I've got this." His phone buzzed as he took it out. Suzanne again.

Did you get the candlesticks?

No. And you don't want them. They got broken.

He tapped the button to bring up the phone, but she responded again. *Completely?*

Yes. Many pieces. Honestly, what was the point of this?

Did you see them get broken? Was there anything else that happened?

He made a face at all her questions. But then, he supposed a repaired family heirloom might still be valuable for the memories it held. He took a picture of the remains of the candlesticks and sent it to her. There were still some large pieces left, but repairing them would only make the candlesticks uglier. *You can see what's left for yourself. Do you want me to try to get the pieces for you?*

More seconds ticked by. Like she was thinking. Then finally, *Yes.*

Marigold's arm and hand hurt, but her pride was a bit bruised, too. Those men had come after her and she'd done nothing. And it wasn't like she was defenseless. She was a witch, for crying out loud.

She could have stopped them in their tracks with a simple spell. One word. *Stagnacio*. And they would have been paralyzed where they stood.

But it had all happened so fast, she'd been the one to freeze up.

She sighed. Worse than her lack of action, she was going to have to explain to Newt that his $6,500 candlesticks were rubble.

At least her seatmate at the auction had been in the right place at the right time and come to her assistance.

That very handsome man walked over to her. He'd been giving a statement to Deputy Cruz, who'd shown up to handle the incident. "How's your arm?"

"Still hurts. And my palm stings." She looked at him, trying to figure him out a little. She wasn't sure why he'd been in the parking lot at the same time she was, but it was nice of him to have called the cops for her. And because he'd yelled at the men and charged after them, they'd run away. No doubt saving her from worse injury. "I'm Marigold, by the way."

"Nice to meet you. I'm Wyatt." He was studying her hand. "You should let me take you to the hospital, just to be sure."

"That's kind of you, but it's just a flesh wound." Wyatt was a nice name. Sort of cowboy adjacent. "And I can drive myself."

"Can you?" His brows lifted. "With your hand like that?"

"Driving with one hand isn't hard."

"Not under normal circumstances, but you're also in pain and possibly a little shock. Plus, I don't mind. I don't have anywhere else to be or anything else to do." He grimaced slightly. "And I feel a little responsible."

"In what way?"

"I didn't get to you in time."

"I'd say you got to me in plenty of time. Just in time, actually. And what happened wasn't your fault."

He shrugged. "I know. But my instinct to help makes me wish I'd done more. Been there in time to keep you from falling. Something. Hard to feel that and know I failed."

"You didn't fail. You yelled at them. That made them run away."

"I suppose."

Deputy Cruz joined them. "The auction house has a few security cameras. I'll see if any of them caught the assailants. In the meantime, Ms. Williams, you should get that hand and arm looked at."

Wyatt lifted one shoulder. "I offered to take her to the emergency room."

"I'm fine." For one thing, she couldn't afford whatever that bill would be. Plus, she had a salve at home (that she'd made herself) that would heal these scrapes in less than twenty-four hours. Green witches were good with stuff like that.

"All right, your decision." Officer Cruz closed his notebook and tucked it away. "If we find out anything, we'll be in touch."

"Thanks. Tell Roxy I said hi."

He grinned. "You got it."

Another happy couple. No doubt she'd be doing their wedding flowers at some point too. With a groan, she got off the back of the SUV and went to survey what remained of the candlesticks. Lots and lots of pieces. Most of them about the size of a quarter. Two larger hunks, the fattest part of each stick, remained mostly intact.

They didn't look fixable, but she wasn't an ugly-candlesticks expert. Regardless, Newt deserved to at least have the shards after what he'd paid. She crouched down, grabbed the box they'd been in, and started tossing pieces in.

"Hey, let me do that." Wyatt knelt beside her. "That's the last thing you need to be doing. Go sit. I'll put the box in the back of your car when I'm done."

"Are you always this bossy to strangers?"

He snorted and looked at her, giving her another chance to inspect his gorgeous eyes up close. "We're not really strangers anymore, are we?"

Sweet fancy snapdragons, he was pretty. "I guess not."

"You sure I can't take you somewhere to have your injuries looked at?"

They were so close. Both huddled together on the pavement. Inches apart. He smelled a little like pine and citrus. It was a nice smell. Masculine, clean, earthy. Just the kind of thing a green witch would like.

And now she was wondering again if her sisters had anything to do with this. Of course, they certainly wouldn't have set up the attempted mugging. "I promise to clean it up when I get home."

"Maybe I should check on you tomorrow." He chucked a handful of pieces into the box. "Make sure you're all right."

She almost fell over. Was he…flirting with her? She wasn't sure, but she covered her surprise by getting to her feet and going back to sit on the SUV's bumper. "I work all day, so—"

"Where do you work?" The box in his hands was almost full.

"Enchanted Garden. It's a flower shop. I own it, actually."

"That's nice—wait. Your name is Marigold. And you own a flower shop. Was your career chosen at birth?"

She smiled a little. It was something people commented on a lot when they first met her. "Marigold is actually my middle name, but I've gone by it most of my life."

"I see." He nodded as he stood. "Well, what time do you open?"

"Nine." Of course, she'd be there earlier to feed Frank, do paperwork, and start on the day's arrangements, but she wasn't telling him that.

He tucked the box of candlestick remains into the vehicle. "I'll see you then."

"Sure." She wasn't positive he was flirting, but she had her doubts about him showing up. If he did, he did. She wasn't going to put much stock in it either way. "See you then."

He didn't walk away like she'd expected. "Do me a favor?"

"What's that?"

"I know someone who would like to have those pieces if that's okay with whoever you bought them for. Maybe you could check for me? And tell me tomorrow?"

She glanced over her shoulder at what was left of the candlesticks and thought about Newt telling her not to say she was working for him. But she had to give Wyatt some kind of answer. "I'll see what I can do, but since they don't belong to me, no promises."

"Totally understand. The person I know would be willing to pay something for them too, so maybe ask your person about a price."

She lifted her chin. "I can do that. Not sure why anyone would want them now, but one person's trash is another person's treasure?"

He laughed. "I guess." He backed away without taking his eyes off her. "Nine."

"Nine." She got up, dug in her purse for her keys, then stood there a moment, watching him. He got into a black SUV that was a lot like hers.

Her phone buzzed, distracting her. It was a Snapchat from Saffie. A picture of her and Charlie. Saffie had a lace doily on her head, a bunch of silk flowers in one hand, and a smile that went from ear to ear. Charlie was at her side, the mostly proud groom.

Marigold let out a little laugh-sigh at the sight of her daughter. "Child, you have got it bad."

She shut the back of the SUV, then climbed into the driver's seat, and one-handed, headed back into Nocturne Falls to pick her daughter up from the Merrows' and end her reign of matrimonial terror.

Marigold knew she should call Newt to explain about the candlesticks, but telling him in person tomorrow seemed like a better idea.

The next morning, Marigold was pleased to see that the healing salve she'd applied to her hand and arm had worked nicely. Very little remained of the scrapes she'd gotten in the parking lot, and there was only minor bruising.

She hadn't bothered to tell Saffie about what had happened. No need for her child to worry.

After a shower, Marigold put on a little makeup, dressed in jeans and a cute floral blouse, then went to see if Mrs. Charlie Merrow was up.

She was. And already in the kitchen fixing herself a bowl of Apple Snaps.

Marigold kissed her daughter's head. "Morning, sunshine."

"Morning, Mom." Saffie added milk to her cereal, then put the carton back in the fridge. "Hey, Mom. Watch."

Marigold turned around in time to see Saffie wiggle her fingers at the refrigerator door. With no further assistance, the door swung closed.

Marigold's mouth came open. "Did you just use magic to shut that door?"

Saffie had the same ear-to-ear grin on her face as she'd had in last night's wedding photo. "Yep."

"How…" Marigold swallowed. "You shouldn't be able to do that. Not yet."

Witches didn't usually come into their powers until about age thirteen. Saffron was eleven.

Saffie shrugged. "But, like, I just did."

"I see that." Marigold made herself smile. Clearly, Saffie was proud of what she'd just shown off. "Great job, honey."

"Does that mean I can get a mentor now?"

Also standard procedure for when a new witch came of age. Someone in the local coven would sponsor her and help guide her through the early days. Marigold nodded. "I'll have to check with the coven, but I don't think that will be an issue."

Saffie's smile grew a little tentative. "Do you think Mimi will do it?"

Marigold kept on nodding. Mimi was Saffie's name for Corette, one Corette far preferred over Grandma. "I bet she would love to. In fact, I'll call her today."

Saffie clapped and ran to her mother for a hug. "Yay!"

Marigold pulled her in and squeezed her tight. She was definitely calling her mother about this.

"Do you think I'll be a green witch like you? Or be able to see auras like Kaley?"

Kaley was Pandora's soon-to-be stepdaughter, and Saffron idolized her.

"Hard to say, baby. We'll just have to see how your powers work out." Marigold kissed Saffie's head again. "Go eat your breakfast, now. The bus will be here soon."

Thankfully, Saffron's school, Harmswood Academy, provided transportation as part of the tuition package. Tuition that was pricey, but worth it. Harmswood was a private school that catered to the supernatural, and it was the best place for a young witch.

Especially one who was blossoming way too fast.

Fifteen minutes later, Saffie was out the door and Marigold was on the phone.

"Mom, you're not going to believe this."

"What is it, dear?"

Marigold took a breath. "Saffron's powers are starting to materialize."

Corette went quiet for a few moments. "Well, just because she thinks she can feel them doesn't mean they're really there yet."

"Mom. She shut the refrigerator door without touching it. She *charmed* it closed."

Corette made a small *hmph* sound. "I'm not surprised."

"You're not? Because I'm flabbergasted. She's eleven, Mom."

"I know, but Charisma's came at twelve and three months."

"Okay, but look at Pandora. Hers didn't come until she met Cole."

"Her gifts came. They were just...unusable. And now her gifts are extraordinary. All of you girls are exceptionally gifted. Who knows? Saffron may be the best of us."

"But at eleven?"

"I understand you're concerned, honey, but Saffron is a good girl. She's not going to do anything to get herself into trouble. And they won't let her at Harmswood. Just because she has powers doesn't mean she's going to use them to do something she shouldn't. Have faith in the child you raised."

Marigold smiled. "I do. I'm just...worried."

"That's called being a mother." Corette laughed softly. "And I had three of you to contend with."

"You did a great job, Mom."

"You are too, honey. Now, unfortunately, I have to get to work."

"Me, too. Love you."

"Love you more."

They hung up, and Marigold got moving. A few minutes later, she pulled into her parking spot behind the shop and headed in through the back door.

She flipped the lights on. Frank the Tank was sitting by his feeding station.

"Morning, Frank. How's the pest patrol going?"

He meowed at her, then moved a few steps closer to his bowl, which she took to mean *feed me now*.

"That good, huh?"

She opened a can of food for him, plopped it into a clean dish, then put it down and picked up the old one. She put that in the sink to wash later, scooped his litter box (the smell of which was probably keeping the mice at bay), gave him clean water, refilled his dry food, then got to work turning the rest of the lights on.

She wasn't looking forward to telling Newt that his $6,500 candlesticks were worthless, so when someone knocked on the shop's door before she had the lights on, she jumped and let out a little shriek.

She peered through the workroom door to see who it was, then exhaled in relief. The figure outlined by the morning sun was Deputy Cruz.

She flipped the lights on, then went to open the door. "Morning, Alex."

"Morning, Marigold. Sorry to bother you before you're open."

"That's okay. Is everything all right?"

He nodded. "Just wanted to check in with you. We'll be running a few extra patrols by here today."

"Because of what happened yesterday?"

"Yes."

"I don't think that's necessary."

"Sheriff Merrow thinks it is. We couldn't ID those two men. They had ball caps on and their faces were hidden from the security cams. Sheriff thought it would be a good idea for us to make our presence a little better known for the next few days."

"If you think so."

"It's a done deal. Just wanted you to know." He started to go, then hesitated. "One more thing."

"What's that?"

"The man who helped you yesterday. Wyatt?"

"Yes?"

"He's human, by the way."

"He is?" It hadn't occurred to her to wonder, really. Most people in town were supernaturals. But then, she hadn't been in Nocturne Falls. "How can you be sure?"

Deputy Cruz tapped the side of his nose. "Feline sense of smell never fails."

"Right. Well, good to know. But won't the town water take care of that?" The town's water supply was fed from the falls, which had been charmed decades ago by one of the most powerful witches that lived here, Alice Bishop.

Because of her spell, any human who drank the water (which was pretty much any tourist who came to town) truly believed that the magic in town was all an act. Ingenious, really.

He shook his head. "It didn't work that well with Roxy. And Wyatt's not staying in town. He's staying in Millersville, by the auction house."

"Well, I'll be on my best non-witchy behavior if I see him again, but I don't think that's very likely."

Men, Marigold had learned long ago, didn't always keep their word.

Wyatt hadn't been to Nocturne Falls since arriving for the auction, even though the touristy town was right next to Millersville. This was a working trip, not a vacation, but seeing as how his work was almost over, a little detour seemed like a worthwhile endeavor.

Especially when that detour took him to Marigold Williams.

But as he drove down Main Street, he realized he should have taken this detour sooner. Millersville was just a regular, ordinary town, and frankly, pretty boring.

Despite being right next door to Millersville, Nocturne Falls, on the other hand, was not even close to ordinary. And about as far from boring as could be.

His first clue was the large pumpkin-shaped sign he passed driving into town that read, *Welcome to Nocturne Falls—where every day is Halloween.*

He'd never seen a place like this in his life. And as a cop, he'd seen some things.

The general color scheme of the whole joint seemed to be black and orange. There was a fair amount of purple, green, pink, and blue too. The colors were bright and true. Even the pastels had pop.

And the Halloween theme was everywhere.

Cobweb-shaped metal brackets held the street lamps off their poles. A few of the buildings were deliberately built to look rickety. Pumpkin shapes were everywhere.

As he drove, he passed a large fountain with an enormous gargoyle at the front of it. The fountain was the centerpiece of a landscaped park that made up the large main square. He blinked as he went by, not sure what he was seeing. Was the gargoyle moving? Talking to people? Had to be animatronics.

He shook his head. This town was something else. Kind of campy and crazy, but cool in a sort of Tim Burton way. He could see why it was such a popular tourist spot. The little kids on the streets wore costumes despite the fact that it was months away from Halloween and early in the morning. He even spotted a few adults in masks. He grinned. Kids must eat this place up.

Just to keep the theme going, the businesses had names like The I Scream Shop and Hats In The Belfry.

The Detective Wins The Witch

Then he saw what he was looking for. A diner. Called Mummy's. The sign had a cartoon mummy on it with the slogan "Our food is to die for!" Based on the number of people at the door, the food had to be good. That was all he needed.

He snagged a parking spot and went inside. A sign for takeout hung over the far end of the counter. He got in line. He grabbed a menu while he waited and quickly deduced that cinnamon buns were the way to go. Not just because of the menu, but because a server went by with one and it was about the size of his head.

Outstanding.

When it was his turn, he ordered two, plus two coffees. The food came up fast, neatly packaged. This place obviously did a tremendous business. He was back in his car in less than ten minutes.

The Enchanted Garden was his next stop, and thanks to the trip to Mummy's, he arrived at nine thirty. Plenty of time, he assumed, for Marigold to get her shop open and her day underway. He didn't want to interrupt her normal routine. And if she was busy, he'd just leave the bag and go. Well, he'd leave his cell number, too.

Takeout bag in hand, he walked in. A bell over the door announced his entrance. He wasn't sure he'd ever been in a flower shop before. He stood there for a moment, trying to remember. No, he didn't think he had. This one seemed nice. Smelled good. He looked around. Had a lot more plants than he'd expected. And more color.

"Can I help you? Oh. It's you."

He turned. Marigold was standing by the sales counter. She must have been in the back when he'd first come in. He could see part of a desk and the ends of some tables through the door behind her. He held up the bag. "Despite that warm welcome, I brought you breakfast."

She laughed. "I didn't mean it that way."

"You didn't think I'd show, did you?"

She leaned against the counter and crossed her arms. "Nope. I didn't."

He walked over and set the bag next to her, but then squinted to study her forearm and hand. "Those scrapes are almost gone. I don't even see any bruising. How is that possible?"

She jerked her arm away. "I, uh, I put some good stuff on it. So, what's in the bag?"

He knew enough to know when someone wanted a subject dropped, but what was the big deal? No one healed that fast. Even so, he let it go. "Coffee and cinnamon buns. That seemed to be the thing to get at Mummy's."

"It is, it definitely is. Their pancakes are outstanding, too. But you didn't need to do this. Or is this part of you trying to persuade me to give you those candlestick pieces?"

He wasn't. He'd just wanted to put a smile on her face. Impress her a little, maybe. He shrugged. "Is it helping?"

Her smile was a nice little reward. "It's not hurting. But it isn't up to me if you get those pieces or not."

"Right. It's up to the man you were buying them for. Any chance you talked to him yet?"

"How do you know it was a man?"

He shrugged. "Good guess?"

"Very good." She gave him a look as if she wasn't sure about his answer. "I did talk to him. He was in here right before you were." She grimaced like the next thing she had to tell him wasn't going to be such good news. "He said he'd sell you the pieces for a thousand dollars."

Internally, Wyatt winced. But it wasn't his money. Suzanne wanted those pieces and was willing to pay. "Done."

Marigold's brows shot up. "Really?"

"Really."

"I should tell you that they're in a few more pieces than they were originally. The guy I was buying them for dropped the box when he was getting them out of the back of my SUV."

Wyatt shrugged. "I don't see that it makes a difference. Broken is broken, right?"

"Right."

He took the coffees out of the bag. "I had them dump a bunch of creamers and sugars in here since I don't know how you like your coffee."

"That's great. It was really nice of you to bring this." She pulled a tall chair from around the counter and positioned it at the end for him. "There. Have a seat."

"While you stand? No, thanks."

"I have to stand. I have to be able to wait on customers in case someone comes in."

He looked around the otherwise empty shop. "Yes, I can see the crowd is nearly out of control."

Her smirk looked less than happy. "I actually have an unbelievable amount of work to—"

The bell over the door interrupted her, and a pretty redhead came waltzing in. "Mari, did you get those—well, hello there."

The redhead stuck her hand out. "I'm Pandora, Marigold's sister. Who are you?"

He put his coffee down to shake her hand. "Wyatt West."

Pandora's eyes were just about sparkling with interest. "You must be my sister's date for my wedding."

"Pandora!" Marigold glared at her sister.

Pandora shrugged. "If you're not, no big deal." Her gaze shifted back to Marigold. "Phil Crenshaw told me he'd go with you, Mari."

"Phil who sells life insurance?" Marigold's upper lip curled.

"Yes. Why do you look like that?"

"Phil Crenshaw has all the sex appeal of a pocket calculator."

"Oh, come on now, he's not that—"

"His favorite color is mediocre."

Wyatt snorted, drawing Marigold's attention. She sidled up to him. "Besides, I can't go with Phil anyway. I mean, Wyatt already said he'd go with me. Didn't you, Wyatt?"

He hadn't known until now what a ping-pong ball felt like being swatted back and forth between two paddles. Something pressed against his side. It was Marigold's finger, poking him. "Uh, yes. I sure did."

Marigold looked at her sister. "See? I have a date."

Pandora crossed her arms. "Really?"

"Really," Marigold said. There was a grave seriousness to her voice that told Wyatt he'd best play along.

Pandora stared him down a little before looking back to her sister. "So when I leave, you're not going to tell him he's off the hook? That this was just a ruse to get me off your back about having a date?"

"No. Because I have a date. Wyatt."

"Then why haven't I heard of him before?"

Wyatt clenched his teeth to keep from laughing. Pandora would have made a great interrogator.

"Because," Marigold said, "we're newly acquainted."

Pandora still looked skeptical. "Feels very scammy to me."

Wyatt sipped his coffee like a boss. "Would I have brought her breakfast if this was a scam? I am clearly trying to make some time here." Then he gave her what he hoped was a very convincing do-you-mind look.

She pursed her lips and stepped back, hands up. "All right. If you say so. And you know what? Just to be on the safe side, I'm officially inviting you to my wedding this Saturday, Wyatt. You got that? It's official. Right from the bride." She pointed at her sister. "That way, that one can't uninvite you."

He laughed. "Thanks." These two were nuts. In a fun way. Never having much of a family himself, he liked the interaction.

"You got it," Pandora said. "Now, you two go ahead with your breakfast there. Mari, call me later."

"No."

"Excellent. Talk to you then." With a wink, Pandora was out the door.

Marigold heaved out a sigh. "That woman is like a dog with a bone. You'd think she'd have enough to worry about with her wedding four days away."

"What's the dress? Semi-formal? Casual? I'll probably have to buy something." He wasn't a fan of shopping, but being her date gave him a reason to hang around her a bit longer and make sure those men from the parking lot didn't come back. He had to admit, he was also partially doing it just to see the look on Pandora's face when he showed up as Marigold's date at the wedding.

She stared at him like he'd sprouted horns and a tail. "For what?"

"The wedding."

She snorted. "Yeah, about that. We're not going. I mean, I am. I'm a bridesmaid. But you're not. Going, that is. Obviously, you know you're not a bridesmaid."

"Ah, but I've just been invited by the bride. Can't really turn down such a personal invitation, can I?"

"Yes, you can. She won't even notice."

He clutched his chest. "I'm wounded."

A sweet, small smile bent her mouth. She fished out one of the cinnamon buns in its enormous container, put it on the counter, and opened it. The warm scent of cinnamon and sugar filled the air. She licked icing off one finger. "You really want to go?"

"You really need a date?"

"No one *needs* a date." She attacked the pastry with a plastic fork, nearly breaking the utensil in half in her effort to get a bite free. "But it would be nice not to go alone."

"Then I'm your man."

"I don't really know you. Sure, you seem nice enough, but..." She waved a fork-speared hunk of bun at him before popping it in her mouth.

"I could be completely psycho."

She nodded as she chewed. "Yep. That."

"You're right. I could be. I'm not." He pulled out his wallet, took out his private investigator's license, and placed it on the counter. "Before I was a PI, I was a police detective. Homicide, actually."

She studied the small rectangle of paper. "Wow. From homicide to a private eye, huh? I've never met either one of those before."

"You have now. What do you think?"

She made no effort to hide her teasing smile. "I think credentials are pretty easy to fake."

He rolled his eyes and laughed softly. "This isn't fake. And I guess my attempt at impressing you failed miserably."

"No, you being a detective—homicide or private—is very impressive." She dug in for another bite of cinnamon bun. "But I think if you are a psycho, based on your work experience, there's no chance the cops will ever find my body. Still, you're more interesting than Phil the insurance salesman, so I'll take my chances."

Wyatt shook his head. "You're a tough nut, Marigold."

"Just a realist. Being a single mom will do that to you."

She had a kid. Interesting. "Well, since we're putting all of our cards on the table, I should tell you I'm not relationship shopping. I like being single. But I'm happy to be your plus-one."

"Then it's a date."

For a moment, it seemed like the light in her eyes dimmed a little, but she turned away so fast he wasn't sure what he'd seen. She was bent over, rummaging under the counter.

Why did he get the feeling he was being dismissed? Had she already been making future plans for them? Why did women do that? Why did they attach a future to every guy? He sighed and got out of the chair. "I should get going. I need to follow up with my client, let her know about the grand for the candlesticks."

"Oh. Aren't you going to eat your bun?" She straightened, a roll of paper towels in her hand. She put them on the counter. "These things are super messy."

"They are, but don't you have work to do?"

She laughed. "So much it would make your head hurt to hear about it. But I have five more minutes to eat some of this cinnamon bun and drink some of this coffee. Or were you trying to bolt because you changed your mind about the wedding?"

"I didn't change my mind." Except, he was now thinking he'd been wrong about whatever he'd thought he'd seen in her eyes. He picked up a pen off the counter. "I should probably give you my cell number, too. And you should give me yours."

"That'll make it harder if you decide to ditch me." She sipped her coffee, smirking slightly. "Or if I turn out to be a psycho."

Leah, Marigold's employee, came in at ten. Wyatt was gone by then, and Marigold was glad. The fewer people who knew about him, the better. The less explaining she'd have to do about why things hadn't worked out when he was gone after the wedding. Or whatever it was that people would assume had happened.

She was fine with him being a one-off. It helped her out a lot. Her sisters would have nothing to rib her about at the wedding, she'd avoid being set up by them, and she had a strong suspicion that Wyatt would be a fun date.

He was funny, handsome, and so far, very kind. She liked him. Anyone would. And she could easily like him more, but she wouldn't let that happen. For one *big* thing, he was a normie. A human. That wasn't something she wanted to mess with.

But also because he'd been so honest about his feelings when it came to relationships. He didn't want anything permanent. She could respect that.

Really, she admired his honesty. It was refreshing. Sad. But refreshing. At least she didn't have to wonder if it was going anywhere. It wasn't.

He wouldn't even need to meet Saffron. Except for at the wedding, of course. After all, what was the point?

"Morning, Mari." Leah came around the counter and put on her green Enchanted Garden apron.

"Morning."

Leah looked around. "Smells like Mummy's in here."

"Oh, a, uh, customer brought me a coffee and a cinnamon roll." Not a lie, but better than explaining the complicated truth.

"That was nice! Does that mean there's coffee and a cinnamon bun for me somewhere, seeing as how you're on the no-wheat-sugar-and-caffeine bridesmaid diet?"

Marigold frowned. "I took a temporary break from that. But there is half of a bun left in the fridge if you want it."

"Heck, yes, I want it." Leah grinned. "How's wedding prep going?"

"Flowers are due in any moment, then it's going to get intense."

Leah rubbed her hands together. She loved her job, something Marigold was intensely thankful for. But then, Leah was a wood nymph and, much like a green witch, was especially suited to working with plants. "Yeah, it is."

The back doorbell rang. Marigold headed toward the rear entrance. "That's either Joe to pick up deliveries or Pandora's flowers arriving."

She opened it and found the driver for the wholesale supply house. "Hey, George."

"Hi, Marigold. I've got a big order for you today." The balding man smiled. "Your sister's wedding flowers."

"Right on time." She propped the door open so he could come and go easily. The bell over the front door jangled. It was going to be a busy day. "You need help?" She knew he didn't, but she always asked.

"Nope, I've got the dolly. Be in with the first batch shortly."

"Sounds good." She went back to the counter.

Wyatt was at the front of the shop, talking to Leah.

Marigold double-timed it to where they were standing. "Leah, you want to see if George needs a hand? You could inventory the boxes for me as they come in."

Leah gave her a curious look. "Sure."

As she headed for the back room, Marigold spoke to Wyatt. "What can I do for you?"

He held out a cashier's check from a local bank, and it was made out to cash for one thousand dollars. "Here's your check."

"Great. The box is under the counter." She walked behind it and grabbed the box of candlestick pieces that had accidently become even more of a mess than they'd been before. Although to her, the accident hadn't looked that accidental. It was almost like Newt had dropped the box on purpose when he was getting them out of her car. "Here's your puzzle."

Wyatt took the box, then leaned one elbow on the counter. "I was thinking, since we're going to your sister's wedding and all, maybe we should go to dinner. You know, get to know each other a little."

She could feel a look of skepticism coming over her. The man who didn't want any kind of relationship now wanted to get to know her better? "I can't. I have so much wedding prep to do that time off is out of the question."

He frowned. "What kind of wedding prep do you have to do? Your sister is the one getting married."

She laughed at him. "Hello, look around you. Who do you think is doing the flowers?"

Realization washed over him. "Clearly, I'm an idiot."

She laughed some more. "No, you're not. Guys don't think about stuff like that."

He nodded thoughtfully. "Well, I'm disappointed you won't get to show me around town. This place is a lot different than Millersville."

"That it is. But you don't need me to show you around. Just pick a direction on Main Street and walk. You won't be disappointed, I promise."

His eyes narrowed. "You realize that was my way of saying I was hoping to spend more time with you."

"Oh." Yeah, she hadn't gotten that. Daisy doodles, she was out of practice.

Leah popped her head out of the workroom. "Everything's here. You want me to go ahead and sign off?"

"Yes, thanks." Marigold looked into the back. Boxes of flowers were everywhere. She blew out a breath. The work that awaited was…staggering. But she'd enjoy it. Her hours of labor were for the love of her sister, and each bloom would be placed with that thought.

"What's in all those boxes?"

She turned around to see Wyatt peering into the back room too. "All the flowers I have to arrange for my sister's wedding. Actually, not all, but most."

His brows lifted. "You have help, right?"

"I have Leah."

His brows went higher. "The two of you are going to handle all of those? How many…bouquets or whatever do you have to do?"

"One bridal bouquet, four bridesmaid bouquets, one flower girl basket, two corsages, eight boutonnieres, six swags, ten aisle markers, one arched trellis—well, that will actually be done on site—fifteen centerpieces, and one toss bouquet." She paused, mentally checking her list. "I think that's it."

His mouth was open, and he was blinking, but otherwise she wasn't sure he was still with her.

"Wyatt?"

He took a breath. "That seems like a lot."

"It is, but thankfully it's a small backyard wedding, so—"

"That's a small wedding?"

"Yes. Well, maybe not that small. About a hundred and fifty people. But small in terms of the number of arrangements necessary. Church weddings with receptions at another venue usually need a lot more. Pandora's wedding will be contained to the backyard. They're having the ceremony and the reception there. In tents. The reception part, not the ceremony."

"You make it seem like it's no big deal. How many weddings do you do a year?"

"In this town? I try not to do more than twenty a year, but sometimes it's a little more than that."

"Wow." He breathed out the word like it was all he could come up with.

She leaned in, ready to blow his mind just a little. "And in two more weekends, I have another wedding. One of my friends."

"I thought being a cop was hard."

"Oh, I'm sure that's still harder. I've never been shot at."

He smirked, seemingly snapping back to reality. "I certainly hope not."

A new thought occurred to her. "You know, if you don't have anything else to do until the wedding, I could always use some help here. You did say you wanted to get to know me better."

He blinked. Hard. "I don't know anything about arranging flowers."

"Oh, yeah, no, that is not *at all* what I had in mind. I was thinking you could just sit here and help customers. You know, answer the phone, take orders. Get us lunch." She did her best not to laugh, because the thought of him being her errand boy made her giddy for reasons she couldn't name. "Just stuff like that. Then Leah and I could focus on the wedding prep uninterrupted."

"For real?"

She shrugged. "Unless you think that's more than you can handle."

"I...could do that." He seemed to be thinking a little more. Then he nodded. "I need to mail this box to my client first, but then I'm all yours."

Frank jumped up on the counter and lay down, paws crossed in front of him.

Marigold smiled. "Good. You're hired. Come back after you hit the post office, and I'll show you how to properly unbox and store these stems."

Thanks to directions from Marigold, Wyatt walked to the post office instead of driving since it wasn't too far. He got the box mailed out, then headed back. On the return walk, he realized he really had no idea what he'd gotten himself into. Not with Marigold, but with Suzanne.

The moment he'd talked to Suzanne about getting the grand for the candlesticks, and she'd told him that there was another auction she wanted him to bid on in a couple days, he'd gotten that funny feeling in his stomach.

That feeling happened only when something hinky was going on. When he was about to figure out a case, or stumble onto some shady dealings, or discover that a good guy was actually a bad guy.

The new item he was supposed to bid on was coming up in Thursday night's auction. He'd agreed, because the money was good, and he had no other cases. It was also part of why he'd signed on to be Marigold's wedding date. He was already going to be here until Thursday now, so what was two more days?

This time, the item up for auction was bookends. Suzanne claimed they were more family heirlooms, also accidentally sold off by the same family member.

But after what he'd seen with the parking lot attack on Marigold, he knew there was something more going on. Okay, maybe he didn't *know* it, but his gut—and that feeling—were seldom wrong.

His gut was telling him that those men hadn't gotten what they'd come for. It wasn't the candlesticks. He just couldn't believe that. And if they weren't satisfied, then Marigold might not be safe.

So he'd agreed to two things he might not have otherwise. To be her date for the wedding and to help her in the shop.

He couldn't leave her unprotected. Being by her side as much as possible was the only way to keep an eye on her without seeming like a creep.

Didn't hurt that she was gorgeous and smelled nice, either.

But flower shop duty? That was a new one. He lived in a one-bedroom apartment in Atlanta. He didn't even have a yard.

He walked back into the Enchanted Garden. "I'm here."

Marigold smiled at him. "Just in time. Here's what I need you to do."

She showed him a couple of things, and he went to work. Despite his reservations, nothing so far was beyond his ability. Unpacking the boxes and putting the flowers into water buckets, then storing them in the big coolers was just grunt work. A trained chimp could have done it. Or in his case, an untrained chimp.

Leah, Marigold's employee, was a sweet kid and currently working on wedding centerpieces. She was a little chatty, telling him about her dog, Rollo, and how Rollo was a failed drug-sniffer dog. Apparently, he could detect drugs, but also French fries, candy wrappers, and animal crackers. Pretty much anything that qualified as a carb.

Mostly, Wyatt just nodded and said, "Huh" or "How about that" a lot. He didn't mind the conversation at all, but Marigold was far more interesting. She was occupied at the moment with taking a phone order.

He was finishing up the last of the boxes when a customer came in. He peered through the door to make sure it wasn't one of their parking lot friends.

It wasn't, but he knew the man all the same. Mr. Carnation.

What was he doing here? But Wyatt knew instantly. That's who Marigold had gone to the auction for.

Was she really working with this guy?

She gave him the thousand-dollar check, confirming she was.

Frank, the shop cat, was lying on the workbench near Leah. Which was also closer to the front of the shop.

Wyatt went to scratch him. Leah kept talking, unaffected by his move, but it put him in a good position by the door. Closer to where he could hear the conversation. Especially when he turned so that his deaf ear was to Leah and his good ear was toward the front of the shop.

Even so, he missed a few words. Leah's constant chatter spilled over a little. He got the gist of what Mr. Carnation wanted, though.

Another auction.

Marigold didn't want to do it. She had too much to do for the wedding, and her sister's rehearsal dinner was the night after the auction, meaning Thursday was her last full evening to get ready.

Mr. Carnation offered her three hundred dollars and assured her the items would come up early in the docket. She'd be in and out in no time.

Marigold said she'd think about it. Mr. Carnation offered her five hundred. She said again she'd think about it and that she'd call him soon. He left.

Wyatt smiled at Leah, who was still talking. He interrupted as soon as she took a breath. "Excuse me just a sec."

He joined Marigold at the counter. "What did that man want you to buy at the auction?"

She made a face at him. "Eavesdropping isn't very polite, you know."

"What did he want you to buy?"

She frowned. "I shouldn't do it."

"Marigold, please. Tell me. Was it bookends?"

She jerked back slightly. "How did you know?"

A weird light passed through Wyatt's eyes, and his gaze shifted to the door.

Marigold poked him in the arm when he didn't answer. "How did you know what he wanted me to buy?"

"Something's going on."

"Yeah, he wants me to go bid on more crap for him. And I could really use the money, but that's my last full night for wedding prep. I'll still end up working after the rehearsal dinner on Friday, but by that point I need to be doing final touch ups, not full-on prep." She sighed. "Five hundred dollars is a *lot*, though."

"It is. But for that kind of money, he can get someone else to do it."

She chewed on her bottom lip. Five hundred bucks would cover the down payment on Saffie's braces. "I'm sure, but I could really use that money."

"What if those guys come back?"

She looked at him. "You really think that's going to happen? What are the chances that those guys want candlesticks *and* bookends?" Her brows rose as she gave him an appraising glance. "Are all ex-cops paranoid?"

"I'm not being paranoid." But the look in his eyes said he suddenly realized he might be coming off that way. "Just cautious."

"I appreciate that." It was sweet that he was so concerned. "Look, I'll get there earlier so I can park in the front. And I'll be quicker getting to my car after I check out."

"And I'll be with you."

"You will, huh?"

He shrugged. Then let out a sigh. "The reason I think something's going on is because the same client who wanted me to buy the candlesticks also wants me to buy the bookends."

Okay, that was strange. Or was it? "So they're valuable, right? We already know that. And just because more than one person wants an item at an auction doesn't mean something shady is going on. That's the whole point of auctions. To get lots of bidders."

"True. But my gut says it's not all on the up-and-up. And my gut is rarely wrong."

"More ex-cop stuff, right?"

He made a stern face at her. "A honed instinct is nothing to ignore."

"No, it's not." Especially when her witchy ones were telling her that Wyatt might be right. Newt was claiming that his presence would make the price go up, but that had still happened on the candlesticks without him there. Why not just go to the auction himself?

Wyatt nodded in agreement. "Hey, did you see a picture of the bookends?"

"No. He said he'd text one to me if I decided to go. Which I guess I basically have."

"Then text him and let's see for sure if they're the same ones my client wants me to buy."

"Okay." She got her phone out and sent Newt her confirmation.

He responded quickly and was apparently thrilled, if the six smiley face emojis were anything to judge by. The picture of the bookends came next.

She stared at them, shaking her head. "Why on earth anyone would want these is beyond me."

Wyatt pulled out his phone and brought up a picture. "Want to compare notes?"

She held her phone next to his. The same dark brown, bird-shaped bookends were in both photos.

He snorted. "What is that? A pelican?"

"I was going to say duck. Except the head is...not right."

"Yeah, the head is really off. You know, I don't think it's a duck or a pelican. It might not be a bird at all."

"Maybe it's a platypus." She laughed. "Or a beaver."

She held the phone in front of Frank. "What do you think, Franko? You're a bird expert."

Frank opened his eyes, glanced at the picture, and hissed.

Wyatt chuckled. "Your cat has better taste than our two bidders."

Leah came out from the back holding the centerpiece she'd been working on. "Marigold, do you want to have a look at this? See what you think?"

"Sure." Marigold studied it. "That's really close. It needs more, though. It needs to be a little looser. You know what I mean? A little wilder. More natural. More in keeping with the spirit of a backyard wedding."

Leah put the centerpiece on the counter, then stepped back from her creation. "I think it'll be wilder with the roses open more. A couple of days will help. Or you could—"

Marigold interrupted before Leah could complete the thought. "I'll work on it later. Just stick it in the cooler and go on to the next one." She gave Leah a look of warning. Leah must not realize that Wyatt was human. They couldn't very well go and use magic in front of him.

Leah frowned, then her eyes widened. "Gotcha." She scooped up the Mason jar bouquet and returned to the workroom.

Wyatt watched her go. "I thought it looked nice. But then, what do I know about flowers?"

"Thanks." Marigold patted the tall stool behind the register. "You're on duty as counterman. Think you can handle that?"

"I'll do my best. But is that really all you want me to do? Just sit there? I'm capable of a lot more."

"I appreciate your enthusiasm, but I don't have the time to train you to do arrangements."

"I was thinking more along the lines of sweeping. Or dusting. If you dust a floral shop. And I can still answer the phone."

Was he serious? He wanted to clean? "Um...sure. This place can always use sweeping. Or dusting. Or the windows washed. Shelves wiped down. Trash taken out. Coolers cleaned. Boxes broken down for recycling. Bathroom scrubbed."

He held his hands up. "Whoa now. I draw the line at toilet duty."

"Naturally." She grinned. "Come on, I'll show you where we keep the cleaning supplies."

Once she got him sweeping, and he was busy at the front of the store, she went back to the workroom and filled Leah in. "Wyatt's human. We can't use our magic in front of him."

"I figured it was something like that." Leah glanced toward where Wyatt was working. "Too bad. He's super cute. But I'm not into humans. I suppose you're not either."

Marigold didn't answer. Just smiled. In theory, no, she wouldn't choose a human partner on purpose. For any kind of supernatural, a human partner came with all kinds of extra complications. She had enough going on in her life without that. "Give me that arrangement. Let's see what we can do."

Leah's eyes brightened. "You got it." She pulled the centerpiece out of the cooler and set it in front of Marigold.

With a quick check that Wyatt was still up front, Marigold cupped her hands around the flowers and spilled magic into them, envisioning the kind of changes she wanted.

As her green magic twined around the stems in the arrangement, the blossoms opened, the ivy sent out a few wild tendrils, and leaves grew and curled. Thirty seconds of gentle, persuasive power and the arrangement went from sweet and staid to wild and gorgeous. Marigold pulled her hands away. "There."

"That is perfect."

It was good. And exactly what she wanted for Pandora's reception. "Think you can reproduce that?"

Leah shook her head. "I don't know. My nymph magic is better on trees than plants."

Marigold knew that was true. No one could get pussy willow or forsythia branches to sprout and bloom like Leah.

"But I can certainly get those centerpieces done, then you can add your touch and we'll be good to go."

"Teamwork makes the dream work." She winked at Leah.

"Wow, I see what you mean now. That one looks a lot better than the first one."

They both looked up to see Wyatt standing in the workroom door.

Marigold's stomach sank. How much had he seen? Couldn't have been much, right? Not if he thought this was a different arrangement. She swallowed and moved toward him. "Did you finish sweeping the floor already?"

"No, but there's a customer here who wants a single red rose."

She looked past him to see a young man at the counter. She hadn't even heard the bell above the door jangle or Wyatt talking to the customer, but then, using her magic often made everything else disappear for a few seconds. "Thanks, I'll take care of it."

Wyatt went back to sweeping while Marigold got the young man his flower. It was nice to have Wyatt's help, but she couldn't afford to be the reason a human discovered what was actually going on in Nocturne Falls.

The coven would kick her out.

Worse, the Ellinghams would not be happy. And the Ellinghams owned this town. It was because of them that Nocturne Falls even existed. Everything from Marigold's shop to her home to Saffron's attending Harmswood depended on this place.

She finished the transaction, and as the young man left, her gaze went to Wyatt. No matter how much she liked him, he was a normie. And until she was sure he was under the spell of the town's waters, she had to be very, very careful around him.

Or maybe she just shouldn't be around him at all.

Wyatt went back to his spot near the front of the shop. He'd swept this area twice now, but it gave him a good view of the street. If those guys from the parking lot were going to come back, he'd see them before they saw him. Or got to Marigold.

It also gave him a perfect place to watch her. From here, he could see the counter and through the door into the workroom. He shifted toward the street again, taking a few moments to think while he swept. He worked the broom with short strokes, not gathering much more into the pile he'd already made.

He might be partially deaf, but his eyesight was perfect. Even so, he wasn't sure what he'd just seen going on in that workroom. Had those flowers really been growing under Marigold's touch? How was that possible?

It wasn't. He knew that. Just like the scrapes on her arm and hand that had healed overnight.

Neither of those things made sense. And neither of them could be explained. Not immediately.

But being a cop had taught him there was *always* an explanation.

So what was it? He worked his way to the back corner of the shop. Maybe the scrapes hadn't been as bad as he'd thought. Even though he'd seen them up close, blood made things look worse a lot of times. He frowned, not buying his own best reason.

How did he explain the flowers?

He couldn't.

Something touched his shoulder. He whipped around, instinct putting him on guard.

It was Marigold. He took a breath, realizing his reaction was a little more than what the situation called for.

"You okay? I called your name a couple times."

"I....must not have heard you." If she'd been on his deaf side, he definitely hadn't heard her, but he didn't want to tell her he couldn't hear on that side. It was a weakness. His weakness. And he didn't like to talk about it. "Need something else cleaned?"

"No, I was just thinking." She tugged at her apron, even though it was already in place.

When she didn't immediately say more, he prompted her. "Are you going to tell me what about?"

She smiled a little, but it didn't reach her eyes. "I'm not sure this is a good idea. You working here, I mean."

That felt like it was out of left field. "Did I do something wrong with that customer?"

"No, it's not that." Again, she hesitated.

"Then what is it?"

She frowned, hemmed and hawed a little, then sighed. "You know what? We should go to lunch."

That wasn't at all what he'd expected to hear, but he wasn't about to turn down a meal with her. "Sure."

"Good." She seemed more sure of herself suddenly. "I know just the place."

Howler's was busy, but since it was a little early for lunch yet, Marigold had no trouble snagging them a booth. That was good. Booths were more private. At least they felt that way to her. And while she needed to get some more local water into Wyatt (she couldn't count on the coffee from Mummy's being enough), she didn't exactly want to put their lunch date, such as it was, on display. So yeah, a booth was good.

They settled in and got their menus. For once, Bridget Merrow, owner of Howler's and Charlie's aunt, wasn't behind the bar. Maybe she was just in the back.

"What's good here?" Wyatt asked.

"Everything," Marigold answered. She'd be getting a salad, regardless of the day's special. She hadn't planned on eating out at all, but when she'd chickened out on telling Wyatt she didn't want him in the shop anymore (because she did want him there, actually) making sure he drank some good old Nocturne Falls H2O seemed like the next best thing. And Howler's made a great salad.

And great peach cobbler. Which she would not be eating.

She would, however, be getting some water into him. At least that way, she could keep him around.

A server came by. The woman's name tag read Jolie. Marigold didn't recognize her. "I'm Jolie and I'll be taking care of you guys today. What can I get you guys to drink?"

"Water for me." Marigold responded with enough enthusiasm so that Wyatt would want water too. She hoped.

"Do you have ginger ale?" Wyatt asked.

Marigold ground her teeth together in frustration.

Jolie nodded. "We have a full bar."

"Then I'll have a ginger ale."

Jolie gave them a smile. "I'll be right back with your drinks and to take your order. Oh, and today's special is pot roast with mashed potatoes and green beans."

Wyatt gave her a big smile back. "Thanks."

As Jolie left, Marigold stared over her menu at Wyatt. "Don't believe in hydrating?"

He moved his menu to the side to see her better. "Hydrating?"

"Don't you drink water?"

He blinked twice. "Sure, I guess so."

"I mean, it's your body after all, but soda is loaded with sugar. Just saying." She went back to her menu, even though she knew what she was ordering.

"So was that cinnamon bun you scarfed down." He snorted.

She looked at him again. "I only ate half of that."

He smirked. "I can tell you're a mom."

"Why? Because I told you to drink water?"

"Instead of soda? Yes. It's a very mom thing to do."

Jolie came back with one water and one ginger ale.

Wyatt smiled up at the woman. "I'll have a water too, when you get a chance. I've been told I look parched."

Marigold frowned at him. "I did not say that."

Mischief sparkled in his eyes. He was enjoying this. So let him, if it got him to drink some water.

Jolie pulled out a notepad. "You got it. Do you know what you'd like to eat?"

Wyatt looked at Marigold. "Go ahead."

"I'll have the garden salad with grilled chicken. Vinaigrette on the side."

Jolie made a note of that, then went back to Wyatt. "And for you?"

"I'll have the pot roast special."

"Perfect. Gravy on your mashed potatoes?"

"Yes."

"You got it." She took their menus and went off to ring their order in.

Wyatt leaned forward. "Garden salad? Grilled chicken? Are you on a diet all of a sudden?"

"I've *been* on a diet. That cinnamon bun was nice, but not on it. I have a bridesmaid dress to fit into."

He ran a quick, appraising gaze over her. "That explains the water, but you don't need to diet. You look good the way you are." One of his brows rose, and he mumbled, "Better than good."

She wasn't sure if she was supposed to hear that last bit, but parts of her got a little toasty in a way they hadn't in a long while. "Thank you, that's very kind. But Pandy picked out strapless dresses that are a little body conscious, and I'd like to look my best."

"Pandy?"

"Pandora. My sister."

He sighed. "Well, you look any better than you do now and the groom might think he picked the wrong sister."

Now she was well and truly blushing. Her cheeks were as warm as if the sun was shining down on her. She dipped her chin, causing her hair to fall around her face. "Cole is absolutely dedicated to my sister. He would never think such a thing."

"I'm sure he wouldn't. I'm sure he's a tremendous guy. But you *are* a very attractive woman, Marigold."

Where was all this coming from? It was nice, but not something she was used to hearing, and it was throwing her. She was about to start fanning herself with the menu.

Thankfully, Jolie came back with his water.

Marigold quickly grabbed her glass and raised it. "To new friends." It was the only thing she could think of, but it was a pretty weak toast.

He raised his glass of water and clinked it against hers. "To new friends."

Then, finally, he drank.

One sip.

He put his glass down, peeled the paper off his straw, and stuck it into his soda.

So much for that.

She sighed. She might have to cast some kind of spell on him. The coven frowned on that, though. But if it was for the sake of the town, she could probably get a pass. She couldn't have him discovering that Nocturne Falls was full of supernaturals.

"What should I wear to the wedding? In all seriousness."

The wedding! She almost fell out of her seat. It would be *full* of supernaturals. In fact, Wyatt and Alex Cruz's girlfriend might be the only humans there, and Roxy wasn't technically a hundred percent human anymore. Not thanks to the special magic that had been created to allow her to shift into a panther like Alex could.

Crap. Crap. Crap. This was not good. In fact, it stank like the water in a vase where the flowers had been left to rot.

"Paging Marigold, are you with me, Marigold?"

She looked at him, once again cursing his handsomeness for making her stupid. "Sorry, yes. Just lots of wedding stuff on my mind." Which was absolutely the truth.

"I'm sure there is. I was just asking what you think I should wear."

"Do you have nice pants, a dress shirt, and a sport coat? I think that would be appropriate."

"No sport coat." He paused. "No dress shirt and nice pants, really, either. But I'm happy to buy some things. Can you direct me to a shop?"

"Men's clothing isn't really my specialty. But I'll ask my mom. If anyone knows, it's her. She owns the bridal boutique in town."

"Wow, you're the florist, and she owns the wedding-dress shop? You guys have the wedding biz sown up in this town, huh? Anyone else in the family a caterer? A minister, maybe?"

She laughed. "No, but Pandora is a real estate agent, so she can get the happy couple a starter home, no problem."

"Nice." He sipped his dumb ginger ale again. "How did you get to be a florist?"

She couldn't exactly tell him she was a green witch and it was a natural fit, but working as close to the truth as she could seemed best. "I've just always had a green thumb. Always loved plants and flowers and herbs and learning about them. Seemed like the way to go."

He nodded. "Did you ever consider being a flower grower? If you have a green thumb, that would have been a way to go, too."

She grinned. "All of the potted herbs and plants I sell in the store I grow myself. Even the exotic stuff. I have a small greenhouse in my backyard."

"Really? That's impressive. Again, I know nothing about plants, but the stuff in your shop looks almost unnaturally good." He made a sad face. "I had a plant once."

"Let me guess, you killed it?"

He laughed. "Did you know a plant can lose all of its leaves in less than twenty-four hours?"

"Sounds like overwatering."

"Well, it sure wasn't from underwatering. And hey, at least I tried."

Jolie returned with their food, which looked delicious. She put their plates in front of them, then left them to eat.

Marigold was happy for the interruption. As much as she liked talking about plants, it was too close to who she was. She was afraid she'd slip up and say something witchy. When your mom and your sisters were witches, that kind of talk just came natural. But that side of her wasn't something Wyatt could find out about.

Turnabout was fair play. She drizzled the vinaigrette over her salad. "How did you become a cop?"

He shrugged. "I liked the idea of helping people. And it was a way out. When I was a kid, I—never mind. That's not important."

"No, tell me. What were you going to say?" She really wanted to know what he'd needed a way out of, too. It made her curious about what his childhood had been like.

He poked at his food for a few long moments, making her think he wasn't going to answer. Then he spoke. "I was raised in foster care. It was sometimes okay and sometimes—a lot of times—not. The feeling of not belonging was always there."

Foster care. The poor guy. She didn't say anything, just nodded, hoping he'd continue.

He glanced at her, then went back to his plate. "A police officer came to talk to our school for career day one time."

Things were starting to make sense now. Her mother's heart hurt for him. Being in the system had to have been so hard. It also meant he'd lost his parents somehow. That made Saffie's life seem extra blessed. She might have only one parent, but she had lots of other family.

Wyatt's gaze grew distant and his fork stopped moving. "He looked like a superhero in his uniform. And everyone—the teachers, the other parents there, the kids—they all looked up to him and treated him with respect. He talked about how the force was a family. How the men and women treated each other as brothers and sisters, and how they looked out for each other."

She nodded, completely understanding. "And you wanted that."

"A family? Hell yes, I wanted that. I got to talk to him after class, and it changed the direction of my life. I worked harder in school, got my grades up, and eventually went to college. I got a degree in criminology. As soon as I graduated, I joined the force."

"Was it everything you'd hoped?"

He smiled, finally looking up from his plate. "It was. It was also harder than I'd imagined, but worth it. I loved being a cop. I made detective in less than ten years. And that was amazing, too."

She could picture him in a uniform. Very handsome. Not surprisingly. "You know, when I first sat next to you at the auction, I thought you might have been a cop."

"You did?" He laughed. "It'll always be a part of me, I suppose."

She mustered the courage to ask the question she really wanted an answer to. "So why aren't you a cop anymore?"

His smile disappeared, and a sad, almost angry look came over his face.

She dug into her salad, feeling bad that she'd made him uncomfortable after he'd just shared such personal history with her. "You know what? It's not my business. Forget I asked. How's your pot roast?"

He sat there, fork in hand, not moving for about four seconds. Then he put his fork down and looked at her. "There was an accident. My gun misfired. I got a couple of powder burns, but I also lost the hearing in my left ear."

She sucked in a breath. "That's terrible."

He nodded. "I thought I could come back. That it wouldn't be a big deal. But it was. I'm not as sharp as I used to be, and that's not a good thing for someone who carries a gun." He cleared his throat. "Carried."

Again, she hurt for him. It must have been a huge loss. After everything he'd told her about how being a cop had changed his life, not being one must have changed it too. "I'm so sorry."

He took his fork up again and dug into his food. "Don't feel sorry for me. I don't like that."

She didn't know how to respond to that, but she tried anyway. "I'm not pitying you. But I don't see why it would bother you that I feel sorry you lost the job you loved."

"Being a private detective is fine." He smiled the fakest smiled she'd ever seen.

She reared back. "Okay, that's horrifying."

His eyes widened. "What?"

"Your pretend smile." She shook her head and stabbed a piece of cucumber. "You should never do that again."

He laughed, a sound she was very happy to hear. "I'll remember that. Sorry to have frightened you."

"It's okay, I'll recover."

They ate a little bit in silence, then he spoke again. "I sounded harsh earlier. I didn't mean to. I'm sorry. The accident is still a pretty sensitive subject for me. Obviously."

Something, maybe her mothering instinct, maybe her general concern for people, made her reach out and grab his hand. "It's okay. I get it. Life is hard sometimes. Don't worry about how you reacted. It's understandable."

"But it wasn't nice." He turned his hand over so he could squeeze hers back. He had a nice grip and slightly callused palms. "Thanks, though. You're all right, you know that?"

She smiled. "Even for someone who thinks you don't drink enough water?"

"Yes, dear." He laughed and picked up his glass to take a big sip. "Better?"

"Better." She kept smiling, even though he was patronizing her. As long as he was drinking the water, she didn't care.

She'd much rather have him around than have to wipe his mind clean with a spell and cause him to forget all about her.

Her skin was velvety soft, and that surprised him. He turned her palm over to inspect it more closely. "How do you do that?"

"Do what?"

"Keep your hands so soft when you work with flowers and plants? You said you had a greenhouse. You can't tell me that doesn't involve dirt under your fingernails."

She laughed, slipping her hand out of his. "I wash!"

"But how do you not have rough spots? Or is that an indelicate thing to ask a lady?" Before she could answer, he turned his own palms upright. "Look, I have calluses, and that's just from time in the gym."

She tipped her head, her mouth bending in a coy smile that told him she was both flattered and a little embarrassed. "I wear gloves. And I use a very good hand lotion."

"I'll say." He wanted to hold her hand again. Especially now that she was blushing. The pink in her cheeks was charming beyond description. She was like a drug he knew he should stay away from for his own good, but couldn't.

So be it. There were much worse things to be addicted to.

Plus, he *wanted* more. Of her. But that would be leading her on, wouldn't it? Because this was never going to go anywhere. He was never going to marry her. Which wasn't anything against her. He was never going to marry anyone. Just like he was never going to have kids. The world had too many of those already and not enough families for them all.

And he imagined that a woman with a child was most likely looking for something long term. Marigold clearly didn't need a man to take care of her, nor did she seem to want one, but she must be thinking about a stepdad for the little one. He didn't blame her. He applauded her really, for wanting to provide that for her child.

Of all people, Wyatt knew what it meant to grow up without parents who cared. How hard that could be around holidays and school events and…all the time, really.

But he wasn't about to discuss that with her, so he changed the subject. Mostly to distance himself from the distracting thoughts she put in his head, but also to keep the conversation from turning back to him and his sad past. "How did you end up going to that auction for Newt in the first place?"

"Newt comes into the flower shop all the time when he's in town. And when he asked me, he also offered to pay me, just like he did this second time."

Wyatt thought a few beats, his detective brain always rolling through possibilities. "The first time I saw him, he had a red carnation in his lapel. He got that from you, didn't he?"

She nodded. "Yes. And I'm surprised you knew the name of that flower."

He narrowed his eyes at her. "I'm not a complete Philistine."

The light in her eyes said she was on the verge of laughter. "Jury's still out on that one."

He gaped at her in mock injury. "What have I done now?"

Her gaze went to his soda. "You do like your sugary drinks…"

He picked up his water and downed half the glass, then wiped his mouth with the back of his hand. "Better?"

She laughed. "Yes. Don't you feel better?"

He went back to his pot roast, shaking his head. He wasn't sure what her thing was with water, but if it made her happy, whatever. He forked up some mashed potatoes. "Tell me about your kid."

"Why?"

At her strange tone, he looked up. Her eyes were a little wide, and all trace of amusement was gone. "Just making conversation. If you don't want to talk about him, that's fine with me."

"Her." Marigold picked up her fork. "I don't usually involve my daughter in any of my... personal relationships until I know they're going somewhere."

He understood that. And respected it. No point in getting the kid to like a guy who wasn't going to be around for long. "But won't I meet her at the wedding?"

Marigold chewed a bite of chicken, then drank a little water. Finally, she answered. "Yes, you will." Then she sighed. "Maybe you shouldn't go after all."

"You could just tell her I'm an old friend. She doesn't need to know anything more than that."

She flicked her eyes at him before digging through her salad for a hunk of tomato. "I don't make a practice of lying to my child."

He smiled.

"What?" Her tone was laced with defensiveness.

He shook his head. "I like your parenting style."

A hint of confusion clouded her gaze. "You do?"

"Sure. Protect the kid, but be honest with her. If more parents did that, this world might be a different place."

She relaxed, making him realize she'd stiffened up. "It's hard."

"I'm sure it is. I can't imagine what it's like to be a single parent. Or just a parent."

"Don't you want kids of your own?"

He grunted softly. "No."

Her brows shot up. "Really?"

"Really. No reason for me to bring more kids into this world when there are plenty of them out there already who need homes."

She nodded slowly. "You're right about that."

Jolie came back with a water pitcher and refilled their glasses. "You guys need anything? Are you saving room for dessert? There's a fresh peach cobbler just out of the oven back there."

"That sounds—" Wyatt glanced at Marigold. "Terrible. Nope, no dessert here."

Marigold laughed. "If you want peach cobbler, have some. It's amazing."

"No, that would be unkind of me with you dieting." He glanced at Jolie. "I'll be back for that when I'm alone."

Marigold snorted. "Make sure he has a glass of water with that when he does."

Wyatt shook his head. "Just the check, please."

Jolie nodded. "You got it."

Marigold dug her credit card out.

"Put that away."

She looked at him. "I'm not paying for the whole thing. We're going Dutch."

"No, we're not. This is my treat."

"This isn't a date."

Wasn't it, though? He shrugged. "I don't care what it is, I'm buying."

"Wyatt, you're already helping me out at the shop."

So help him, he loved the sound of his name on her lips. He'd probably love his lips on her lips too. Okay, that line of thinking was going to cause him to make bad decisions. "No arguing. It's done. The client I'm working for is paying me very well for doing very little. So please, my treat."

"Okay." There was still some reluctance in her voice. And she was frowning at him.

He imagined it was the same look she gave her daughter when the kid misbehaved. It scared him a little that he found it rather sexy. "I guess I'll get the rest of the shop swept up when we get back."

"Actually, you should probably go buy that sport coat." She got her phone out. "Let me text my mom real quick and ask her where you should go."

While she did that, Jolie returned with the bill. Wyatt handed her his credit card and she left again.

Marigold was concentrating on her phone. "Okay, my mom says Guildman's on Main and South. How did I not think of that? Guildman's is right by my mom's shop. Anyway, they're having a private sale. Just say you're a guest going to the Williams-Van Zant wedding, and they'll give you twenty percent off."

"Sounds good."

She looked up. "That is a pretty sweet deal."

"It is. I'll head down there and take care of it as soon as we leave. And you point me in the right direction. Or should I drive?"

"No, it's walkable."

Jolie returned with the check. He added a nice tip, signed it, and grabbed his card. "All right, I'm ready if you are."

"Sure." She slid halfway out of the booth, then stopped. "Hang on." She picked up her glass of water and started drinking, her eyes on him the whole time.

"All right, I get it." He picked his glass up and took a drink too. Women. Amazing how the crazy didn't bother him when they were so drop-dead beautiful.

Marigold pointed Wyatt toward Guildman's, then headed in the opposite direction to the flower shop. She walked faster than she might have if Wyatt had been with her. No slow, leisurely stroll. She needed to make the best use of his time out of the store to work on magically enhancing whatever work Leah had finished.

But when she got into the shop, Leah was behind the counter ringing up a man buying a birthday bouquet complete with a big Mylar balloon. She nodded at Marigold. "Nice lunch?"

"Nice lunch."

The man headed for the door with his goodies. Marigold tipped her head toward the back. "How many centerpieces did you get done?"

"One and a half." Leah smiled apologetically. "It's been busy."

"That's okay. Busy is good."

"Thanks again," Leah called after the customer. Then she shrugged at Marigold. "I really thought I'd get more finished."

"We'll get them done."

Leah looked past Marigold. "What did you do with Wyatt?"

"He went to buy some clothes for the wedding. I'm guessing we have forty-five minutes or so to do whatever magical stuff we need to, but then we'll just spend the rest of the day working on getting those centerpieces done. Then I can do my thing to them tomorrow morning when I get in."

Leah pulled up a screen on the counter computer. "We also have a dozen red roses, another birthday bouquet, two get wells, and a thinking of you. Plus, Mrs. Duncan ordered sixteen pink happy birthday balloons. All of which have to go out tomorrow."

"We'll do them, no problem. Has Joe been in for deliveries?"

Leah bit her lip. "About that. No. He called and said he'd be late because the van got a flat."

Marigold sighed, but kept a smile on her face. "When it rains, it pours."

The bell over the door jangled. She turned to see who it was and almost lost that smile. "Newt. How are you?"

"Not well, not well. We must talk."

She glanced at Leah. "See if you can knock out that other half of the centerpiece. I've got this."

Leah gave her a thumbs-up. "Got it." And went off to the workroom.

Marigold met Newt in the middle of the shop. "What's going on? You seem upset."

"There are dark forces at work, my dear. Dark forces."

Marigold reacted as appropriately as she could, but the truth was, wizards were known for their dramatic flair, and Newt was no different. "Why? What's happening?"

He looked around like someone might be listening in, but the only other person in the shop beside him, Marigold, and Leah was Frank. And he technically wasn't a person, despite what he thought.

Newt spread his hands for extra emphasis. "The spirits have contacted me."

"Mm-hmm." Also like a lot of wizards, Newt believed he had connections in the afterlife. Now Pandora, on the other hand, had an *actual* ghost living in her attic, but hey, to each their own. "What did they tell you?"

His eyes grew gravely serious. "That you're in danger, my dear. Well, perhaps not you. But possibly your sweet child. There is an agent at work against you. An agent in league with the man you never thought you'd see again. They want to take her away from you."

A chill shot down her spine, and a shiver ran through her before she could stop it. "What are you talking about?"

He shrugged. "That's all the spirits told me. But I had to warn you. I do hope you'll be careful. This agent could be anyone. But whoever he—or she, I suppose—is, they mean business."

"Thank you for telling me." She nodded, numbed by the thought that was her secret fear. The deep, dark terror that woke her up at night.

Saffron's father had changed his mind.

11

Guildman's was a nice store with nice things.

The clothes ranged from funky hipster to English gentleman, which surprised Wyatt, because from the look of the outside, he'd expected it to be more…retired dude who golfed and dined at the country club. Sure, the place had those kinds of clothes, but they had a lot more, too. And from what he could see, everything on display was *sharp*.

"Hello there, son."

Wyatt looked around to see who the deep voice had come from.

A couple racks away stood a large man with graying hair and goatee. He was built like a retired linebacker. Burly, but also kindly. Like a grandfather. If Wyatt had had a grandfather to compare him to.

Linebacker. *Guildman's*. Suddenly, it hit Wyatt. "Are you Dexter Guildman? The Wrecking Machine?"

The man smiled. "Yep, that's me." He folded his hands in front of him. "Don't get called that much these days."

The Wrecking Machine had been an integral part of the Atlanta Thrashers in the early nineties. He'd gone to three Super Bowls with them and come home with two championship rings. Wyatt realized he was about to have a fanboy moment. "You're one of football's greats. You're a legend."

Dexter gave a little shrug. "Not so many people know me now. But that's all right. Life is good. Now, what can I help you with?"

Wyatt stuck his hand out. "First, I have to shake your hand. I was a big fan of the Thrashers. Still am. But you were one of my heroes growing up." No matter what home he'd been placed in, he usually got to watch football. And Dexter Guildman had been one of his favorites to watch.

Dexter shook his hand. "You're all right, son. What's your name?"

"Wyatt West. If you don't mind me asking, what are you doing in this town?"

"Nice to meet you, Wyatt. I retired here. My granddaughter goes to Harmswood Academy." He smiled. "Gotta be near my grandbaby. Now, what can I do for you?"

"You know, makes sense you own a shop like this. You always were a sharp dresser. I guess that means I came to the right place. I'm going to the

Williams-Van Zant wedding, and to up the ante, I'm Marigold Williams's date."

Dexter whistled. "You have *got* to be on point."

"You're right. I do." The plan of just getting the bare minimum changed. Wyatt needed to impress Marigold. And her daughter. And the rest of her family. He also wasn't going to walk away from an opportunity to have Dexter Guildman help him pick something out.

Dexter stroked his goatee as he made a slow circle around Wyatt. He paused. "You know, you have a little undercover vibe going on. Not sure if you're aware of that."

Wyatt laughed. "That's because I was undercover. And in uniform. But I'm retired from the police force. I'm a PI now."

Dexter's brows rose. "Is that right? Are you packing?"

Wyatt held his hands up. "No, not anymore."

"All right. Just trying to figure if we need room for a holster." He narrowed his eyes and studied Wyatt some more. "You and Marigold…is that a new thing?"

"Very."

"Uh-huh, I see." He stroked the goatee a little more. "I think I have just the thing."

Almost an hour later, Wyatt had a new friend and a new suit. Tan in a linen-silk blend with a pale lilac shirt underneath. He had a new belt and shoes, too. Dexter had thrown in a casual, cotton pocket square he promised would take the look up a notch.

Wyatt had to admit he'd never worn lilac in his life, but he'd never looked this good before either. He handed over his credit card, not caring how much it was going to scream even with the wedding discount. "Thank you for your help. I feel a lot more confident about the event now."

Dexter smiled. "Then my job is done. Well, it will be after my tailor makes those final adjustments. You're going to look sharp, my friend."

"I'll be back Friday morning to pick everything up."

"We'll be ready." He ran the card through, then handed it back.

Wyatt tucked it away in his wallet. "I have to say, I've never worn a lilac shirt before. It looks good. And I trust you. Just new ground for me."

A spark lit Dexter's eyes. "You want to impress Marigold and her mama? Then that shirt is how to do it. It's the exact shade of her bridesmaid dress."

"Are you sure? I could have sworn she told me there were three colors of bridesmaid dresses. And she didn't tell me which one she's wearing."

Dexter tilted his head toward the shop window and the other side of the street. "See that bridal boutique over there? Corette Williams owns that.

She's the girls' mother. Trust me when I tell you I know what color Marigold is wearing."

Wyatt's brows shot up. "That's impressive. You're like the secret agent of fashion."

Dexter laughed and extended his hand. "You're all right, man. You come back here any time, you hear?"

"Thanks again, I will. See you Friday." After the handshake, Wyatt left. He was smiling and feeling remarkably good about himself. He'd never paid much attention to clothes. Being in uniform had meant he hadn't thought about them much for a big part of his life. Being a detective meant he'd switched to a different kind of uniform. Jeans and a button-down and a black leather jacket.

But Dexter was right. Wyatt was going to look sharp on Saturday night.

He took his phone out to make sure he hadn't missed anything. He hadn't. That was good.

When he looked up, he was staring across the street. Straight at the Ever After bridal shop sign. He looked both ways and crossed, unable to stop himself from walking in.

The place was exactly like what he imagined a bridal shop would be, not that he'd spent much time imagining such a thing, but he had handled a case once where a bride had stabbed one of her bridesmaids to death with a stiletto. The Bridezilla Murder, they'd called it.

He shook his head, in that moment not missing the force quite as much.

"Can I help you?"

A handsome older woman in a pink suit greeted him. She had the same smile as Marigold. The same sparkle in her eyes.

He was momentarily struck dumb. Why had he come in here?

She continued to smile at him. "Are you looking for someone? Or something? Need a tuxedo?"

"I...no, I was just..." He cleared his throat. "I'm your daughter's date for the wedding. I just thought I'd come introduce myself."

For the briefest of moments, a look of shock passed over her face. Then she composed herself. "You must be Paolo Mardini. Charisma has told me all about you. How lovely to finally meet you."

"No, I'm Wyatt West. And I'm Marigold's date."

The look of shock returned. "Marigold has a date?"

He stuck his hands in his pockets and grinned. "Yes, ma'am. Me. Lovely shop you have here."

"Thank you." She straightened a little, which seemed impossible, given her already perfect posture. "I apologize for my reaction, but Marigold..."

"Doesn't date much, does she?"

"No, she doesn't." She put a hand to her throat and smiled. "I'm Corette, her mother, as you must already know. How kind of you to stop by and introduce yourself."

"It's very nice to meet you, Ms. Williams."

"Please, call me Corette. We're all adults here."

He heard giggling and realized there were customers in the store. "I don't want to interrupt your day. I'm sure you're busy. I have to get back."

"Oh? Where do you work?"

"I'm actually helping Marigold out at the shop."

She laughed softly, like she was pleased, not like he'd suddenly become the punchline. "That is so sweet of you. I'm always telling her she should hire more help."

He shrugged. "I don't mind. I don't have anything else to do."

She lifted her chin, and the tiniest bit of concern came into her eyes. "Are you unemployed, Wyatt?"

"No, ma'am. I just...I'm a private detective and I have a lot of downtime."

Her smile returned. "I see. Well, how very nice of you to give Marigold some of that time."

More giggling came from the back of the shop.

Corette glanced that way. "If you'll excuse me, I should check on my bride. I'll see you Friday night at the rehearsal dinner, then?"

"I'm...not sure. I'm just a date. I didn't think dates went to those, just family."

"Dates can come. If they're invited. And Jack Van Zant might be paying for it, but I'm inviting you. See you then."

"I guess you will." He watched her go. She was a beautiful woman and somewhat intimidating, which was saying something. It took a lot to intimidate a former homicide detective.

He stepped outside and sighed up at the Guildman's sign. Then he shook his head and went across the street.

Good thing Dexter had said come back anytime. Wyatt had no idea what to wear to a rehearsal dinner.

By the time Wyatt was on his way back to the flower shop, he'd spent more on clothing in Guildman's than he had since he'd retired from the force. It felt like a worthy cause, though, and he knew he was going to look good for Marigold. That mattered.

More than he'd expected it to.

But he wanted Marigold to think he looked nice, and not to be embarrassed by him in any way in front of her family. And if he was being very, very honest, he desperately wanted her family to like him.

He walked at a quick pace, covering the distance to the shop with his long, easy strides while he thought about what was going on.

The truth was, he wanted to be a part of a family like hers. A family that cared for each other and did things for each other and made each other a priority.

He couldn't imagine what it would be like to be a part of a clan like that, but from the small glimpses he'd already had of the Williamses, it was something special.

And it filled him with a longing that made him ache in a way he hadn't since he'd been in foster care. It was a soul-deep kind of yearning that stuck in him like a dull pain. If he thought about it too much, about that hole inside of him that had never quite been filled, then the edges of his world started to cave in.

Darkness lived in that empty place. Darkness that had never been diminished by the right kind of light. And if he let himself dwell on it, he would very quickly come to a place where everything was *not* all right.

Buying those clothes was an attempt to make him seem like the right kind of man for Marigold. The kind her family would embrace.

He stopped cold on the sidewalk, almost causing a woman to run into him.

She scowled at him. "Watch where you're going," she muttered as she walked around him.

"I'm trying," he answered. Where was he going? What was he thinking? He didn't want to get married. Didn't want to be involved with a woman with a kid. He wasn't equipped for that. He was screwed up when it came to personal relationships. Foster care had seen to that. People left. People lied. People were awful.

But Marigold wasn't. She was kind and sweet and patient and strong and funny.

So why would she want a guy like him?

She wouldn't, the dark place said.

Or would she? What if he told her what a mess he was? Told her he was willing to try? Maybe she'd be...he snorted. He was an idiot. No woman wanted a project. Especially not right before her sister's wedding.

At most, Marigold wanted a nice guy to keep her company at the reception. To make sure her family didn't try to set her up with anyone.

That was proof right there she didn't want a guy, wasn't it? Otherwise, wouldn't she let her family, who loved her and knew her best, introduce her to the men they thought she might like?

He shook his head. A pretty face had turned his brain into yearning, pitiful mush. What a sad, lonely—he sighed. Enough.

He started walking again. He could see the shop's sign from here. Marigold wanted a nice guy for the wedding, she was going to get a nice guy. He'd be polite and charming and the perfect date.

Then he'd be the other thing she wanted.

Gone.

Marigold hadn't told Leah what Newt had said, and she didn't plan to. Not yet anyway. When she got home, she'd do some scrying for herself. It was one of her special witchy gifts, and although it wore her out, it might help her determine if Newt was telling the truth.

It might also help her see who this agent was.

Because the only possible agent that she could think of was Wyatt. She didn't like thinking such awful things about him, nor did she like giving Newt's terrible warning any real credence until she had proof. But still...how much did she know about Wyatt?

She'd originally thought their meeting was a setup by her sisters. Now she had to wonder if it hadn't happened because someone else had put it together.

Someone like Saffron's biological father.

But why would he suddenly be interested in the child he'd walked away from? They hadn't been in contact since that day. She didn't even know where Tim was. She had no reason to keep tabs on him.

He'd made his thoughts on her pregnancy clear. He wanted nothing to do with getting married or being a father. If Marigold kept the baby, it was going to be her responsibility.

Could he have changed his mind? Did he suddenly want to get a hold of Saffron before she came into her powers? Why would he want that?

The thought caused a small amount of panic. She didn't want to put so much emphasis on Newt's words when she had no idea if there was any truth to them, but her first instinct was always to protect Saffie. That made Newt's warning, no matter how crazy, impossible to ignore. She needed to know more about Wyatt without him knowing she was digging.

And in this town, there was only one real resource for that kind of work.

But it might not be an issue if Wyatt had decided he wasn't interested in helping out anymore. He'd been gone a long time. Maybe he knew his cover had been blown. But how would he know that? And why was she paying so much attention to Newt's drama?

Because of Saffie, that was why.

Marigold took a breath. She had too much work to do to get wrapped up in speculation right now.

At the sound of the bell, she peeked through the workroom door to greet the customer who'd walked in. But it was Wyatt. At last. She smiled. She had a hard time believing he was out to do Saffron any harm. He hadn't pushed to meet her. And he was a former cop and a current PI. If he wanted to get his hands on Saffron, he would have done it by now. "Hey there. I was starting to think you'd run away."

He laughed, his smile easy as he strolled in. "I just needed more clothes than I realized. Sorry for leaving the counter unattended for so long. I'll understand if you dock my pay."

She snorted and came out to meet him. It was hard to think bad thoughts about Wyatt. He just seemed so nice. This guy couldn't be out to ruin her life, could he? "No, I think I'll keep paying you exactly what I've been paying you."

"Good, because I'm pretty sure I just spent it all anyway." He winked, which sent a little thrill through her she refused to pay much attention to. "What can I do to help?"

She hesitated. Subterfuge was not one of her great strengths. "There is something you could do for me. For the shop, I mean."

"Anything. What'll it be?"

"I need a bouquet delivered."

His eyes narrowed. "You trust me to do that even though I don't know the town very well?"

"You can use your map app if you need to."

He rubbed his hands together. "Okay, where am I going?"

She pursed her lips. He was so *eager* to help. "You're sure you want to do this?"

He nodded. "Absolutely. It'll be fun. Hey, do I get to keep the tip?"

She laughed, amused despite her misgivings. "Sure. If there is one. Let me get the bouquet."

He drummed his fingers on the counter while she went back into one of the coolers and got the arrangement she'd whipped up. This might be the silliest thing she'd done. Or the smartest. Only time would tell.

She'd already wiped the vase down when she'd put it in the cooler. Now as she removed the bouquet, she was careful to hold it by the neck as she carried it out. She offered it to Wyatt. "Here you go."

He took hold of the body of the vase, just as she'd hoped. "Very pretty. And where's it going?"

"You probably won't need your map at all. Just go out to Main Street and head back the way you came. Past the Main Street park with the fountain, past Guildman's, and a few more blocks after that. You'll see the Nocturne Falls Sheriff Department. These are for the receptionist, Birdie Caruthers."

He gave her a nod. "I can handle that." He started for the door. "I'll be back as soon as these are delivered."

"Take your time. I don't want you to drop them."

He backed through the door. "I won't."

"Good," she said, even though the door was closing and he was well out of earshot. "Because I need Birdie to run your fingerprints."

Wyatt had been on Main Street enough now that it was starting to feel comfortable. He paid less attention to where he was going and more attention to the shops and people around him. This town continued to entertain him. The people were the most interesting, though. Every once in a while, he'd pass one of the crazy character actors who were part of the town's Halloween theme.

The one that caught his eye today was a witch. It seemed curious to him that while she was wearing a flowy purple dress and a pointed hat, which seemed pretty witchy, she hadn't opted for the phony hooked nose or a press-on hairy wart. He liked that, actually. Made her seem more real.

If there were such a thing as witches, he was sure they wouldn't go around looking like they'd just stepped out of a story meant to scare children.

He slowed as he walked by the young witch. A group of tourists clustered around her while she made a coin float in midair. He shook his head and smiled. Now that was a magic trick he'd like to learn. Had to be clear fishing line. Maybe connected to her hat.

He couldn't see how she was doing it, making the trick that much more convincing. Really added to the whole magic thing going on. But there had to be an explanation that wasn't witchcraft. Because there was an explanation for everything.

That was just how life worked.

Even though he still hadn't figured out how Marigold had made those flowers grow in the centerpiece. He looked down at the vase in his hands and gave them a little shake. No, that didn't look like they were growing. Just shaking. Very different.

And why would she shake the flowers anyway?

The only thing that really would explain what he'd seen was, well, witchcraft. He laughed. That was crazy. And probably the influence of this town and all its theatrical put-ons. He snorted. No way was Marigold a witch. Witches weren't real. Not in the magical sense of the word.

He kept walking and thinking. About Marigold and her growing flowers. About how she'd healed so fast. And how she had a black cat.

But those were all just coincidences.

A minivan drove past with a bumper sticker on it that read, "My other car is a broom."

It was just this town. All the woo-woo nonsense was leaking into his brain.

A man in a black silk cape strolled by and smiled, revealing fangs.

Wyatt did his best not to stare, but turned at the last moment to get a second look. The man had stopped to take pictures with some of the tourists.

Wyatt stood there for a moment. Wasn't there something about vampires not showing up in pictures? Or was that mirrors? Or both.

Oy. Why was he even thinking about vampires? That guy wasn't a vampire, he was an actor. For one thing, vampires couldn't be out in the sun.

For another, it was this town. He had to let all these crazy ideas go and just accept that in Nocturne Falls, you were supposed to believe in the unbelievable.

He started walking again. The sheriff's department was just up ahead. It would be good for him to be in a place like that. It would be grounding. It would remind him of his time on the force. When everything was by the rules and had a reason.

He pushed through the doors.

Birdie Caruthers found him before he even had a chance to look for her.

"Well, hello there." An older woman stood behind the curved reception desk, smiling at him. "You must be Wyatt."

"I am." He wasn't sure how she knew that unless Marigold had called ahead. "Are you Birdie Caruthers?"

She turned her head, smiling like she was about to have a photo taken. "The one and only."

He hadn't expected the blue hair. Not old-lady blue, but sort of robin's egg. Not that he'd ever describe the firecracker in front of him as an old lady. He held out the flowers. "These are for you."

She clapped her hands together. "Aren't they lovely? My beau just spoils me silly." She pointed at the top of the reception counter. "Just set them there, will you?"

"Sure thing." He put them exactly where she pointed.

She stuck her hand out. "Nice to make your acquaintance, Wyatt. I have to say, I'm surprised to see a cop delivering flowers."

He shook her hand. Her grip was surprisingly firm. "A cop? I'm not a, well, I was, but—"

"Once a cop, always a cop. Am I right?"

"I suppose." Marigold must have mentioned that when she called Birdie about the bouquet. But why would she do that? "How did you know that I was a cop?"

Birdie shrugged, eyes twinkling. "I work with enough LEOs to know one when I see one."

Her use of the abbreviation for law enforcement officer made him feel right at home. Maybe Marigold hadn't called. Maybe it was just Birdie's familiarity with the type. He looked around. The place was neat and modern. "This is a nice station you have here."

"Would you like a tour? Not much to it. Won't take more than five minutes."

He had five minutes. And Birdie didn't seem like the kind of woman who took no for an answer. "Sure."

"Good." She pressed a button on the desk phone, bending a little to speak into it. "Hank, you'll have to get the phone for the next few. I'm busy."

A grumpy voice responded. "Doing what?"

Birdie ignored the question to smile at Wyatt some more. "Right this way. I'll show you the holding cells."

He joined her and they walked back together. She leaned toward him slightly, and for a second, he thought she might be sniffing him. But that would be weird.

He cleared his throat. "Um, so you've worked here awhile?"

She nodded. "My nephew is the sheriff."

That must have been the grumpy voice on the intercom. "I see."

She pointed spokesmodel-style to the holding cells, which were pretty much like all the other holding cells he'd ever seen. Maybe a tad larger. "Nice, huh?"

"Yes. I'm sure your detainees are very happy."

She laughed, then crossed her arms and leaned against one of the sets of bars. "So, tell me all about your intentions toward Marigold."

He shot her a hard look. "My what?"

"You heard me. You're a tourist, right?"

"Yes, I live in Atlanta."

"Then what happens when Marigold falls for you? You're going to leave and break her heart? The poor woman's had enough aggravation with her crumb bum ex."

He felt sideswiped. "I'm just going to the wedding with her so she can avoid being set up by her—"

"She's got a daughter, too, you know."

"I know."

"One of the sweetest little girls you'll ever meet."

"I have no doubt."

"Neither she nor her mother need another disappointment in their life, you get me?"

Something in her gaze, a kind of animalistic wildness, unsettled him. Like she might suddenly bare her teeth and snarl at him. He'd never been looked at like that before. Not by a human, anyway.

The Detective Wins The Witch

He nodded. "I'm not going to hurt either one of them, I swear. Marigold is fully aware this is a temporary thing. We're both in agreement on that. As far as her daughter goes, Marigold's going to tell her I'm just a friend. I understand about not getting the kid's hopes up or anything like that."

The feral look was gone, replaced by a big smile. "I'm so glad to hear that."

He rolled his shoulders, still slightly unsettled.

She pushed off the bars and tipped her head toward the exit. "C'mon, I'll show you the armory."

13

When Wyatt returned, he seemed to be in a different headspace. Like he was deep in thought about something. Maybe even a little upset. Maybe not upset but at least unsure of something.

Could be a case he was working on. Could be something personal. Whatever it was, Marigold left him alone. She had enough work to do without playing therapist. That was really Charisma's job anyway. Or at least, that's what Marigold thought life coaches did.

Most men weren't talkers anyway. If he wanted to be quiet, she was okay with that. Plus, she liked quiet when there was a lot to be done. Living with an eleven-year-old often meant silence was a rare commodity.

She adjusted the last rose she'd just added. "These really need that *special* touch," she said softly to Leah.

Leah nodded and whispered back, "I know."

Leah was working on shop orders, but Marigold was focusing on centerpieces. They had six more to go.

She fussed with the centerpiece for five more minutes before she realized she just couldn't leave Wyatt alone. Maybe it was her maternal instincts kicking in, but her curiosity was overwhelming her. "So," she said nonchalantly, aiming her voice toward him. "How did the delivery go? Did you get a tip?"

He came around to the workroom door and leaned on the frame, making a long, lean line of maleness that was impossible to ignore. Rambling roses, the man was so very well put together. "Oh, I got a tip all right."

His expression said the tip had not been monetary in nature. She held her breath. "Oh?"

His gaze narrowed. "Mostly that I'd better be nice to you and your daughter, or I'll be in big trouble."

Marigold blew out a breath, lifting the hair hanging in her face. "Birdie," she muttered.

"Then you knew what you were sending me into?"

"No. Not exactly." She stuck another rose into the centerpiece. "But Birdie can be a little in your face at times—"

"A lot, you mean."

His arms were crossed, and he was giving her a perturbed look. She smiled, trying to soften the mood. "She's a lot of everything. But very well meaning, I assure you. And really beloved in this town."

"Is that because people are afraid of her? Or because her nephew is the sheriff?"

Now was not the time to tell him that Birdie's other nephew was the fire chief, and that her niece owned Howler's, the place they'd eaten lunch. "I didn't know she was going to give you the third degree. I promise."

All she'd asked Birdie to do was get Wyatt's fingerprints off the vase and run them. Then do a little digging to see what she could find out about him. That was all. Not lecture him on all things Marigold. But Birdie being Birdie, it was no shocker that she'd taken it upon herself to give Wyatt some unsolicited advice.

"I've seen veteran police officers who didn't interrogate with such ferocity." He straightened, dropping his arms to his sides. "Speaking of which, that woman gets a look on her face unlike anything I've ever seen. I swear if I didn't know better I'd have thought she was going to bite me if I said the wrong thing."

Marigold faked a laugh to cover up her sudden horror. "Oh, that Birdie, she wouldn't hurt a fly."

Mostly because werewolves preferred much bigger prey.

Marigold went back to her centerpiece. "Anyway, I'm sorry about all that. I'll talk to Birdie."

"No, don't. I survived. And part of me likes her a lot. I know how hard it can be working with LEOs, so I give her credit."

Marigold tipped her head. "LEOs?"

"Law enforcement officers."

Leah perked up. "So that part of you likes her? What about the other part?"

He laughed. "The rest of me is terrified of her, but let's keep that between us."

Leah snorted.

Wyatt shot her an amused look that clearly said all was forgiven. "I'm serious, missy. Not a word of this."

She crossed a finger over her heart, then held up her hand. "I swear."

"Good." Then he looked at Marigold again. "When's quitting time?"

"You can go any time you like. You've really done enough already today."

His brows rose. "I've swept and made one delivery. That doesn't seem like much help."

"But it was, really."

He nodded slowly. "I see. You're trying to get rid of me."

"No, I'm not. But I feel guilty that you're doing all this and not getting anything in return."

"What else am I going to do? Millersville is pretty boring compared to Nocturne Falls."

"I'm sure most places seem boring compared to Nocturne Falls."

"True. Most places don't have vampires and witches on the streets taking selfies with the tourists."

She stiffened a little, then made herself relax. Those supernaturals were specifically out there to entertain the tourists. If he'd seen them, it was no big deal. They were meant to be seen. And he'd had a little of the water, so maybe he wasn't picking up on anything odd. "You know, there's some great hiking around here. If you're into that. I am, when I can spare the time. The falls are beautiful."

"You *are* trying to get rid of me."

She laughed. "I promise, I'm not. But there's a lot more to see of this town than the inside of my shop."

He shrugged, a sly smile playing on his lips. "I'm pretty happy with the view."

She glanced at him. He was looking straight at her. He was smooth, she'd give him that. "Well, if you're going to stay, I'm going to put you to work."

"Bring it on."

He was going to wish he hadn't said that. She got off her stool and went out to where he was standing. "Follow me."

He did just that as she led him through the shop. "Going back to the cleaning supplies, are we?"

"Not exactly." She opened the door next to the supply closet. This walk-in closet housed all the vases necessary to fulfill the many orders that arrived by phone and computer daily. They were everything from the clear, inexpensive glass ginger jars that were included with a dozen budget roses to the cut crystal vases that proudly held most Valentine's Day bouquets.

And then there were the cheery mugs that proclaimed their purpose through their printed sayings. Get Well, Happy Birthday, It's A Girl…the list went on.

She turned to him, the closet at her back. "All of these need to be cleaned. If dust is left to accumulate, it builds up and clouds the glass. Plus, it makes more work for us when an order needs to be filled.

He stared at the inventory behind her. "All of that looks very breakable."

She nodded. "It is. So I suggest you take your time and do it carefully."

"Maybe I should call it a day."

She smirked. "A little on the clumsy side, huh?"

"No." He took a beat. "Maybe."

She started to shut the door. "If it's too much for you…"

"No, I can do it." He grabbed for the door and ended up putting his hand over hers.

The warmth of his hand felt nice. And the move put them face to face, so close a daisy wouldn't have fit between them. Her lips parted to tell him…something.

Then his mouth covered hers in a gentle kiss that sent the most delicious ripples of pleasure through her. She couldn't remember the last time a man had kissed her. His lips were as soft as rose petals, and the feel of them made her knees buckle.

She leaned into him, kissing him back just a little. She remembered this feeling. The way her stomach went all light and floaty and the world slowed down and a funny little trilling sounded in her ears. Actually, she didn't remember that last part.

"Marigold." Leah's voice rang out through the shop. "Your phone is ringing."

Marigold jerked back, the moment gone. The ripples of pleasure remained, however, while some of them turned to embarrassment. "I shouldn't have done that."

Wyatt was still mere inches away and seemed in no hurry to change that. "Shown me the closet?"

She pushed some hair off her face. The doorjamb was behind her. There was really no way for her to back up. "You know what I mean."

"I kissed you." He brushed his mouth across hers again. "Like that."

Her next breath was a ragged inhale that must have announced to him how affected she was by his presence. "My, uh, phone is ringing."

He stepped back. "So it is."

Twelve inches. Maybe eleven. That was all the space he'd put between them. And yet, somehow, it was too far.

She was losing it. Over a man who wasn't interested in anything more than passing the time. And who might potentially be working with Tim to get custody of Saffie. Wow, she was desperate and sad. She marched toward her phone. Time to snap out of it.

She grabbed the phone, saw it was Birdie, and hit answer. "Hey. What's new?"

"I did a deep dive on Mr. West."

"And?" Despite being a little angry at herself for that kiss, Marigold held her breath. She didn't want him to be a bad guy.

"He's clean."

She exhaled. "Okay. Good. But how can you be sure?"

"I can't be completely. But I looked into his financial records and—"

"Are you allowed to do that?"

"Did you want to know if he was being paid by your ex to dig up info on you and Saffie or not?"

"Yes, but I guess I didn't realize what that would entail." Marigold also realized that most of what Birdie told her, she was going to have to keep to herself. That or explain to Wyatt how she knew so much.

"Now you know."

"I suppose." Marigold hesitated. What was done was done. "What else?"

"He's working for a woman named Suzanne Anderson. She's a witch. No clue what kind of powers or how skilled. There's not a lot on her."

Marigold walked into the workroom, putting more distance between herself and Wyatt. She lowered her voice a little too. "He can't know what she is. He's human."

"I don't think he knows. He was a very well-respected police officer and detective. He had an accident—"

"I know about that."

"Medical reports show he's deaf in one ear. The left one."

"Holy holly, how deep did you go?"

"You know me. I don't leave stones unturned."

"Apparently."

"He grew up in the foster care system. Did you know that?"

"I did."

"Eighteen homes in thirteen years."

The breath left Marigold's body for a moment. She put her hand on the table to steady herself. "Oh."

"Yes," Birdie whispered, her voice thick with emotion. "That poor boy had no childhood. Not being shuffled around like that."

Marigold blinked back tears. "That's awful."

"The most awful," Birdie confirmed. "His parents were killed in a car accident when he was four. His aunt took custody of him, but found out she had cancer six months later. The fact that this man became a cop instead of a criminal is plumb amazing."

Marigold nodded. "Agreed."

"I'll tell you something else," Birdie offered. "I don't believe in my heart that this man would ever do anything against a child. Your ex might have hired someone to dig into Saffie's life, but it's not Wyatt. You can take that to the bank."

"I believe you." But then, what had Newt been talking about? "Hey, there's someone else I need you to look into."

"Name?"

"Newton Mathers."

14

Wyatt wiped the dust off another vase, returned it carefully to the shelf, and then applauded himself for reaching new heights of stupidity.

Kissing Marigold had been far more pleasurable than he'd imagined it would be—and he'd imagined it quite a few times since meeting her—but it had also been one of the dumbest things he'd done in a long time.

So dumb. But so amazing.

He got another vase down and went to work cleaning it. Thinking about how soft her lips were was not going to help him. He'd been completely set on keeping things platonic. He'd pretty much promised her that's what he would do. He'd *told* her he wasn't interested in any kind of relationship. Because he wasn't. Or hadn't been. *No*, he wasn't.

The thing was she lived here, and he lived in Atlanta. And he'd be returning there soon. Like the day after the wedding.

So why had he kissed her?

Because he really, really liked her. And he'd wanted to kiss her so much that when the moment had presented itself, he'd taken it. The need had filled every cell in his body.

He was a man, after all, and she was a beautiful, desirable, smart, funny, independent woman. And they'd been flirting. Hadn't they? At least, he thought they had.

But he shouldn't have kissed her. At first, he'd thought she was into it, but then how she'd reacted after…not so much.

Which really meant they needed to talk.

He put the vase down, tossed his rag onto a shelf, and left the storage closet behind. Marigold was in the workroom, putting more centerpieces together. "Hey, do you have a minute?"

She kept her eyes on the centerpiece she was making. "Not really."

He smoothed a hand over his hair. She was mad. He'd been a cop long enough to get a pretty accurate bead on people's emotions. Being a cop had also taught him not to be a quitter. "I'd like to talk to you. Please."

She lifted her gaze to him for a long, thoughtful moment, then glanced at Leah. "You want to run down to the Hallowed Bean and get a coffee?"

Leah's mouth took on an incredulous bend. "We have coffee here."

"Not salted caramel lattes with extra whip."

Leah jumped off her stool and grabbed her purse. "Good point. Back in a few. You want anything?"

"No, thanks," Marigold answered.

Leah headed for the door. Neither Marigold nor Wyatt spoke until the bell jingled at her leaving.

Marigold turned toward Wyatt, crossed her legs, and gave him a look that stated pretty clearly she wasn't interested in having a conversation with him, so it had better be short and to the point. "What do you want to talk about?"

No point in beating around the bush. "You know. That kiss."

She frowned and sighed in a way that spoke volumes.

"I know," he said. "I shouldn't have. You obviously didn't like it, and I—"

"I liked it."

That was news to him. "You did?"

"I thought it was fantastic, but I'm not interested in fantastic kisses from a man who's here temporarily and completely uninterested in anything more than a one-night stand, because I'm a grown woman and a mother, and I don't *do* one-night stands."

"I never said anything about a one-night stand."

"It was implied."

"In what way?"

"Really?" She blinked at him like he was a complete idiot, which maybe he was around her. She did something to his brain. He couldn't think straight around her. "It's an established fact that you're not going to be around for much longer, you told me you don't want a relationship, and yet you're flirting with me and kissing me. You obviously think you're going to make something happen. This is why I don't date tourists and I don't date huma—never mind."

"You don't date humans?"

"I was going to say...*new* men. Men I don't know."

That's not at all what he'd heard, but now was not the time to argue over a slip of the tongue. "What other kind of men are there if they aren't new men?"

"I prefer men that have been vetted by a friend or family member. A guy someone already knows."

And yet she hadn't wanted to date the insurance guy, although her sister had recommended him. Marigold was hiding something. He didn't need his cop instincts to figure that out. "Okay, whatever."

"Can we focus on the fact that you're leaving and you've clearly stated you don't want to get involved?"

"Right." He could see her point. Sort of. "Look, Marigold, I'm sorry I gave you the impression I wanted a one-night stand. And I know what I said, but I do like you. Maybe we could just see where things take us?" Even as he said the words, he had to wonder if a long-distance relationship could really work.

Especially when he still wasn't sold on marriage.

Her frown deepened. "Well, it's just great that you like me, but it's still a no from me. I don't think you get that what isn't good for my daughter, isn't good for me. Having a man in my life temporarily might be fun, but those days are gone for me. My carefree single days ended the moment I found out I was pregnant. And I realize that putting a child first as a priority is probably a foreign concept to you, but that's what a parent does." As the last words left her mouth, an odd, regretful look came over her face.

He couldn't focus on it. His past swamped him with a deluge of horrible emotions in a way they hadn't in years. He struggled to keep the pain and anger out of his face. His voice still came out edgy and raw. "Yeah, you're right. I don't have a clue what putting a child first means."

He spun and stalked toward the door.

Her stool scraped the floor with a piercing metal-on-concrete screech. "Oh, Wyatt, no, I didn't mean, I didn't think—wait. Please. I meant because you're single, not because…"

He stopped walking and just stood there, facing the door. The muscles in his jaw ached from clenching down so hard. He realized that she probably had meant because he was single. She didn't strike him as the type to hurt him intentionally by bringing up his past, but it reminded him why he so rarely shared his history with anyone. He swallowed, trying to clear the anger and pain away, but it had come upon him with such ferocity that it wasn't so easily dismissed.

"I'm so sorry, Wyatt." Her voice was filled with regret and sympathy, and somehow, that just made it worse. He didn't want her to pity him. To see him as some child who'd been hurt by the very system meant to take care of him.

He didn't want her to think he was weak, not this woman who had it all together. If she didn't need him at his best, she certainly wasn't going to want him at his worst.

He shook his head and finally found his voice. "I have to go."

Then he walked out and left Marigold behind, knowing he'd just blown any chance with her he might have had.

Marigold wanted to cry. Even as the words had left her mouth, she'd realized how wrongly they could be taken.

Then that was exactly what had happened.

She'd hurt Wyatt. Cut him to his soul, she expected. And she felt like a big pile of manure because of it. Why on earth hadn't she just kept her mouth shut? What had possessed her to say that to him?

Was it really so bad that the man had kissed her? No.

Why wasn't there a spell that could take words back? Also no. Just a complete mind wipe, and that seemed...extreme. She didn't want him to forget her.

She had to find him and apologize again. She had to do something. Because no matter how she wanted it not to be true, she liked him too.

She grabbed her phone and texted Leah. *Get back here. Please.*

I'm still in line at the HB.

I'll make it up to you. Need you back.

Wait, they just called my name.

You have your key?

Yes, why?

The door will be locked. I'll explain later.

What?

But Marigold was already out the door. She closed it and locked it. The only other time she'd locked up the shop during business hours was when Saffie had come down sick at school. That was before Marigold had hired help.

It didn't matter. Leah would be back.

Wyatt mattered now.

He couldn't have gone far. Where was he parked? In the back where she parked? If he'd left already, she might have to drive out to Millersville to his hotel. Birdie would know where he was staying. But going to a man's hotel might be...well, not the best thing to do when she'd just accused that man of being interested in a one-night stand.

She jogged around the corner to check.

Yep, his brand-new, rented black SUV was parked next to hers, making the later model vehicle look a little shabby. She frowned. If his car was still here, then he hadn't driven off.

Obviously.

Good grief, she was losing it. Where could he be? She strode down Main Street, scanning in both directions in the hopes she might find him. He really couldn't have covered much distance if he was still on foot. He'd been gone, what? Ten minutes?

She thought back through the day to see if he'd said anything that might give her a clue to his whereabouts now, but came up with nothing. Unless he was returning the stuff he'd bought at Guildman's. Would a man think to do that, though?

She grabbed her phone and called Birdie.

The woman answered in a couple rings. "Hi, Marigold. What's going on?"

"I had a fight with Wyatt and I need to apologize, but he stormed out. And look, I know this is a huge, crazy long shot, but do you have any idea where he might have gone?"

"Give me a second." Marigold heard clicking in the background. Like a keyboard. "He just opened a tab at Howler's. You want me to call Bridget and tell her to send him back to you?"

"No, but how do you know that? About the tab?"

"I checked his credit card."

That sounded very illegal, but in the moment, she didn't care. "Thanks. I owe you."

"No problem."

Marigold hung up and marched toward Howler's. She hated public scenes. Even worse that she was about to have one with a man. Tongues would be wagging for sure. Well, those tongues could bite themselves.

She owed Wyatt an apology.

She yanked Howler's door open and went in, standing there for a second until she spotted him. He was at the bar, his back to the front of the restaurant. Bridget was setting a beer in front of him.

Marigold hoped she could find the right words. He was probably furious with her. She didn't blame him. If he wanted to make her grovel a little, she'd get it. If he didn't want to talk to her, she'd get that too. She'd hate it, but she'd understand.

Didn't mean she wasn't going to talk to him.

She gathered her courage and walked toward him, heart pounding, and not at all unconcerned by how much this mattered to her. Oh, she liked Wyatt all right. Way more than she should.

She stopped behind him, next to his shoulder, trying to find the words that would make him understand how sorry she was. "Um, Wyatt? I know you're mad. You have every right to be. I would be if I was in your shoes. What I said was insensitive and cruel, and if my daughter had said something like that, I'd probably ground her for a week. I'm really, really sorry. I hope you can forgive me. I honestly didn't mean to bring up your past, but you'd confided that in me, so I knew about it and I should have thought before I spoke."

There. She'd said everything that was on her heart. She stood there, waiting for his response.

And waiting. And waiting.

Meanwhile, he just stared at the beer in front of him. She wasn't even sure he'd drank any of it yet.

"I guess you want to be left alone."

And...nothing.

Great. He was giving her the silent treatment. She'd really been hoping he wasn't that kind of guy. But better to find that out now than—wait, why did it matter when she found out? They were not about to be in a relationship. Not now, not ever. Especially not now, though.

She should just go.

Bridget walked by behind the bar. "Hey, Marigold. What can I get you?"

Wyatt's head jerked up, and he twisted around to look at her. "Oh. Hey. I'm, uh, glad you're here. I'm sorry about losing it back there."

He was apologizing to her? "Did you hear anything I said?"

His eyes clouded in confusion. "You mean in the shop?"

"No, I mean like five seconds ago."

His gaze narrowed. "How long have you been standing there?"

"A good six or seven minutes."

"And you were talking to me?"

"Yes. I made a big apology speech."

One corner of his mouth quirked up. "On my left side."

"Yes. Why?"

He turned his head a little and tapped his ear. "Because I'm deaf on that side, remember?"

She sighed and put a hand over her face for a second. "No, I did not remember that. I guess that makes both of us great listeners."

He barked out a short, sharp laugh, then pressed his lips together in a hard line. "I'm sure it was a great apology. Much better than mine." He patted the empty seat to his right. "Want to join me?"

"I should really get back to the—yeah, sure." She plopped down. A couple more minutes wouldn't hurt. Leah was probably back at the shop by now anyway.

He turned around to join her at the bar, slanting his eyes at her. "So…are we good?"

"I don't know. Are we?"

"I am if you are."

She nodded. "Okay. Good. I'm really sorry. I didn't mean it the way it came out."

"I know. I just…reacted. I'm sorry for storming out."

She wanted to touch him. To put her hand on his arm or her head on his shoulder or something, but that's what couples did. And they were not a couple. They weren't going to be a couple.

That made her inexplicably sad. She held her hand up for Bridget's attention. "Can I get a half glass of cider?"

Bridget smiled at her from the taps down at the end. "Coming up."

15

He couldn't believe she'd come after him. It staggered him emotionally. They'd known each other for a day and a half. And yet she cared enough about how she'd made him feel to come after him and make things right.

It felt like a light shining into the dark place in his soul. His chest constricted with an odd tightness he couldn't explain.

He sipped his beer. He didn't really want it, but he couldn't very well sit at the bar without ordering something and Howler's was the only place in town he'd known to go.

Then a new thought came to him. He looked at Marigold. "Weren't you alone in the shop?"

"No. Frank was there. Why?"

"You know what I mean. You're here." Frank didn't really qualify as an employee. As far as Wyatt knew, you needed thumbs to operate the register.

"Yes, I am."

"Leah must have gotten back pretty quickly."

"No. I locked up."

He stared at her. "During business hours."

"Yep."

"Is that something you do often?"

"Only once before."

"And that was because of your daughter, wasn't it?"

Her gaze narrowed. "How did you know that?"

"Deductive reasoning."

"You're pretty good at that. You might give Sherlock a run for his money."

He just nodded, because his head was spinning over what she'd done. For him. He couldn't just walk away from a woman like this. He realized that. She was a rare individual. A gem. People like Marigold needed to be treasured.

He wasn't sure he was the man to do that. No one in his life had taught him how to take care of a woman this priceless.

But he wanted to try.

"No snappy comeback?" she asked. Then her brow furrowed. "You look deep in thought."

Fear crawled out of the darkness within him. The fear of putting himself out there. Of being abandoned again. Of being not good enough. He tried to swallow it down, but there was so very much of it. "I...I..."

He could chase down criminals, put his life on the line, protect and serve without a care for his own well-being, but he couldn't do *this*. Why should he? Why be hurt again? Why—

"What is it?" She leaned in and put her hand on his cheek. "Are you okay? You look a little pale."

Her touch was enough to bring him courage. He closed his eyes and forced the words out. "I like you. I want to try."

Her hand left his cheek, but there was no laughter, no dismissive snort, so he opened his eyes. She was still staring at him, her gaze expectant.

"You want to try what?"

"Us." The word caused a new wave of fear to rise up.

She didn't say anything for a moment. Then she leaned back. "I like you, too, Wyatt. But you don't live here."

"I realize that. And I know long-distance relationships are hard, but we could at least try it."

She shook her head. "I can't travel. Even to Atlanta. My life is too complicated for that kind of time off."

"I know. I'll do the traveling. My job has some flexibility to it. When I'm not on a case, I'm free. I could spend that free time here."

She seemed to give that some thought, then her gaze dropped to her lap. "That doesn't solve you not wanting a relationship."

"That's what I'm trying to tell you. I think I do want a relationship. That's what I want to try. With you. I've never wanted to try with anyone else until you, so that feels like a feeling I shouldn't ignore." He groaned. "I don't think I'm making sense. I know what I'm trying to say, but this...*stuff* makes me dumb."

"Stuff?" There was humor in her gaze.

He sighed. "Help me out here, will ya? You see me drowning. Throw me a life preserver."

"You want to try dating me and see how it goes. You're willing to make the effort so that the long-distance aspect isn't a deal ender. Right?"

"Right."

"And if things go well, what then?"

"Then...we keep seeing each other. Maybe I eventually move here. I could do that. I'm licensed in Georgia. I can be a private investigator anywhere in the state."

Some of the amusement in her eyes disappeared.

He wasn't sure why. "Was that not the right answer? It felt like the right answer."

"Are you going to change your mind about marriage?"

They hadn't even decided to start dating and she was talking about marriage. But he understood what she was asking. She needed some sense of what the future was going to bring. But no one ever knew that, did they? Still, he wanted her to feel good about this. "I think that I could. And I've never even said that before, so you're clearly having an effect on me."

She nodded. And looked very thoughtful. But stayed silent.

He could wait. He'd been on stakeouts. Nothing taught you patience like a good stakeout. Except...this was Marigold. And he *needed* to know what she was thinking. He said nothing, just cleared his throat.

She smiled at him. Mouth closed, lips pressed together, and the expression only half reached her eyes. That told him everything. She wasn't sure.

He understood. A little. He'd presented himself to her in one very specific way, and now he was trying to backtrack. She had reservations. Who wouldn't?

With all of that in mind, he made himself stay positive. "What aren't you sure about?"

She laughed a little, like she was surprised he'd picked up on what was going through her head. "I just need a little thinking time."

"Okay." Stay positive. "That's wise." She was cautious. He understood that. "How about we take a breather? Say, until tomorrow night's auction?"

"That would be good. That would give me some time to mull this all through." She started to reach for him, then pulled her hand back. "I haven't had a man in my life since Saffron's father walked away from us. You have to understand what a really big step you're asking me to take."

"I do. I get it. I want you to be comfortable with all of this." He also understood she'd been hurt before. In a big way. His world had upended when he'd lost his parents. Hers had upended when she'd become a parent.

Somewhere in the middle of all that, there had to be a place for them to meet, didn't there?

"Are you sure that's right?"

At Leah's question, Marigold's thoughts came back to the work at hand. "What?"

Leah pointed overtop of the arrangement she was creating. "You put a ranunculus where a sprig of lavender was supposed to go."

"I did?" She looked at the centerpiece in front of her. "I did."

She sighed as she pulled the wayward stem out. "Good thing you caught that."

Leah shrugged. "I don't think anyone else would have noticed."

"I would have. At some point." There was an art to flowers, even when they were meant to be a little wild and carefree, as was the case for Pandora's wedding. Marigold took her art seriously.

They both went back to work. Frank sauntered

in for a bite to eat. The sound of him crunching on kibble broke the quiet.

Then Leah spoke up. "Wyatt?"

Marigold sighed. "Yes."

Leah nodded as if that explained everything. And maybe it did. "You like him."

"I do." Marigold added a bloom in exactly the spot where it belonged. "And he likes me. Enough that he's changed his mind about being in a relationship. As in, he wants to try it. He's even willing to do the traveling back and forth from Atlanta since there's no way I can with the shop and Saffie."

Leah sat up a little straighter. "That all sounds good. Like, really good."

"It does." She picked up a peony.

Leah squinted at her. "But?"

Marigold took in a long, slow breath. "He's still human. And I'm still a witch. Neither one of those things is going to change."

"It really complicates things, doesn't it?"

"Hugely." She slipped the peony in between two roses.

Leah lifted one shoulder. "You could tell him."

"I'm pretty sure the coven has rules about that. So does the town. You know humans aren't supposed to know the truth about Nocturne Falls. That's the whole point of the spell in the water."

"Yeah, but this is a different situation."

"Is it?" Marigold asked. "What if I tell him and that's the end of it? He could think I'm crazy. Or worse. Then what? He tells everyone? And I suffer the consequences? I have a lot to lose. My whole life is here. I can't jeopardize that." Especially not with Saffie's powers coming on so young. Saffie was going to need the coven and Harmswood more than ever.

Leah bit her lip. "You do have a lot at stake. Maybe...you could put him under some kind of spell that would allow you to do a test run."

Marigold thought that over. "That's not a good idea. For one thing, I'm just not sure what kind of spell that would even be. For another, putting him under a spell for my benefit like that seems... shady. No, I have to figure this out another way. If only I could scry his future and see if it includes me, but my scrying doesn't work that way." Which reminded her, she still needed to do some scrying about Newt.

"You've helped your family whenever they've needed it. Why not ask for their help now?"

"Now that's a good idea." Marigold picked up her shears to trim another stem. "I need to talk to my mom. She's the coven secretary. If anyone can tell me where the coven stands on telling normies the truth, it's her."

"Go now," Leah said. "You're not getting anything done here anyway."

"Hey! I'm working."

Leah shrugged. "Yes, but you're also super distracted."

"All right, fine." Marigold put her shears down and started to clean up.

"Leave it," Leah said. "I'll finish that one up as soon as I'm done with this birthday bouquet."

"Okay." Marigold smiled. "Thanks."

She whipped up a quick bunch of white calla lilies, blush roses, peach dahlias, a couple sprigs of lilac scabiosa and baby's breath, added some greenery, then wrapped the whole thing in florist paper and taped it up.

Wouldn't do to go empty-handed when she needed help.

And boy, did she need help.

Marigold couldn't remember when she'd been out of the shop so much during the work day. Certainly never when she had a massive wedding order looming. But this situation had to be settled. She needed advice now. She walked into Ever After, hoping to find her mom free.

Thankfully, Corette was just finishing up with a bride.

While Marigold waited, she checked the arrangement on the front table. Her mom got fresh flowers for the shop every week, along with a daily delivery of nibbly things from Delaney's Delectables.

It was a great way to subtly sell brides on where to get their wedding flowers and wedding cakes.

The bride left, and Corette came over to greet her daughter with a hug and a kiss on the cheek. "Hi, honey. How are you?"

"I'm good." Very conflicted, but good.

"It's a lovely surprise to see you."

Marigold handed over the flowers she'd brought. "For you. For your office."

"They're gorgeous. I'm going to put them on my desk." Corette brought the blooms to her nose and smiled as she inhaled. "They seem very much inspired by your sister's colors."

"They are."

"How's that going, the flowers for Pandora's wedding?"

"Great." Okay, not exactly great, but now was not the moment to delve into that. "Do you have a little time to talk?"

"I have an hour before the next appointment, so plenty. Want to go into the office?"

Marigold nodded vigorously. "Yes."

"Come on." Corette linked her arm through her daughter's, and they walked back together.

Corette went to get a vase for the flowers, then returned. She unwrapped the stems and put them in the water, arranging them just so. "All right. What's the matter? I can tell by the look on your face that something is troubling you. Honey, do you need extra help with Pandora's wedding flowers?"

"No, it's not that." Although that wasn't the worst idea in the world. "It's…a guy."

"I see." Corette's always perfect brows rose ever so slightly. She sat to face Marigold, who'd taken the opposite chair. "Is the guy that nice Wyatt that stopped by to introduce himself to me?"

Marigold had to take that in for a second. "Wyatt came to see you?"

"Yes. He'd just been in Guildman's getting some clothes and wanted to introduce himself to me since he's apparently your date for the wedding. That I knew nothing about. He seemed very nice. I thought so, at least."

"Wow." Marigold sat back. What a sweet gesture. And he hadn't said a word about it. "So you like him?"

"I do. Granted, we only spoke for a few moments, but my initial impression was that he's a nice, polite man who's trying very hard to impress you. And your family. Nothing wrong with that."

"No, I suppose not."

"So what's the trouble, then? Or don't you like nice, polite men? Pandora told me you turned down her offer to introduce you to Phil Crenshaw."

"Mom. Phil Crenshaw is an insurance salesman. Which is fine. But we don't click. At all. And I'm pretty sure his idea of a fun night out is a meeting of the local actuaries association. Of which he's probably a founding member."

"Everyone needs insurance, Marigold. It's a solid industry."

"He's not my type. And I like nice, polite men. That's not the problem."

"Then what's wrong with Wyatt?"

Time to lay it out. "He's human."

Only by the slight widening of her mother's eyes did Marigold know that Wyatt's humanity presented an issue. Corette didn't immediately say anything, though.

Marigold thought that was answer enough. She sighed. "I know, Mom. I know. It's not ideal."

"No, it isn't. But then Tim was a second-degree wizard and look how that turned out."

"True. Wyatt's also the first guy who's paid any attention to me in, well, forever."

"That's not exactly true. Dennis Prescott? James O'Neill? Carlos DeMarco? Phil Crenshaw?"

Marigold rolled her eyes. "Okay, Wyatt's the first guy who's paid attention to me who I actually want to pay attention back to. He's funny and kind and deeply scarred in ways that will break your heart, and I think I'm falling for him."

Corette pursed her lips. "He's also movie-star handsome, but I suppose you hadn't noticed that."

"Oh no," Marigold said with a big grin. "I noticed."

Corette's smile was thin, but Marigold understood. Her mother had raised them to look beyond a person's exterior, which Marigold was. But it really had more to do with Wyatt being human.

Corette folded her hands in her lap. "Tell me about the deeply scarred part."

That took the grin off Marigold's face. "Mom, he was in the foster system. Lost his parents at four, then the aunt who took him in passed from cancer a year later. In thirteen years, he was in eighteen different homes."

Corette gasped softly and put her hand to her throat. "That poor baby." She closed her eyes for a moment, then opened them and took a breath, regaining her composure. "I'm surprised he confided all of that in you. Speaks very well of how he's dealing with it all."

"He did tell me about some of it, but the details came from Birdie."

A sharp light entered her mother's eyes. "Spying is a rather dubious way to start a relationship, don't you think?"

"It wasn't exactly spying. And there were special circumstances."

Corette's expression said she remained unconvinced. "Such as?"

Marigold filled her in on Newt's warning. "I didn't know what else to do. And I haven't had a chance to scry for more information yet."

"For Saffron's sake, I'd say what you did was understandable. But at some point, you need to tell Wyatt you know more. Things like that have a way of coming back to haunt you."

"Does that mean you think I should pursue a relationship with him?" That surprised Marigold.

She'd expected her mother to balk at the idea of a human mate.

"I don't know. His being human is one thing. But his meeting Saffron is another."

"And he will meet her at the wedding. There's no way around that. So what do I do?"

Corette thought for a moment. "You could tell him your truth."

"That's part of what I wanted to ask you about. Wasn't there just something in South Carolina about a witch dating a normie that went badly? Where does our coven stand on that?"

"It's at the discretion of the witch, although most covens, ours included, prefer that a witch think long and hard before revealing herself. Because while there are those of us who live long happy lives with human partners, revealing one's true self doesn't always go well."

"I can imagine. What about the town? The town has rules about that kind of stuff, right? And by the town, I mean the Ellinghams."

Corette smiled a little. "It's an unwritten but widely understood rule that the supernaturals in this town should protect each other. Not telling humans who they really are and what Nocturne Falls is actually about fall under that rule. But love is an exception to almost everything."

"I'm not in love with him. Not yet. I do think it could happen, though."

Corette reached out and took her daughter's hand. "Then there's your answer."

"What?"

"You should wait until you're in love."

"What about Saffron?"

"She's eleven. And in some ways, wise beyond her years. Don't you think she'd want you to be happy? Don't you think she'd understand that your dating Wyatt doesn't mean he's going to instantly become her new daddy?"

Marigold thought that over. "Yes to both those things. But I'm more worried about her getting attached to him, then things not working out and her heart getting broken."

"You're right. It's something to worry about." Corette patted Marigold's hand. "But broken hearts heal."

Marigold let out a groan. "Maybe I should just stay single until she's out of the house like you did with us."

"Oh, honey." Corette chuckled softly as she released Marigold's hand. "Do you not remember Uncle Roy?"

Marigold thought back. "Sure, I remember him. Whatever happened to him? How was he our uncle anyway?"

"He wasn't."

Her mouth fell open. "Are you telling me Uncle Roy was your boyfriend?"

Corette nodded. "Yes, for about two years. He was a lovely man, and we had a lot of fun together, but ultimately, he wasn't ready to be daddy to three precocious witchlings. Our parting was amicable, though. And he helped me through a very lonely time in my life."

"Two years? But I remember him being around more than that. Or…was he? He sent us Christmas gifts, didn't he?"

"Yes. He sent you Christmas gifts for two more years after we broke up. Even though he wasn't ready to be an instant father, he cared for you girls very much."

"Huh." Marigold sat back. "All this time I had no idea."

Corette adjusted the lapel of her suit. "You don't have to tell Saffie everything. Just what she needs to know. Be truthful, but be circumspect. Adults are allowed to have adult lives separate from their children."

"I guess so."

"Does that help?"

"Yes, it does. Thanks, Mom. You did a great job raising us, you know that?"

Corette's smile was broad and unrestrained. "I do know that. Every time I look at you girls, I am reminded of how wonderful you are and how well you turned out." She stood. "Now you should get back to work. You have a lot left to do."

Marigold got to her feet. "How do you know that?"

Corette's smile turned sly. "You just told me."

Wyatt sat in his SUV, staring through the windshield at the cars passing by on Main Street.

He wasn't ready to return to the hotel in Millersville. What would he do there? He could go to the fitness center and work out, he supposed, but then what? Get a shower and have dinner by himself? Watch a little mindless television? That all sounded so sad.

Staying in Nocturne Falls seemed like a better idea. Especially if he was entertaining the idea of moving here. He snorted. How things changed. He'd always considered himself a city guy, but Nocturne Falls might be all right. It seemed to be a fairly hopping place, what with the tourist industry.

Would he get enough PI work here to pay his bills? That part he wasn't sure of.

He sat for a bit longer, watching cars and people. He didn't really know what to do with himself. Odd as it seemed, he missed being in the shop with Marigold and Leah. It had nothing to do with the flowers, but everything to do with the company.

Of course, he'd see Marigold tomorrow at the auction. But then he might never see her again.

He tipped his head back against the headrest and exhaled. He didn't want to think that way. Not when he'd put himself out there to her like he never had before.

But it *was* a possibility. She could absolutely decide she didn't want to take things further than their platonic wedding date. Or maybe she'd think it was best her daughter didn't get to know him for fear she'd get attached and he'd flake.

He wouldn't flake. She had to know that, right? He might have some serious baggage, but that baggage was the exact reason he wasn't going to up and disappear. Especially not when there was a child involved. She'd get that, wouldn't she?

He hoped so. He liked being with Marigold. He liked the way he felt around her, the way things were so easy with her. Even if there was some strange stuff going on with her. And this town. He could overlook all that if she gave him the green light.

His thoughts took a new direction. What was her daughter like? What had Marigold said, that the little girl was eleven? He had no idea what eleven-year-old little girls were like.

Would she like him? He grimaced. That might be a long shot. What kid was going to look at him and think, yeah, there's my new best friend?

Maybe he should get her a present. That might help tip the scales. He wasn't above bribery for a good cause.

But what did you get for an eleven-year-old girl? And where did you shop? He might as well have been contemplating life on Mars for all he knew about the subject.

He straightened up and grabbed his phone. He typed into the search bar: *gifts for girls nocturne falls*. Then he hit enter.

The first place on the list was Santa's Workshop. Apparently, Nocturne Falls had a toy store. Perfect. They'd be able to help him in there. He hoped. He checked the address and laughed.

The shop was right by Howler's, which wasn't far from Marigold's store, which meant he'd already walked past the place a few times. He jumped out of the car and headed over.

The shop was really something inside. The air even smelled like Christmas, or what he imagined Christmas smelled like. Holidays were sketchy when you were a foster kid and nonexistent when you were a homicide detective with no family. At least for him, they'd been nonexistent, but then, he'd always picked up holiday shifts so those with families could enjoy them.

The girl behind the counter was cute in an elfin sort of way. Button nose, smattering of freckles, blue hair. He shook his head. The crazy-colored hair thing still seemed odd to him, but on her, it looked almost natural.

"Hi there," she said. "Welcome to Santa's Workshop. Can I help you with anything today?"

"Yes, you can. I need a gift for an eleven-year-old girl. I don't know her tastes at all. Actually, I haven't met her yet."

"Hmm." The girl pursed her lips. "You're not making it easy on me, are you?" Then she laughed. "It's okay, we'll figure it out. Making kids happy is what we do. Can you tell me anything about her?"

"Not really. I only know her mom, and she likes flowers. She owns the flower shop here in town."

"Oh, is this gift for Saffron?"

"Yes. Do you know her?" He'd definitely come to the right place.

"We keep a wish list registry for the locals. Come on, let's go take a look."

"That's a brilliant idea." He followed her to the counter. "I'm Wyatt, by the way. Thanks for your help."

She took out a big leather-bound book from under the counter. He'd expected her to look something up on the computer, but whatever worked. "I'm Juniper. And happy to help."

She flipped the big book open and ran her finger down the page, searching the list of names. "Here we go. Saffron Williams. Looks like she's got two things on the list. A Hogwarts paint-by-numbers set and the light-up terrarium kit."

"Hogwarts is *Harry Potter*, right?"

"Right," Juniper said.

"Sorry. I'm not as up on popular culture as I probably should be." Considering that Marigold owned a flower shop and had told him that she had a greenhouse in her backyard, Wyatt wasn't surprised by the terrarium. But the Hogwarts paint by numbers was a little more interesting. Which one would Saffron like better? "Any idea which one she wants more?"

"I'd say the paint by numbers. It was out of stock last time she asked for it, so she's been wanting it for a while."

"Done." He got his wallet out. "Any chance you can gift wrap?"

Juniper smiled. "We can make that happen."

"How was school?" Marigold wasn't sure how to broach the subject of Wyatt with Saffron, but it wasn't going to be directly. She wanted to work up to it and find the right moment. Dinner conversation seemed like a good time to make it happen.

"Good," Saffron said, taking a bite of her chicken fingers. "I changed the colors of a butterfly's wings today."

Marigold held her forkful of green beans aloft. "You did what?"

Saffron shrugged. "Mrs. Fipple said I could try. I don't think she thought I could do it."

"Mrs. Fipple isn't one of your teachers. Who is she, actually? That name isn't familiar."

"She's the magic lab monitor."

"Does that mean you were in the magic lab?" It was Marigold's understanding that Harmswood's magic lab was for older students. Students whose powers were fully seated.

Saffron rolled her eyes. "Mom, it's not like I can't go in there. I am a witch, you know."

"You're not a witch yet, not fully. At best, you're a fledgling. Were you in there alone?"

"No, I just told you. Mrs. Fipple was in there."

Marigold didn't like this at all. "But you went in alone?"

"No, Miss Boschman took me in there because I told her my powers were starting to come in, and she said we should go to the magic lab and see."

Miss Boschman was Saffie's pre-spells teacher. "Uh huh. Okay." This was all happening too fast. "So you changed the colors on a butterfly's wings? How did that go?"

She shrugged like it was no big deal. "It was easy."

Easy was relative, and Marigold was sure Saffie wanted to show off a little in front of her mother. "How many tries?"

"One."

Marigold swallowed. Sweet snapdragons. "One try."

"Yep."

"Did the butterfly live through it?"

"*Mom.*" Saffron sighed. "Yes."

"Just asking." Marigold shook her head. "That's...impressive."

"That's what Mrs. Fipple and Miss Boschman said. My guidance counselor wants to have a meeting with you to discuss my placement in some new classes. I brought a note home."

"I'll read it right after dinner." And so it began. Marigold wasn't sure if she was ready to have a gifted fledgling witch in the house. On one hand, it was amazing. On the other, Saffie was growing up faster than Marigold could stand. She changed the subject. "Are you excited about Aunt Pandie's wedding?"

"Yes!" Saffron grinned. "Of course I am. After all, Kaley and I are junior bridesmaids, and Charlie is the ring bearer, so it's basically like Charlie and I are practicing for our wedding for real."

"No, it's not like that at all." Marigold laughed. "You need to calm down or that poor child is going to run screaming for the hills. Or howling. Whatever werewolves do."

"No way," Saffie said. "Charlie loves me."

"I have no doubt he does. You are very lovable. But you might still want to lay off the marriage talk just a little." Marigold took a breath and dove in. "Speaking of the wedding, I have a date."

Saffie looked up from her mac and cheese. "You do? With who?"

"A nice man you haven't met yet. His name is Mr. West."

"He sounds old."

Marigold pursed her lips. "He's not old. He's about my age."

Saffron made a face. "So he's old."

"Saffie, behave."

She grinned. "Do you like him?"

"Yes, I like him."

"Are you going to marry him?"

Marigold almost choked on a green bean. "Slow your roll, missy. I'm not about to marry him any more than I'm going to marry anyone else."

"What does that mean?"

"We're friends, sweetheart. That's really all that's going on between us right now."

Saffron tipped her head. "Have you kissed him?"

Marigold was *not* answering that. "Eat your green beans."

"Ew, you *have* kissed him." She stuck her tongue out.

Marigold just smiled. If Saffie still thought kissing was gross, then maybe Charlie was safe for a little while longer.

Wyatt wasn't going to be, however, because if he and Marigold were going to be a couple, kissing was going to be high up on the list of activities.

At long last, she was moving out of Singletown and looking at a lease in Datingville.

Wyatt stood at the back of the auction house, looking for a seat. And Marigold, although she'd texted him to say she wouldn't be there for a few more minutes, so he didn't expect to see her just yet.

He was very much aware that she'd given him no indication of her answer, either. But he wasn't freaking out about that at all.

He went back to looking. His spot near the wall was gone. He was going to have to sit somewhere else. Maybe that third aisle would be—someone poked him in the back.

He turned. And smiled. Marigold. "Hey."

She answered by leaning up and kissing him on the lips. It was half a second of contact, but it almost knocked him over. She smiled as the kiss ended. "Hey."

It took him a moment to reorganize his thoughts. "I, uh...hi."

She laughed. "Did you get us seats?"

"Whoa. Hold up. You just kissed me. I can't ignore that. Does that mean—"

"Yes. I'm willing to try."

He almost yelled. He wasn't the kind of guy who yelled, but this was something that felt worth yelling about. He didn't. Well, maybe a little internal yelling. Externally, he grinned. Hard. "That is good news. Really good news."

"I guess we'll see, won't we?"

He nodded. "You look beautiful, by the way." She did. She was wearing a little sundress with yellow flowers and a jean jacket and sandals. Her toes were painted pink. Like bubblegum. He was nuts about how perfect she was.

"Thanks. You look nice too."

He'd shaved, but otherwise he was wearing pretty much the same thing he always wore. Jeans and a T-shirt with a jacket and boots. He might need to work on that. "You're just being kind. We should find some seats."

"Wherever you want to sit is fine with me. I'm only staying as long as it takes for the items to come up, then I'm taking them home and going to the shop to work on wedding flowers."

She seemed pretty confident she was going to win the bookends. Poor thing. "How about those two on the end of the third aisle?"

"Perfect." She started forward.

He put his hand on the small of her back to follow her, and a sudden, possessive thrill ran through him. This beautiful woman had agreed to go out with him. And he wanted other men to know it. Apparently, being around Marigold made him a caveman.

The urge to grunt and pound his chest must not be far behind. Was that what love did to a man?

Not that he loved her. Not yet. It was way too soon for that. But he liked her very much. Too much, maybe. He'd better dial it back or she'd think he was a stage-five clinger.

They settled into their seats, and he put his arm around her, mostly on the back of her chair, but still touching her.

She glanced at it, smirking with blatant amusement. "You sure stake your claim fast."

He shrugged. "You greeted me with a kiss there, speedy."

She giggled. "Okay, good point."

He settled back, unable to remove the smile from his face and not wanting to. This was going to be fun. Scary. But he could do this, because he wanted to do this. Marigold was a beautiful woman, a solid citizen, a savvy business owner, and no doubt, a fabulous mom. All of that made him positive she was going to be an excellent girlfriend, too.

He was not going to screw this up. If this went south, it would be her doing. Her decision.

She leaned over. "You know I'm going to win these bookends."

He shook his head slowly. "Sorry, sweetheart, can't let you do that."

Her expression turned sly. "Oh, really? And how much do you have to spend?"

Suzanne had bumped him up to ten grand, but he didn't want to give that away and end the little game going on here. "I'm afraid that's confidential detective-client information."

"Is that actually a thing?"

He answered with another question. "How much do you have?"

She crossed her arms and shot him a smug look. "More than you."

He snorted. "You do not."

"I might."

"True. But you don't."

She wrinkled her nose. "I'm going to win."

He straightened up a little. "Let's make this interesting. Winner makes the loser breakfast."

An odd light filled her eyes, and she whispered, "Is this a sex thing? Because I'm not ready for that."

He almost choked on his own breath, somehow managing not to fall out of his chair. "No. I meant as in going out for breakfast. Like for those pancakes at that diner."

"Oh." Her eyes widened, and she laughed. "Okay, let's do that."

The auctioneer banged the gavel and got things underway. The bookends didn't come up until forty-five minutes in, but Wyatt had his paddle at the ready.

Marigold put hers on her lap, then shot him a flip look. "Winning," she whispered.

"Nope," he whispered back.

One of the auction house employees walked back and forth with the bookends in his hands, and the auctioneer got the bidding started. "Next up is an interesting pair of antique bookends. These bookends were said to have been in Ben Franklin's home at one time, although we have no provenance on that."

"What are they supposed to be?" someone from the audience shouted.

"Ugly," another person answered.

Laughter filled the room, and the auctioneer brought things back to order with his gavel. "My description says they're winged frogs."

Wyatt and Marigold responded in unison, "Oh."

"Do I hear fifty dollars? Fifty to get us started."

Wyatt stuck his paddle up.

"There we go, fifty in the third row. Do I hear fifty-five? Anyone with fifty-"

Marigold's paddle went into the air. "One hundred."

The auctioneer looked at Wyatt. "Do I hear one twenty-five?"

"One thousand," Wyatt answered.

The crowd gasped, but Marigold just narrowed her eyes and lifted her paddle again. "Two thousand."

Wyatt smiled and raised his paddle high. "Three."

The auctioneer stared at him. "Are you saying three thousand?"

"I am."

"Ma'am?" The auctioneer directed his attention to Marigold. "Would you like to counter?"

"Four," she answered. "Thousand."

The audience was dead silent and hanging on every word.

Before the auctioneer could ask, Wyatt said, "Five."

"Six," came Marigold's reply.

Wyatt shook his head. "Seven."

Marigold let out a sigh. Wyatt smirked. He'd done it. He'd won.

"Nine," she said.

"What?" He looked at her. "Nine?"

She nodded. "Nine. You have any other questions?"

"Sure," he answered. "How do you feel about nine thousand five hundred?" His cap was ten. He was hoping she'd already hit hers.

The audience seemed to be collectively holding its breath.

"I feel like it's five hundred too little." She waved her paddle at the auctioneer. "Ten thousand."

Wyatt sat back, almost unable to keep from laughing out loud. He put his paddle down and held his hands up. "I'm out."

"Yes," Marigold hissed.

The auctioneer looked a little blank. He glanced around the room. "Do I hear ten thousand five hundred?"

Not a peep.

He banged the gavel down. "Sold to the blonde in the third row."

The audience started clapping.

She grabbed Wyatt's hand. "Are you mad?"

"Not one bit. My client isn't going to be happy, but hey, that's on her, not me." He tipped his head toward the checkout desk. "Let's get these hideous things and get out of here."

"You got it."

They went together to collect the bookends, then he waited while she paid. He picked up the box that the bookends were in. "I'll carry them for you."

"In case I get knocked down again?"

"No one is touching you. But yes, something like that."

She smiled and looped her arm through his as they left the building.

Dusk was fast approaching. He did a quick scan of the parking lot, but saw no one suspicious. "Where's your car?"

She clicked the button on the key fob, causing the lights to flash. "Right there."

"Okay." They walked over together, then while she got in, he secured the box on the passenger seat.

Something felt off. He did another scan of the parking lot. His gut was telling him they were being watched.

She put her seat belt on. "I guess I'll see you tomorrow for the rehearsal dinner."

"Reneging on the bet, huh?"

"Oh! Breakfast! The excitement of winning made me forget—hey, are you paying attention to me?"

He nodded. "Yes, but something's not right."

Her smile vanished. "Like what?"

"Not sure. I'm going to follow you home. Make sure you're okay."

"You're scaring me a little."

"I don't mean to. I just want you safe."

"You really think something's up?"

"I do." He took his eyes off the parking lot to look at her. "But nothing's going to happen to you."

She nodded, the concern in her eyes evident.

"Lock your doors as soon as they're closed, then pull out. Wait at the exit until I'm behind you, then head home. Don't get out of your car until I'm there."

"Okay." She closed her door, the snick of the locks engaging the next sound.

He walked to his SUV, his head on a swivel.

Nothing happened in the parking lot, and nothing happened on the drive back to her house, but the feeling in his gut had yet to abate. She parked in her driveway.

He pulled in behind her and got out. A quick perimeter check revealed nothing out of the ordinary. He walked to her car door.

She rolled the window down. "Everything good?"

"Seems to be."

"You know, I was just going to drop these off and go back to work."

He nodded. "I know. I don't think that's the best idea. Unless you want me to come with you. I don't like the thought of you being alone."

She sighed. "I guess I can stay home. Just means more work I have to make up tomorrow."

"I'll do whatever you need me to. I'm all yours tomorrow."

"Okay."

"Good. Let's get you inside and make sure the house is secure." He doubted that would be enough to satisfy him. Whatever was setting off his instincts wasn't going away.

Marigold woke up disappointed in herself. After thinking all day yesterday about how much she wanted to kiss Wyatt some more, she'd kissed him only once at the auction house. Once wasn't enough. Not with a man that handsome with lips that soft.

Last night, he'd smelled better than she'd remembered, too.

But the events after the auction had distracted her from all thoughts of kissing. She'd been a little scared. She wasn't ashamed to admit that, but having Wyatt follow her home, then check the outside of her house had given her a lot of peace.

It was kind of hot how serious he'd gotten. He'd suddenly turned into this all-business protector man. Like her safety was the most important thing in his world.

She'd never experienced that before. It was heady stuff.

Almost enough to make her forget how much wedding prep remained.

With happy thoughts of her new guy and less happy thoughts of her to-do list, she got up, brushed her teeth, put on her robe, and went to wake Saffron up for school.

But Saffie wasn't in her bed. "Saff? Where are you?"

"In the living room."

Marigold walked in to see what the kid was up to. Hopefully not levitating the furniture.

But Saffie was leaning on the windowsill, staring intently out the front window curtains.

Maybe there was a rabbit on the lawn. Saffie loved animals. "What are you doing, kiddo?"

"Watching the man in our driveway."

Marigold stopped breathing for a second. Then she leaped forward, grabbed Saffron, and pulled her back from the window.

"Mom!"

"Saff, go stand in the hallway."

"Why? What's—"

"Go. Now." Marigold rarely snapped at her daughter, but this wasn't the time for a debate.

Saffron went to the hallway. "What's going on?"

"I'm not sure." Marigold peeked through the curtains. She sighed and shook her head in amusement. "Never mind. It's nothing. Go eat your breakfast."

"But—"

"Please, Saffie. Go get your breakfast. You know how fast the morning goes."

"All right." Saffie started walking in that direction.

Marigold took another look outside. Wyatt was asleep in his SUV in their driveway. And by the looks of the clothes he had on, he hadn't made it home last night. But she'd checked around the house (through the windows) before going to bed and his SUV hadn't been there.

"Who's that guy, Mom?"

Saffie hadn't gone more than three steps. Marigold moved away from the window as she tied her robe a little tighter and gave her daughter a stern look. "Kitchen. Breakfast. Now."

With an exasperated sigh and a massive eye roll, Saffron went.

Marigold ran her fingers through her curls, using the mirror by the front door to see if she could tame them a little. She failed and gave up. The upside was if the shock of seeing what she looked like first thing in the morning didn't scare Wyatt off, she'd know he was a keeper.

She unlocked the front door and slipped outside. The air was cool and still. She padded barefoot down the driveway to rap her knuckles lightly on Wyatt's car window.

He blinked rapidly as he sat up and cleared his throat. He looked through the window at her, blinked a few more times, then smiled.

She lifted her eyebrows. "You okay in there?"

He turned the car on enough to power the window down. "I must have fallen asleep."

"I see that. But why are you sleeping in my driveway? Did you get kicked out of your hotel?"

He rubbed his face. "I was keeping an eye on your house."

Very sweet. Maybe a little overcautious, but she wasn't about to tell a former cop that. "What time did you get here?" Had to be after ten. That's around when she'd turned in last night and the only car in her driveway then had been hers.

"About midnight. I went back to the hotel, had some dinner, but I couldn't shake the feeling that something was wrong. I ended up driving back here."

"And you've been here since."

He nodded.

"And here I thought you were just making sure I fulfilled my end of the bet."

His expression perked up. "That's right. You owe me breakfast."

She shook her head. "Not right now I don't. I have a child to feed and get to school, and I have to get ready myself and get to work. And after not doing any work after the auction last night, I have a *lot* of work to do today. A lot. Buckets of work. More work than you can—"

He snorted sleepily. "I get it. You're busy. I told you I'd help. How about I meet you at the shop at nine and I'll bring breakfast? Then I'll take up my counter-watching duties so you and Leah can get all that wedding stuff done."

She mulled that over. With him there, she was going to have to be very careful about using her magic to finish off the arrangements, but there were ways of distracting him. And having him at the counter would buy her and Leah all kinds of time.

She wasn't stupid. His help would be invaluable. "It's a deal."

He leaned his arm on the window. "What would you like, then, sunshine?"

She smiled. "Veggie omelet, light on the cheese, wheat toast dry."

"How very healthy. No pancakes? No bacon?"

"Bridesmaid dress, remember?"

He seemed to suddenly wake up a bit more. "That reminds me, I will need a little time off today to pick up my clothes from Guildman's."

"No problem." That would give her a chance to work her magic. Literally. "See you in the shop."

The rest of the morning went by in a blur. She got Saffie off to school and herself halfway to work when she remembered she'd left the bookends at the house. Newt was coming to get them at the shop this morning, and with what he'd spent, she really wanted to hand them over as soon as possible.

She ran into the house and grabbed them, then headed back to the car. Her cell phone rang as she was walking out. She shifted the box to get into her purse, lost her grip on the cardboard, and dropped the box on the driveway.

It landed with a sharp crack.

She stood frozen for a moment, ignoring her still ringing phone. "You have got to be kidding me."

She didn't want to open the box. Didn't want to find out she'd just broken a ten-thousand-dollar pair of bookends. After what had happened with the candlesticks, Newt was going to think she was doing this on purpose. She already felt sick to her stomach, knowing that crack had not been a good sound.

With a sigh, she bent and opened the box.

The left bookend was perfect. The right one was in two pieces. She closed her eyes and groaned. If Newt expected her to pay for the one she'd broken, she was sunk. "I can't afford this. I *cannot* afford this."

Maybe she could glue it back together. With magic. Except Newt was a wizard and he'd pick up on that. Of course, there was always the possibility that he'd think the damage had been done pre-auction.

But that would be dishonest, and that was not who she was.

She carefully lifted the box and went back into the house to examine the pieces. She eased the broken bookend out to see if the crack was all the way through.

It was. The bookend came apart cleanly.

And a small, muslin-wrapped package fell out.

Intrigued, she put the pieces aside to examine the package. It was heavier than she expected. The fabric was frayed but seemed new. She unwrapped the linen and found a silver chain with an odd pendant dangling from it.

The pendant was shaped like an eye, and the iris and pupil were made from an amber stone of some kind.

She had no idea what it was or how much it was worth, but there was magic in it. Strong magic. Enough that it gave her some pause.

Newt had been willing to spend six thousand dollars on those ugly candlesticks and ten thousand dollars on these hideous bookends. Men had tried to steal the candlesticks, and Wyatt had felt sure someone was watching her last night.

Then there was Wyatt's client who'd also been willing to spend big bucks for the candlesticks and bookends.

It was all starting to add up in a way that could mean only one thing. This was no coincidence. Whatever was going on had very little to do with some ugly home decor and everything to do with the magic pendant in her hands.

Wyatt walked toward the Enchanted Garden with mixed feelings, but he'd finally decided not to tell Marigold what he'd seen last night.

When he'd arrived at her home, there had been a dark sedan parked two houses away. He'd driven around the block, and when he'd returned to her place and pulled in the driveway, the sedan had taken off.

His gut had been right. She was being watched.

She didn't need to know he'd been right, though. Not today, not when she had her sister's wedding flowers to finish and then the wedding itself tomorrow.

Until that wedding was over, he planned on being with her as much as possible. No one was going to harm her.

Because she might have been buying those candlesticks and bookends for Newt, but whoever was trying to get them might not know that. And that meant she still wouldn't be safe, even after she turned those bookends over to Newt.

He didn't like that. At all.

But he put a smile on his face as he rolled into the Enchanted Garden. She was safe, and she was going to stay that way.

Frank was sleeping in the front window, nestled into a basket of tulips. Wyatt leaned in. "I don't think you're supposed to be sleeping in those, buddy."

Frank covered his face with one paw.

Wyatt chuckled. The cat was something else. Wyatt liked him. He liked all of this. Now he just had to protect it. And he would. Because he'd finally found a place that felt right.

Not only that, but he was nailing this boyfriend thing. He was bringing Marigold breakfast, and he was going to be helping her out by handling the counter while she got the wedding flowers done.

Small-town life was apparently his jam.

Marigold and Leah were in the workroom, deep in conversation. He held up the two takeout bags. "Breakfast, ladies."

Neither one of them looked at him. He cleared his throat. "No one's hungry?"

Marigold glanced his way. "That feeling you had in your gut about something being off? I think you were right."

A sharp jolt went through him, the need for action, the need to respond and make things right. He dropped the bags on the counter and went into the workroom. "What happened? Are you okay? Did those men come back?"

"I'm fine, it's nothing like that. Listen, what do you know about your client? The woman who hired you to bid on the same stuff as me?"

That wasn't the response he'd expected. Had Suzanne done something? "She's a wealthy woman. Deep into real estate from what she's told me. Why?"

Marigold looked at Leah, and Wyatt got the distinct feeling they weren't telling him something. But what? She shifted her attention back to him. "Is that all you know about her?"

"I know a little more. But why? You've got to tell me what's going on. I'm as involved in this as you are."

She chewed at the inside of her cheek for a moment. "I dropped the box that had the bookends in it this morning. Broke one of them right in two."

"That isn't good."

"That's not the half of it," she said. "I found this." She pulled a chain from the pocket of her jeans and held it up. A weird eye-shaped medallion hung from it.

He peered closer. "What is that? You say you found it? Where?"

"I don't know what it is, but it was inside the bookend that broke. Fell out when I picked the pieces up. I was going to see if they could be mended. This pendant was inside, wrapped in fabric. I'm thinking it's what this whole thing was really about, not those ugly knickknacks."

He nodded, the elements coming together in his head the way they did when a case was about to be solved. "You're right. I'm sure of it. But why? That thing doesn't look like it's worth much. But I admit, I don't know much about jewelry."

"Me either." She tucked it back into her pocket. "I have a friend here in town who does. I was hoping you could help Leah mind the store while I go see her this morning."

"Yeah, sure. But I don't like the idea of you going by yourself."

"I'll be fine. I appreciate your concern, but nothing happened last night, right?"

"Actually…" He rubbed the back of his neck. "Do any of your neighbors own a dark sedan?"

Marigold squinted a little as she thought. "Silver Camry, blue Explorer, black Tahoe, silver F-150, tan Pacifica…and one yellow Corvette. Nope, no dark sedans." Then she squinted at him. "Why?"

So much for not telling her. "There was a dark sedan a few doors down from your house last night. I rolled by your place, then ran the block and came back. When I pulled into your driveway, the sedan took off."

"Oh…crap."

He nodded. "So I'd really prefer if you not go see your friend alone."

She nodded. "Agreed. But the bookends are here. I'm not sure how I feel about you coming with me and leaving Leah alone with them."

"Is Newt coming to get them today?"

"Yes. Right before lunch."

"And when are you going to see your friend?"

"Pretty much now."

"Is there anyone else you can call to sit with Leah? Can that woman Birdie get a deputy to come up here? Just the visual of a patrol car parked out front would go a long way."

Marigold picked up her phone off the worktable. "That's a great idea. Birdie can get anything done."

Taking Wyatt with her to see Willa wasn't Marigold's ideal plan, but she didn't want to go without him either. Not after what he'd told her about the car parked outside her house last night. What if those men showed up again? She'd much rather have Wyatt at her side.

She also liked being with him. The way he looked at her, the way he wanted to take care of her. She was happier around him than she'd been in a long time, and he made her feel special.

Feeling safe was just an added bonus.

She felt safe with Deputy Jenna Blythe at the shop, too. Besides being an outstanding officer of the law, Jenna was an honest-to-goodness valkyrie. Leah looked up to her like she was Wonder Woman. As a result, the two got on pretty well.

As Marigold and Wyatt walked, she pondered her new problem. How could she buy some private time with Willa to discuss the magic surrounding the pendant? She had an idea, but she wasn't sure if Wyatt would see through it or not. If he went for it, she and Willa would be able to talk about the pendant's magic without spilling the beans in front of him.

But just in case her plan didn't work, she'd also texted Willa that the man with her was human.

Talking about the pendant in front of Wyatt wouldn't help much, though. Marigold needed to know what powers this thing had.

As they got closer to Illusions, Willa's jewelry store, Wyatt seemed to be scanning their surroundings and assessing every person they passed. It was obvious that he hadn't lost any of the skills he'd learned in the police department.

"That's the shop up ahead." Marigold angled her head toward Illusions. That felt more discreet than pointing just in case someone *was* watching them. "I was thinking once we go in and I introduce you to Willa, you might want to come back out and do a perimeter check. The way you did at my house."

He nodded. "I was planning on doing that, actually. Does she have a back entrance the way your shop does?"

He'd bitten. That had gone easier than expected. "Yes, but it's unmarked as an extra safety precaution. And it's always locked. It's the door under the steps that lead to the apartment upstairs. She lives up there. For now."

"For now?"

"When she and her fiancé get married in two weeks, they're going to move into his house. Not sure what she'll do about the apartment. Maybe keep it." Marigold shrugged. "It was kind of a package deal with the shop."

He was still studying every face that came by. "Seems like an unnecessary expense. Especially for newlyweds."

"I think she can afford it. She was the queen of—" Marigold shut her mouth. She couldn't very well explain that Willa had very briefly once been the Queen of Rhoswynn, the fae kingdom hidden in the mountains of Arkansas.

"The queen of what?" Wyatt asked.

Crappity crap. Think fast. "The queen of jewelry design. Her stuff is really sought after." Wow, worst save ever.

"She *was* the queen of jewelry design?" Wyatt stopped looking at the passersby long enough to glance at Marigold. His expression said he thought something wasn't right about that answer. Him and his dang gut instincts.

"Well, the shop keeps her so busy. I don't think she pursues the competitions and stuff like she used to." Marigold hurried forward to grab the door to Illusions and pull it open. "Here we are!"

Thankfully. Her ability to cover her slipups was horrible. And frankly, she hated lying to him. She wanted to tell him everything. She was just a little scared. Okay, maybe a lot scared.

But there would be time for truth telling later. Much later.

With Wyatt following, she went inside, blinking at the cool air and glittering showcases. Illusions was one of the best places in town to window shop. So many pretties. There were no customers in the shop yet, just Willa and one of her employees, Ramona.

Ramona was a brownie and a bit of a flirt. Marigold gave both women a little wave. "Hi, Willa. Hi, Ramona."

Ramona was cleaning the glass top and front of one of the showcases. "Hey, Marigold. How are you?"

"Great, thanks."

Willa came out from behind the counter. "Good morning, Marigold."

"Morning, Willa. Thanks for making time for me."

"Of course."

Marigold put her hand on Wyatt's arm. "This is Wyatt West, the guy I was telling you about. Wyatt, this is Willa Iscove, my friend and the best jeweler in town."

He nodded at Willa. "Nice to meet you." Then he grinned at Marigold. "You were telling her about me?"

"Maybe a little. Settle down." She winked at him.

Ramona was giving Wyatt an approving gaze, then she caught Marigold watching her and grinned. "You go, girl."

Marigold laughed softly. She wanted to tell Ramona she was, but thought that might embarrass Wyatt.

"Why don't you come into my office?" Willa gestured toward the back room, visible slightly through an open door. A big window next to the door looked like a mirror, but it was actually two-way glass that allowed whoever was in the office to keep an eye on the shop. "I'll see what I can do to help."

Wyatt jerked his thumb toward the outside. "I'm going to make sure everything's good with a once around, then I'll be back in."

"Perfect." Willa smiled. "We'll see you in a few then."

He left and Marigold followed Willa into the office. Marigold pulled the pendant from her pocket even before Willa had the door shut.

As the pendant swung free, Jasper, Willa's cat who often came to work with her, hissed from his spot on her desk. He sat up and let out a low yowl, swatting at the eye-shaped medallion. The hair ridged up along his back.

"Wow, he doesn't like this thing at all, does he?" Marigold asked.

"Now, now, Jasper. It's not going to hurt you," Willa said. She put her hand on his back to calm him down as she spoke to Marigold. "That's not a good sign."

"No, it's not. Animals can sense dark magic. Some witches even keep pets for that reason. As a sort of first-alert system against hexes and such."

"Interesting," Willa said. "Did Frank react to it?"

Marigold shook her head. "No, Frank didn't have any response to it. Although he hissed at the picture of the bookends this was hidden in. He saw it on my phone. But the pendant itself…" She thought for a moment. "I think he was asleep in the shop window when I had the pendant out this morning. And I was in the back room."

"Enough distance that it may not have registered. Especially if he was sleeping." Willa held her hand out. "Let's have a look before Wyatt comes back in."

Marigold held it out.

With a throaty growl, Jasper jumped down and ran into the front of the store.

Willa glanced at him. "He *really* doesn't like this thing." She took the amulet. "And I understand why. I can feel the magic in the metal. Feels prickly. Like dark magic would."

"That confirms what I felt." Marigold exhaled. This just got better and better. "Do you have any idea what it does? Is it for protection against something? Is it cursed?"

Willa turned it over, looking closer. "It's sterling. The stone is golden topaz. You can tell Wyatt that much. Tell him too that I'm going to research it some more. See if I can find out when it was made and by whom."

"Sounds good. Now, what else can you tell *me*?"

Willa closed her hands around the pendant and went silent for a moment. Then she shook her head. "This isn't fae magic. This is strictly witchcraft. *Old* witchcraft. There might be blood magic involved, too, but I imagine one of your coven members could answer that better than I."

Marigold grimaced. Blood magic wasn't always dark, it depended on the spell and the intent. But when it *was* used in dark magic, it was bad news. "This is so not my area. Plants, sure, all day long, but this kind of stuff? Nope. I need to talk to my mother about this. And soon. Like, I should go now."

Wyatt walked in. "Go where?"

Willa glanced at Marigold as she handed the pendant back. "I should go find Jasper before he crawls into one of the showcases and takes a nap in it."

"Who's Jasper?" he asked as Willa left.

"Her cat." Marigold stuck the eye pendant into her pocket. She didn't like having it so close to her knowing what might have been involved in its creation, but she couldn't explain that to Wyatt either. So into her pocket it went.

He glanced back toward the storefront. "She has a shop cat too? Is that a thing here? I know it is in some places. New Orleans has some shop cats."

"Jasper isn't really a shop cat. He's Willa's pet, he just comes into work with her a lot. Since she lives upstairs and all."

Wyatt nodded. "So what did you find out?"

"Willa couldn't tell me much about the pendant, unfortunately." Not much that she could share with him. "She did say it's sterling and the stone in the center is a golden topaz."

"Sounds fancy. Did she say what she thinks it's worth?"

"She's going to do some research on it. See if the age of it and the designer affects its value." She had to get to her mother. And she had to do it without telling Wyatt why. She contemplated putting the truth out there, but if he freaked out, she was going to be on her own for this. She didn't want to lose him.

Not when there was so much possibility for them. Not when she was sure she could find a way to explain who she really was in time. When he loved her and wouldn't care.

"What's going on?" he asked with that keen look in his eyes. "What aren't you telling me?"

She shook her head and forced a smile she didn't quite feel. "I need to run down to see my mom. Wedding stuff. Do you mind?"

"Not at all. In fact, I can go over to Guildman's and pick up my clothes while you talk to her."

Her smile turned genuine. That worked out well. "Perfect. Let's go. I don't want to leave Deputy Blythe on flower shop duty for too long."

They said goodbye and hit the sidewalk again. This time, Wyatt reached over and took her hand.

He glanced at her. "Is that okay?"

She smiled and squeezed his hand. "Yes."

It was more than okay. It was strange and wonderful and perfect.

They walked like that all the way to her mom's shop, then Wyatt kissed her cheek. "I'm only right across the street. Call me if you need me. I'll be there instantly."

"Okay. See you in a few."

"You got it." He headed to Guildman's, and she went into the bridal shop.

The soft sounds of conversation reached her ears. Her mother must be busy, but this was an emergency. She followed the voices back to the dressing rooms.

A young woman was on the podium in one of the many, many dresses the store had available. Marigold smiled. It was impossible not to with a radiant bride in front of her. "Oh, that dress is beautiful."

The woman, her entourage, and Corette all turned. "Thank you," the woman said, smiling. "I think this might be the one."

"I can't imagine a more perfect dress. You look like a million dollars. And I'm so sorry to intrude, but I need to talk to my mom for a couple of minutes. My sister's getting married tomorrow, and well…" Marigold shrugged and smiled like they would understand. "Wedding stuff."

The young woman's eyes lit up. "Is Corette your mom?"

Marigold smiled. "Yes."

"You lucky duck. And yes, please, go ahead and talk to her. Wedding stuff always comes first," the young woman said. "I'm going to twirl around in this gown for another ten minutes anyway."

Corette walked toward Marigold. She was smiling, but Marigold knew that smile. It was the something-had-better-be-on-fire smile. Corette did *not* like to be interrupted when she was working with a bride.

They were back into the main area of the salon before Corette spoke. "What's going on? Did something happen to Pandora's flowers?"

"No, Pandora's flowers are fine. I just—"

"Then why did you drag me away from my bride? You know how I feel about that."

"I do, but this is very important. We need to go into your office. I don't think we should talk about this here."

"Talk about what?"

But Marigold was already halfway to her mother's office. This couldn't wait. Wyatt would be back soon enough.

Corette strode after her.

As soon as her mother was in the office, Marigold shut the door and locked it.

"What on earth are you—"

Marigold pulled out the pendant.

Corette sucked in a sharp breath and put her hand to her heart. "Stars preserve us. Where in all of creation did you get that evil thing? Why do you have that?"

"Mom, I don't even know what this is. That's why I'm here."

"You don't know? I guess that's good." Corette swallowed. She'd yet to take her eyes off the pendant.

"What is it? Tell me."

Corette let out a ragged exhale and shook her head. "It's a tool of evil. A cunning device used to trick and sway. I thought they had all been destroyed, but apparently they weren't."

"Mom, *what is it*?"

She swallowed. "That, my dear child, is a piece of blood and ash magic called the jaundiced eye, and it is the worst kind of trouble you can imagine."

"The jaundiced eye? Sounds like a disease."

Corette frowned. "It's worse. Whoever wears that pendant gains the ability to see a person's weaknesses, and the power to use those weaknesses against them. But it takes a little piece of the wearer too, making their own weaknesses worse with each use."

"Why would Newt want this? He seems like such a nice old wizard."

"Power," Corette answered. She held out her hand. "You have to give it me."

"I can't. How would I explain that to Wyatt? What good reason do I have to turn it over to you? Unless I tell him the truth."

Her mom thought for a few long seconds. "Then tell him the truth."

"Right before the rehearsal dinner?"

"Honey, if he can't handle it, then he's not the man for you."

"But you're the one who told me to wait until we were in love."

"I know. And I wish you could. But this…this is a special circumstance. That pendant cannot be allowed to fall into the wrong hands. It needs to be destroyed."

"So destroy it." Marigold held the offensive thing out toward her mom.

"It's not that easy. It requires a ritual. You can't just let that kind of magic loose into the world. I'll contact the coven, and we'll start preparations, but there's no way it can happen before the wedding."

"Are you going to tell Alice about this?" Alice Bishop was the head of the coven and the most powerful witch Marigold had ever known. She was responsible for the spell that gave the water of the falls the ability to hide the truth of Nocturne Falls.

"I have to. We'll need her for the ritual. Why?"

"Because she'll figure out that I've told Wyatt the truth."

"Don't worry about that. He's already shown himself to be a good person. I'm sure he'll understand once you explain things to him. It won't be an issue."

Corette seemed so sure, but Marigold wasn't. Finding out the truth of the world, that there were shapeshifters and vampires and witches and a whole host of other creatures who lived and worked alongside you, that wasn't the kind of thing everyone could accept.

Wyatt had been a police officer. They relied on truth to do their jobs. Maybe, just maybe he would be okay with it.

Then again, he'd only just changed his mind about even being in a relationship. What if being in a relationship with a witch (who had a whole witchy family) was more than he could handle?

Corette put her hand on Marigold's shoulder. "Do you want to tell him together?"

"No. If this goes poorly, I'd rather not have witnesses." She smiled as best she could. "I'll do it as soon as we get back to the shop."

As much as Wyatt would have loved to hang out and chat with Dexter Guildman, he didn't like leaving Marigold alone. Not even if she was just across the street in her mother's bridal salon. Where technically she wasn't alone. But *he* wasn't there to protect her.

And that's what really bothered him.

So he hustled through trying on the clothes, which all fit perfectly, then got everything wrapped up and headed back to Ever After.

No one was around when he walked in. He adjusted his new garment bag over his arm. Dexter had given him the bag to hold all of his new clothes. "Marigold? You here?"

He didn't want to just traipse through the store looking for them. It felt like a very feminine space and not one he should interject himself in.

A few moments later, she and her mom came out from a back room. Marigold made eye contact immediately. "Did you get your clothes already? That was fast."

"The tailor did a great job," he said. From their body posture to their expressions, they both looked stressed. Whatever wedding stuff was going on, it must be serious. "Everything okay?"

Marigold's smile was weak. "It will be. We need to get back to the store."

"Sure thing. I'm ready when you are."

She glanced at her mother. "I'll call you later."

Corette nodded. "Please do."

Wyatt raised his free hand. "See you at the rehearsal dinner tonight, Ms. Williams. But if there's anything I can help with in the meantime, you just let Marigold know and I'll take care of it."

"That's a very kind offer, thank you. Marigold will fill you in. Now if you'll pardon me, I have a bride waiting." She went off toward the other side of the salon.

Marigold looked so pensive. "Let's go."

He hoisted his garment bag over his shoulder, then took Marigold's hand with his free one. "You sure you're okay?"

"We'll talk about it at the shop, okay?"

"Okay."

It was a long walk back, mostly because he couldn't stop wondering what was going on. He couldn't think of anything that would make Marigold and her mother so anxious. The wedding was still on, wasn't it?

He was sure the two women would have been much more emotionally distraught if the wedding had been called off. They'd probably have rushed to Pandora's side. That seemed to be what families like this did, they supported each other. But that wasn't happening, so that couldn't be it.

What, then?

He had no idea and was no closer to figuring it out when they arrived at the Enchanted Garden. Apparently his skills of deduction didn't extend to matrimonial affairs.

Marigold thanked Deputy Blythe for staying at the shop while they'd been gone. Deputy Blythe left, then Marigold checked in with Leah to see if anything needed her attention.

It didn't and Leah seemed to have made good progress on the wedding flowers while they'd been gone. The workroom was a mess, but in that busy, productive, organized chaos kind of way.

Marigold went over the list of arrangements needed for the wedding, then nodded. "We're pretty much on track. Great job, Leah. Would you watch the counter for a bit? I need to talk to Wyatt alone."

"Sure. I can finish these boutonnieres out there." Leah picked up her tray of supplies and headed out, leaving Marigold and Wyatt in the workroom.

He stood facing her, ready for anything. He hoped. "Is this about the wedding?"

"Not exactly." Marigold smiled the same weak smile again as she looked at Wyatt. She took the garment bag from him and hung it on one of the coat hooks by the door, then came back to him. He was on one side of a worktable, she was on the other. "We need to talk."

He hadn't expected to hear that for a long time. If ever. He'd thought he'd been doing all right in the boyfriend department, but maybe not. Whatever was wrong, he'd fix it. "Okay. What's on your mind?"

She hesitated. "I don't know how to say this."

Everything in him chilled. Was she breaking up with him? They'd barely begun. But this definitely sounded like she was about to end things. A knot formed in his gut. "Just say it. I can take it."

That might not be completely honest, but being a homicide detective had taught him to compartmentalize things. He knew how to suppress his emotions until there was a time and place to deal with them.

"I haven't told you the full truth about who I am. I haven't lied to you deliberately, I don't want you to think that, but there's more to me than just what you know."

He frowned. Maybe she wasn't breaking up with him, but it still wasn't good news. "That sounds ominous."

"It's nothing bad, I swear. Not for me anyway. But revealing this side of myself is hard." She drew in a long, unsteady breath and put her hands on the table between them. Bits and pieces of flowers, stems, and leaves covered its surface. "I like you a lot, Wyatt. I sincerely hope what I'm about to share with you doesn't change the way you feel about me, but if it does…I understand."

He couldn't give her any reassurance without knowing what she was going to say, but he had to say something. "I'll do my best to keep an open mind."

"Good." She smiled a little, but now she was twisting a few of the loose leaves together. She was nervous, clearly.

Whatever this was, she was fretting over it. Seeing her like this, so worried, so unsure, hurt him. He went to her and took her hands. "Hey, I'm sure it'll be fine."

"I don't know…"

He made himself smile. Not because he was happy about any of this, but because she needed it. "Just tell me."

She nodded. "Okay." Then exhaled. "I'm a witch."

He stared at her, trying to process what she'd just said. And why she'd said it. "I don't think that's true at all. I think you're very sweet. Why would you say that about—"

"No, I mean I'm actually a witch. A spell-casting, magic-wielding witch."

He stared at her a little more. Then laughed as he tugged playfully on her hands. "Come on, stop fooling around. I know this town is all about the illusion that Halloween and the creatures that go with it are real, but this is taking things a little too far."

Cold, hard seriousness shone in her eyes. "Wyatt, I'm not kidding. I'm a witch. My mother and my sisters are witches, too. So is my daughter, but her powers are just beginning to manifest."

He dropped her hands and backed away. "Why are you telling me this?"

"Because the pendant I found in that bookend? It's steeped in dark magic. You're involved in this whole mess, and you deserve to know the truth. But there's more."

"More? What else could there be?"

"There are supernaturals of all varieties in this town. That's the reason this town exists. To give those of us with supernatural abilities a safe place to live. Where we can be ourselves and not have to hide."

He laughed defensively. "All varieties? What's that supposed to mean?"

"Besides witches, there are vampires, werewolves, shapeshifters, fae, nymphs, mermaids, dryads…the town is home to all sorts of creatures.

None of them mean you or any human harm, I promise. We live in peace and harmony. You're in no danger."

"No, I'm not," he said, shaking his head at the craziness filling it. "Because none of it's real. I don't believe in any of that. Just like I know magic is a trick. There's a reason for everything. An explanation. I might not know what it is just yet, but there's *always* a reason. The only thing I can't figure out is why you're telling me all this."

But even as he spoke, the things he'd recently seen—the flowers growing under Marigold's touch, the witch on the street performing magic, the strange feral gleam in Birdie's eyes—said Marigold was telling the truth.

He didn't want to believe that truth, because believing it meant questioning everything. He'd come to rely on absolutes in his world. If there was a crime to solve, there was a way to solve it. Clues that led to concrete evidence.

Magic meant there might not always be concrete evidence. And that upset everything he knew.

"Wyatt, I'm telling you this because of the pendant. It's dangerous. And I won't be able to get rid of it until after the wedding. The ritual that can destroy magic that powerful takes time to prepare."

He stood there, listening, but not fully accepting. "I don't know how to react. I don't know what to think. Except that I don't want to believe any of this. I *don't* believe it. But then…maybe I do."

He shook his head and paced to one end of the workroom, then back. "You understand how crazy all of this sounds."

"I can only guess." She shrugged apologetically. "I've lived in this community all my life, so it's as natural to me as being a witch is."

"A witch," he muttered, testing the word for the weight of truth the way he'd always done with witness statements. "How is that possible? It's not. It shouldn't be."

"It is," she said softly.

Then, as if to punctuate the moment, Frank sauntered by on the way to his food bowl.

Wyatt stopped dead in his tracks. "A black cat. You have a black cat."

"Frank's just a shop cat. He's not my familiar. And black cats aren't really a witch's favorite pet. They can have whatever kind of pets they like. The whole black cat thing was made up by…whoever made it up."

Wyatt finally looked at her again. "How can this be real? How am I supposed to believe that everything I've come to think of as a fairy tale is suddenly true?"

"Do you want proof?"

He couldn't answer her until he'd thought that through. Proof would mean he'd have to believe. Or he'd have to run.

That's why this bothered him so much. Either he believed and he stayed, or Marigold was a liar and he left.

He didn't want to believe, but he wanted even less for Marigold to be a liar. He liked her. Even with this new development.

He wanted to stay. "Okay. Show me proof."

A small light entered her gaze. As if she suddenly had hope. "I won't do anything too intense, all right?"

"Whatever you want to do is fine with me." He crossed his arms and waited.

She wiggled her fingers toward the table in front of her. It lifted off the floor.

His mouth came open. He knew it could be rigged. But when would she have had the time? And why go to such great lengths?

Then she lifted one hand a little higher and all the plant debris on the table rose into the air and whirled around in a small vortex.

There was no rigging that. This was real. And if that wasn't intense, what would she consider intense? "You're a witch," he breathed.

It wasn't a question, but a statement of truth.

She nodded and set the debris and the table back down. "I am."

He shook his head. "How is this possible?"

"I was born this way."

He shoved a hand through his hair and thought over everything she'd said. "So is everyone in town…something? When I saw you with the flowers, what was going on? The flowers looked like they were growing."

"First question first. No, not everyone in town is a supernatural. But a lot are. Leah is a tree nymph."

"I don't even know what that is."

"Tree spirit. Basically." Marigold tucked a blond curl behind her ear. "Birdie, the woman you met at the sheriff's department, is a werewolf."

His mouth came open again. "That explains so much."

"There will be a lot of supernaturals at the wedding, too. In fact, you might be the only normie. I mean, non-supernatural human. Well, there should be one other human there, but she's kind of a special case."

He put a hand to his head. This was a lot of new information. Then something else occurred to him. "Dexter, the man who owns Guildman's, said he retired here because this is where his granddaughter goes to the school. Some place called Harmswood. Is he also here because he's…not human?"

That might explain some of his incredible football skills.

Marigold nodded. "Harmswood is the same school my Saffie goes to. It's for supernatural children. And I don't know the Guildmans very well because they just moved here about a year ago, but I'm pretty sure they're tiger shifters."

He collapsed into one of the work stools. The Wrecking Machine was a tiger. It was almost funny because his cat-like grace had often been written about. Wyatt heaved out a breath. "This is nuts. You know that, right? How crazy this all sounds?"

She nodded. "I get it. I do. I'm sure it'll take a few days for it to all sink in. Maybe longer." She took a few steps toward him. "I've never told anyone human about my being a witch before. Are you...okay?"

He wasn't sure, but he liked that he was the first non-supernatural she'd shared her true self with. "That must have been hard for you to share."

"It was."

"I appreciate the effort it took." But he wanted to know more. "Tell me about the flowers."

"You mean why they looked like they were growing?"

He nodded.

"After we put the arrangements together, I use my powers to grow the flowers and plants in them a little. I'm a green witch. Plants and flowers are my specialty. That extra touch is what makes my arrangements so big and beautiful and natural looking."

"I see. I guess it makes sense that a green witch would work with flowers and plants. What about the witch and vampire I saw on the street? Were they actors playing parts or...the real thing?"

"The real thing. If you saw a vampire during daylight hours, it was probably Julian Ellingham or Greyson Garrett. There's only a handful in town who can handle the sun. The rest are strictly night shift."

He sat there, staring at nothing and thinking about everything. "Wow."

She bit her lip. "Are...we..."

She didn't finish, but he heard the question in her voice and understood. She wanted to know if they were good.

He had to tell her the truth. Especially after what she'd just shared with him. "I don't know. If you have all these powers, why would you be interested in a regular non-magical guy like me?"

She smiled. "Well, I'm a woman and you're a man. Attraction is attraction. Plus, I think you have your own kind of magic, Wyatt. And as long as I haven't scared you off, I am still very much interested."

Then she hesitated. "Have I scared you off?"

"I still like you," he said. "I just feel a little lost right now."

"I understand that. Do you want me to leave you alone?"

He laughed. "This is your shop. If one of us is going to leave, it has to be me. But no. Don't go. I can handle this. Talking about it helps. Speaking of, tell me about the pendant. Where is it?"

"Still in my pocket, and frankly, I hate having it that close to me." She pulled it out and set it on the table. "We have to find somewhere safe to keep it until it can be destroyed. My mother offered to take it, but I don't like dumping this on her. Or possibly putting her in harm's way."

The pendant looked innocent enough to him. Kind of like something some bohemian hippy chick might wear to a music festival. "It's really evil, huh?"

"Its purposes are. And the magic attached to it is very dark. Blood and ash magic, which are almost always used for nefarious motives."

The phone rang, and a few seconds later, Leah knocked on the door. "Sorry to interrupt, but there's a call for you Marigold."

"Coming." Then she patted Wyatt's knee. "Be right back."

He nodded, eyes still on the pendant. As she left, he picked it up to look at it more closely. It didn't feel evil. It didn't feel like anything but metal and stone. Maybe you had to be a witch to know there was magic involved.

A strange impulse made him loop the chain over his head.

His last thought was that wasn't something he should have done.

Marigold was happy that Wyatt hadn't run screaming, but she felt bad that she was the reason he looked like he'd been hit by a truck. She understood, though, and she felt pretty optimistic that everything was going to be okay.

Finding out the truth about her—and Nocturne Falls—was a big shock, she knew, but maybe being a cop had helped him learn to deal with big shocks. Whatever the case, he seemed to be handling things with a surprising amount of calm.

She took the phone from Leah. "Hello, this is Marigold speaking. How can I help?"

"You're not answering your texts. I got concerned."

"Everything's fine, Mom." She covered the mouthpiece to whisper at Leah, "Why didn't you say it was my mom?"

Leah held up her hands. She had moved into the shop to give Marigold space behind the counter. "She said not to."

Corette continued. "Did you tell him the truth?"

"I did." And it had been the hardest conversation she'd ever had, outside of telling Saffron the truth about her father.

"How's he handling it?"

"Pretty well, I think. He didn't storm out or run screaming, so that's something. But I should probably get back to him."

"You should, but I also wanted to tell you that I spoke to Alice about the pendant. She's putting things in motion for the destruction ritual, but she thought I should tell you that it's imperative no one puts the pendant on."

Marigold nodded. "Trust me, that is not going to—"

Wyatt walked out of the workroom looking very, very different. His eyes were dark and wild, and there was a dangerous air about him.

Then Marigold saw something else. The pendant.

Around his neck.

Marigold stared as her pulse shot up and her blood went cold. "Mom, what happens if someone puts the pendant on?"

"They become the owner of the pendant until their death. Which, according to Alice, takes until the dark magic completely possesses that person. A strong witch or wizard could last for years. A lesser being, maybe only one year. Or just months."

Marigold swallowed. "And a human?"

"Days. So you see, it's paramount that no one—"

"I gotta go." She hung up on her mother, something she'd never done before in her life. "Wyatt, take that pendant off right now."

He smiled a terrible grin that made her shiver with revulsion. It was almost like the evil spilling off him had become visible. There was no doubt the darkness in that pendant was in charge of him.

He shook his finger at her. "You're a naughty girl. You've been keeping all this power from me. That's not very nice."

"Um…" Leah made a face. "What's going on here?"

"Leah, get out of the shop and lock the front door behind you. Then call my mother back and tell her Wyatt put the pendant on. Tell her to bring the coven here. We have to help him. Fast."

Leah didn't move. "What pendant? What's going on?"

"Leah," Marigold yelled. "Just do it."

Wyatt kept advancing, trapping Marigold behind the counter. "You're afraid of me. I can see it. I can see all of your weaknesses. You thought you might be falling for me, and now you're afraid. It's so sad. Boo hoo." He rubbed at his eyes like he was crying, then sneered at her. "You're so pathetic. So needy."

She raised her hands even as she retreated farther, but she was reluctant to use magic against him. What if the pendant caused him to lash out? What if Wyatt got hurt because of it? "That's just the pendant talking. I know you're still in there, Wyatt. I'm going to get you free. I promise."

But how? He was a human being controlled by powers that would be daunting even for her, a seasoned witch, to command. She had to figure this out. Had to save him.

After all, this was her fault. She never should have agreed to help Newt.

Newt! He'd be arriving soon. Maybe he could help get Wyatt free.

Wyatt took another step toward her. Any closer and he'd be able to touch her. She wasn't sure what he'd do, but she didn't want to find out. She hopped up onto the counter and scrambled over it. That put him behind the counter and her in the main area of the store. Behind her, Leah was on the phone explaining things to Corette.

She had to protect Leah. She snapped her fingers to get the woman's attention. "Get out of here. Lock the door behind you. Go. I don't want you hurt."

Leah shook her head. "I'm not leaving you." Then she pointed at the phone. "Your mother says I shouldn't leave you either. She's getting Pandora and Charisma and coming over. And she's calling the rest of the coven from the car."

Wyatt was out from behind the counter and headed for her again. "Pretty, pretty Marigold," he purred as he moved toward her.

She lifted her hands again. "Wyatt, stay back. I don't want to hurt you."

He laughed long and hard. "You sweet, dumb child." Then he spread his hands wide. "You can't hurt me. Not now. Not with the power of the jaundiced eye flowing through me. I see your flaws. I know how to control you."

"That pendant can't control me."

He dropped his hands and stalked forward. "You don't think you can be loved, do you? Not after your ex left you alone and pregnant. So sad. Sadder still is how lonely you are. So lonely. But that's because you're not good enough, are you?"

His words cut into her like blades. She reminded herself that this was not the Wyatt she'd gotten to know, but the Wyatt held in the sway of some dreadful dark magic. But the pain of the truth he was speaking made her heart ache.

She lifted her chin, as determined to fight as she was not to break down. "I'm going to free you, Wyatt. I promise."

He laughed again. "I've never felt this free."

As he walked past a display of ivy topiaries, he reached out and picked up one of the large pots. It must have weighed fifty pounds, but he lifted it like it was nothing.

She braced herself for him to smash it or something, hoping he didn't. She'd grown all of those from cuttings. Nurtured them into shapes with her magic. Stars, hearts, spheres.

He'd picked up a simple circle. He held it before him so he could look through it at her. "But you, you're trapped, aren't you? Trapped by your ineffectual gifts." He snorted. "A green witch. What good is that?"

"I'll show you," she hissed. She lifted her hands and tapped into her magic, calling for the plants to help her. The ivy responded by snaking their tendrils forward and wrapping around him. The vines thickened and grew with such incredible speed it caught him off guard.

"Now who's trapped?" she asked.

His only answer was a growl as he struggled, but the vines continued to mature and twine around him, pinning his arms to his sides and tying his legs together.

She urged the vines on, spilling more magic into them. Round and round him they went.

"Let me free, witch." The anger in his voice gave it a gravelly, unnatural edge, almost like the pendant was speaking. But so far, her magic was winning because he seemed unable to break free, despite the power of the pendant.

"I don't think so." She pushed the vines a little more so that they knotted up and took him to the ground. He was almost mummified now, having basically become a human topiary. At last, she eased off, letting the ivy rest.

"Wow," Leah said.

Marigold glanced at her. "I wasn't sure what else to do."

"I'd say that was perfect." Leah's eyes were wide. "Holy cannoli, that was amazing."

"Except the pendant is still on him." But at least he wasn't a threat to himself or to them anymore.

She went to him. His eyes flashed with anger. The ivy had covered his mouth, muffling him. She crouched down beside him. "I'm sorry, Wyatt. But this is for the best until we can figure out how to get you free of the pendant's magic."

He growled out more words she couldn't understand.

The shop door rattled.

Marigold looked up to see her mother and Pandora on the other side of the glass.

"Got it," Leah yelled. She scrambled for the lock, letting the two women in.

"Charisma's on her way. I also let Alice know what had happened, and she's researching the situation." Corette's eyes rounded as she saw the green mummy on the floor. "Well done, Marigold. I take it he's contained?"

"Yes."

Wyatt growled and tried to move, but succeeded only in shaking the leaves a little.

Marigold stood. "We can't leave him here."

"No, we cannot." Corette stared at him a little longer.

Marigold pointed at Leah. "Lock the door, but stay by it to let the rest of the coven in. We'll put up a sign that says we're closed to handle wedding business until further notice. No one in town will question that."

"Done." Leah went back to the door.

Then Marigold got her sister's attention. "Pandora, grab his feet. We'll carry him into the workroom. Mom, make that sign for the door, will you?"

Pandora hustled forward as Corette nodded and went around them to the counter. Pandora grabbed Wyatt's feet, then dropped them and straightened. "Why not just let me levitate him back to the workroom? Move, I've got this."

"No," Marigold snapped. "We can't. The pendant has control of him. We have no idea what will happen if we use magic on him."

"She's right," Corette said.

Pandora gave them both a look. "But you wrapped him up in ivy and nothing happened, did it?"

"No, but I used my magic on the ivy, not on him. He was sort of a bystander for that."

"Oh." Pandora shrugged and grabbed Wyatt's feet again. "All right. Ready when you are."

Marigold got his shoulders. "One...two...three." She hoisted him up as Pandora lifted.

"Wow," Pandora said. "Your boyfriend is heavy."

Marigold huffed out a breath. "He works out."

They shuffle-walked him to the back room, positioning him between the two big worktables.

Pandora straightened, brushing her hands off. "Hey, are these the corsages for my wedding? They're gorgeous. Can I see my bridal bouquet?"

Marigold put her hands on her hips. "Could we maybe deal with the evil magic that's currently possessing my date for said wedding first?"

Pandora shrugged. "I just figured while we were waiting..."

"Hello?" Charisma called out from the front of the shop.

"Back here," Marigold answered.

Her sister walked in looking like the cover of a fashion magazine. That was standard for Charisma. No one had it together quite like her. Sleek, dark bob, perfect makeup, ivory linen pants and jacket that were somehow not wrinkled. "Hi, Mari, Pandy. Mom filled me in."

She peeked past the table at Wyatt. "I take it that's the poor normie stuck in the middle of this mess?"

Marigold sighed. "Yes."

Charisma pursed her lips. Which were the perfect nude, probably because of some exclusive lipstick. "That poor man. He needs some help."

"Which is why," Corette announced as she joined them, "we are here."

Marigold looked past her mom toward the front of the shop. "What about the rest of the coven?"

"Alice didn't think alerting everyone was a good idea. Not with this kind of magic. She thinks the news about the jaundiced eye best be kept to ourselves for the moment."

Marigold stared at her mother. "Wyatt is in desperate shape. Who cares who knows?"

Corette sighed. "I understand how you feel, but I can't go against Alice. She's in charge. You know that. We all know that. And Alice might be right. What if word got out and some unscrupulous person tried to take control of Wyatt in order to get the jaundiced eye? We have to protect him while we save him."

Marigold nodded reluctantly. "I guess you're right."

Charisma put her arm around Marigold. "We're going to fix this, Mari. I know you like this guy. We're not going to let him be collateral damage. This is all going to work out."

"Thanks." Marigold made herself breathe calmly. Charisma's words helped. Probably why she was such a successful life coach.

Corette's pocket buzzed. She took her phone out and answered it. "Yes?" She looked at her daughters. "I see, Alice. Thank you. I'll let them know."

She hung up and tucked the phone away. "Alice knows how to break the pendant's hold on him." Corette hesitated, clasping and unclasping her hands. "But I don't know how we're going to do it."

Marigold took a step toward her mother. "Just tell us. I'll do anything. How do we save him?"

Corette smiled thinly. "If he was a supernatural, we'd have to perform a ritual that would strip all magic from him. It would leave him human."

That made sense. "But since he's already human?"

"We have to turn him into a supernatural. We have to force enough magic into him to displace that which has its hooks in him already."

Marigold shook her head. "How do we do that? And how do we do that without his consent?"

Pandora glanced at Wyatt. "Do you think he could actually give consent? The pendant wouldn't let him, would it?"

Marigold followed her sister's gaze. Wyatt glared at them, his eyes the only visible part of him. "No. I don't suppose it would. But shouldn't he have some kind of say in the sort of supernatural he becomes?"

"It would be best if that was possible," Corette said. "But under the circumstances, I don't see how it could happen. Like your sister said, the pendant isn't going to let him speak on his own behalf. We have to do this for him. And hope he understands."

Marigold's throat constricted, tight with emotion. And a lot of guilt. "How on earth are we going to generate enough magic to turn him into a supernatural?"

"That," Corette said softly, "is the most difficult part of all. It must be a gift. Given selflessly. A sacrifice."

Marigold looked at her mother. "Meaning what exactly?"

"Someone must volunteer their powers to save his life."

There was no hesitation, no question, not even the slightest moment of doubt in Marigold's mind. "Of course. I'm happy to do it."

Well, maybe *happy* wasn't the perfect word to describe what she was feeling, but she had no reservations that it was what she needed to do.

"Marigold." Her mother looked at her, aghast. Her sisters seemed stricken as well.

"What?" Marigold asked. "He's in this condition because of me. Who else is going to help him if I don't? It's not even a question."

The rightness of it didn't mean her heart wasn't breaking over what she'd be losing. But it was absolutely what had to be done. And she was the one who had to do it.

Pandora was practically sputtering. "B-but you have a child to raise. A fledgling witch who's going to need your guidance and direction. The kind of nurturing that only another witch can give her."

Marigold shrugged. "I agree, so it's a good thing I have two sisters and a mother who fit that description. And that's why we have the mentorship program in the coven."

"But you're her mother," Pandora argued.

"That's not going to change just because I'm no longer a witch."

Charisma shook her head. "You can't do this, Mari. You barely know this man. That's too much to give up for him. Even if you think you're falling for him. There's no guarantee he's going to feel the same way about you once he's transformed."

Marigold knelt beside Wyatt. "This isn't about my feelings for him or his feelings for me, whatever those might be. This is about doing what's right."

"My dear, caring child," Corette said. "Your kindness and generosity are without question. But you need your gifts not just for your daughter, but for your business." She gestured around the shop. "This place was built on your abilities as a green witch."

"Then is one of you better suited to lose your powers? I don't think so. Charisma relies on her ability to see auras to help her clients. You use your gifts to aid brides in finding their perfect dress, plus you're the secretary of the coven. And Pandora only just got her gifts working right, so there's no way she can be expected to give them up."

Her mother and sisters just stood there silently. Probably because they knew she was right.

Marigold smiled to keep from crying. "My green thumb isn't going to disappear because I can no longer speak to the flowers with my magic. I can still be a florist. My business won't be affected very much. And Saffron has all of you to guide her."

She put her hand on Wyatt's ivy-covered chest. Angry magic stung her hand like wasps, but she held the contact, hoping he could feel it and understand she was there with him. And on his side. "I am the only one who can do this. And it's my responsibility anyway. Now we're not discussing it anymore."

Her mother and sisters continued to hold their tongues, but the looks they were exchanging weren't lost on Marigold. She knew they disagreed with her. But the matter was decided. She pushed to her feet. "Where are we doing this?"

Corette swallowed before she spoke. "Alice said she would handle all the setup and we should bring him to Elenora's."

Marigold nodded. "Then that's what we need to do."

Wyatt was being held underwater. That's what it felt like anyway. Being held underwater, but being able to breathe at the same time. Sort of. He was floating. Or drowning. No, he was sinking. Into darkness.

That darkness covered him like oil and was just as impossible to be rid of. There was no freeing himself from it, no matter how hard he fought and struggled and shoved against it.

No stopping the terrible things the darkness pushed from his mouth.

And as if being deaf in one ear wasn't bad enough, sounds were even more muffled with whatever was going on.

He wasn't sure what was happening, but he was aware of enough to know that it wasn't good. The darkness wasn't just the lack of light in his world, it felt very much like a living force that was trying to wrest away his self-control.

It was winning. Not quickly, not as long as he fought. But he was ever so slowly losing his grip on…himself.

The words the darkness had caused him to say…terrible things…and the things he had threatened… But it wasn't him. It was the malevolence gnawing at him. He shuddered and vowed to fight harder.

Fighting was getting more difficult, though. The reasons why he should fight were fading, replaced by an unnatural serenity. The odd calm was being induced by the dark force. He knew that. No matter how much he dug down, he couldn't bring up the things he knew he should be feeling. Anger. Frustration. Fear.

All of those normal emotions were being held underwater with him.

There was the occasional spot of sun. Marigold.

He could see her now and then when she moved into his narrowed field of vision. She looked very far away, but he recognized her beautiful face. He'd also grasped that her mother and sister were around him. Another woman too, but he didn't recognize her voice.

Words were hit or miss, but their tones came through. And once in a while, his name. They were talking about him. And about something very, very bad that had happened to him.

He didn't know what that thing was exactly, but he knew what had caused it.

The pendant. That stupid piece of jewelry was to blame. Why had he picked it up? Why had he put it on? Because it had called out to him. Compelled him. He'd been powerless to stop his own movements.

That wretched pendant. Where was it? He focused on it with all of his energy and suddenly felt it around his neck.

It was the anchor weighing him down. Dragging him deeper.

And he realized with great certainty that if he hit bottom, he would never return to the surface.

That's where life was. Where Marigold was.

He was dying.

The panic he should have felt floated away on a bubble, rising up, up, up until it popped and he forgot what emotion he'd even been thinking about.

The landscape above him changed. Lights shifted. Shadows flitted over him. He was moving. Brightness filled his vision. He was outside. The brightness faded. He was inside again. Something metal surrounded him. It smelled sweet and mechanical.

A thin grumbling sound hummed through him. A motor. The metal surrounding him was a vehicle. The flower shop's delivery van. The women were taking him somewhere. To help him, he hoped.

Their voices echoed against the metal, making them impossible to decipher.

He focused on the pendant again. It burned his skin. Made him feel like something was crawling over him. Into him.

He couldn't move. All he could do was think, and even that wasn't easy.

But there were two things he knew.

Magic was real.

And this pendant was bad.

But the thought registered in the same way that he might think about whether to have his club sandwich on white or wheat.

It was just a fact. Nothing more. Because there was nothing he could do about it. No way to make himself react. The dark force prevented it.

He drifted lower, and the light above him faded a little more. The sounds grew farther away as he sank deeper into the darkness.

He imagined most people would retreat to their happiest memories at a time like this, but he didn't have many of those.

His days on the force. Those were good. Those were happy. But a lot of them were sad, too. That was just part of the job. The people, he thought. The people he'd worked with. They were good. His brothers and sisters in blue.

And then there was Marigold. Bright, smiling, sunshiny Marigold. She was a happy memory. The happiest.

So he thought about her. Marigold the beautiful. Marigold the mother. Marigold the florist. Marigold the witch.

She was a witch. She'd told him that. He tried to understand what that meant. Tried to speak the word. "Witch," he whispered.

But maybe he hadn't said anything at all.

Marigold whipped around to look at Wyatt. "What?"

Across from her, Pandora shook her head. "I didn't say anything."

Marigold frowned. "No, I think Wyatt did."

She and Pandora were with him in the back of the delivery van. Their mother was driving, and Charisma was in the passenger seat. Marigold leaned down, putting her ear to his ivy-covered mouth. "Say it again."

But he was silent.

"Maybe you just thought you heard it." Pandora put her hand on the van's metal side. "It's noisy back here without insulation or carpet to deaden the road noise."

Marigold nodded. "It's a delivery van. No need for that stuff." She put her hand on his chest again. The magic felt stronger. Angier.

Her heart ached. They had better rescue Wyatt fast. In a way, the need to hurry was good. It meant less time to think about what was going to happen.

How she wasn't going to be a witch anymore. She stared at his ivy-covered form, the green blurring as tears filled her eyes.

"Hey," Pandora said softly. "Are you sure you want to do this?"

Marigold nodded. "Yes. I can't let him die."

"No, of course not. We won't let that happen. It's just…"

"I know," Marigold said. She gave herself a mental shake. Lots of people went through life with no powers or magical gifts. Pandora had done it for years. She smiled at her sister. "It's not that big of a deal. You survived without usable magic."

Pandora gave a little half-smile. "Yeah, I did. But I didn't have the added difficulty of knowing what good, working powers were like."

Marigold shrugged one shoulder. "I'll get to live on both sides of things. If I need anything magic, you guys will help me."

Pandora leaned in enthusiastically. "Oh honey, you know it. You just call me any time. I mean it. And if this guy doesn't appreciate what you're doing for him, then I swear, I will turn him into a—"

"Pandy, he doesn't have to appreciate it. I'm sure he will, but that's not why I'm doing this."

Pandora sighed and sat back. "I know. But still. He'd better."

Marigold laughed softly. Sisters were the best.

"I'll mentor Saffie if she wants me to."

"You're already mentoring Kaley."

"I can handle two."

"No," Marigold said. "Kaley is about to be your stepdaughter. You need to give her all your attention. Mom can help Saffie."

Corette looked over her shoulder. "That is a task I will gladly take."

Pandora looked a little weepy again. "You're such a good person, Mari. You don't deserve this."

Marigold spread her fingers in the ivy, feeling the sting of the dark magic but unwilling to break contact with Wyatt. "Neither does he. It's going to be okay."

Pandora reached out and put her hand on Marigold's, then sucked in a breath and yanked it back. She rubbed her thumb against her palm. "Yikes, what is that?"

"The pendant's darkness."

Pandora grimaced. "Do you think Wyatt can feel that or just us because we're already attune to magic?"

"I hope just us. Because otherwise, he's in a lot of pain." Pain Marigold would soon release him from.

Then she would have a different kind of pain to deal with. One that would be with her for the rest of her life.

Alice met them at the side entrance of Elenora Ellingham's large estate. It was the same entrance Marigold brought flowers through every year for the Black and Orange Ball. The grand ballroom was past the kitchen (which was about the size of an entire one-bedroom apartment) and directly ahead. But Alice took them left down a hall and then led them through parts of the house that Marigold had never seen before.

They were headed to what she guessed was Alice's room. Pandora and Marigold followed behind Alice, carrying Wyatt in his ivy wrappings just as they had before. Behind them came Charisma and Corette.

Upon arriving, Marigold realized Alice didn't have a *room*. She had an entire wing.

And once they were through the double doors that accessed Alice's apartment, it was as if they'd entered another dwelling entirely.

While the furnishings were well crafted and clearly fine quality, the luxuriousness of the rest of the house was gone. Elenora's extravagant taste didn't exist here. Alice's rooms reflected her simple, no-nonsense personal style. Clean straight lines, modest fabrics, with a lot of dark wood and stone. Very little existed in the way of personalization, which also seemed very much like Alice.

To most people, including the coven, she was an enigma. She was respected for the power she wielded and for the tragic history she'd escaped in Salem so many years ago, but she was also feared. No one, except maybe Elenora, really knew Alice Bishop.

Or knew what she was truly capable of.

No one seemed willing to be the one to figure that all out, either.

The story that was often shared about her in whispered tones was that when Elenora had saved her from death in Salem, Alice had somehow absorbed all the power of the witches that had already met their fates.

Whether that was true or not, no one knew. And no one was going to ask.

But it certainly gave Alice a status that had remained unchallenged for as long as she'd been in Nocturne Falls. Still, questions remained. How powerful was she? Was she immortal like the vampire who'd saved her?

Marigold didn't think they'd ever know.

"Here." Alice pointed to the center of a large slate-floored room where a rug had been rolled up and set off to the side to clear the space. An enormous fieldstone fireplace occupied one wall. The rest of the walls were lined with wooden shelves filled with books, bottles, and boxes. Near the fireplace sat a chair upholstered in worn tapestry fabric with a small stand next to it that held a slim volume.

But the thing that drew Marigold's gaze was the plain wood worktable, scarred and stained with use, positioned by one of the tall, arched windows that let light in.

Some tools of the craft—a thick leather-bound book, a few bits and pieces of nature, a copper bowl, and a variety of jars, sacks, and containers were scattered over the table's surface.

Marigold realized they were in Alice's practice. The space she used for her craft. Most witches had one. For Marigold, it was her greenhouse. A practice was a sacred space, one rarely shared.

Her mother and sisters must have realized it too, because they were uncommonly quiet.

"Put him here," Alice repeated.

Pandora and Marigold lowered Wyatt to the floor.

Alice went to her worktable and opened the book. It was obviously a grimoire and a very old one, judging by the yellowing of the pages. Marigold peeked over Alice's shoulder just a little. Had she written all those spells herself? It wasn't Marigold's business, but the book was impressive. Her own grimoire was anemic by comparison.

Marigold glanced at her mother and sisters. They shrugged, also unsure of what to do next. Marigold cleared her throat softly. "Should I unbind him?"

"Not yet," Alice said without turning. "Best he's contained until we're ready." She leafed through the book until she came to a page marked with a strip of red leather. She flattened the book to those pages, smoothing her hand over them with care.

Then she faced the women again. "Who among you is going to provide the power to save this man?"

Marigold lifted her chin. "I am."

Alice looked her over, but her gaze was not unkind. "You know what's required of you?"

Marigold nodded. "I do. But he's in this fix because of me."

Alice frowned. "The jaundiced eye was created many, many years ago. That's not even remotely your fault."

"But it's here now because of me. It crossed his path because of me." She shook her head. "I promise that I willingly accept what I'm about to do."

Alice stared at her a second longer, then did something that almost knocked Marigold off her feet. She put her hand on Marigold's arm, her touch gentle. "Your sacrifice won't be forgotten."

Before Marigold could really process what Alice meant by that, the woman took a burlap sack about the size of a five-pound bag of sugar off the table and held it out toward Corette. "Mark the circle."

Corette took it and untied the twine at its neck. Salt. Of course. She started at Wyatt's head and went clockwise, drawing a large circle around him with a thick line of salt.

Alice held another sack out to Charisma. "Seal the circle."

With a nod, Charisma went to work. Her bag held ashes.

Marigold pondered that. Salt was standard. Chalk was too. One or the other was typically used to draw a casting circle, because both were of the earth. Ashes were a strange choice, but her mother had said the pendant was blood and ash magic. Marigold glanced at Alice, almost afraid to ask the question burning in her mind. "Are you going to require my blood?"

Alice smiled a little. "No, child. We want to drive the pendant's magic out, not give it more power."

"But you're sealing the circle with ash."

"So that the pendant's power cannot escape."

Marigold nodded, reassured. "Thank you. I'm a little nervous."

Alice moved to stand by Marigold's side. "I would be too. You're giving up a lot for him. He will owe you. Whether he realizes it or not."

"He's already saved my life." Maybe a slight exaggeration, but in this instance, she didn't care. "This just makes us even. He won't owe me a thing."

Alice made a little argumentative noise in her throat. "Your magic will be in him. You will be bound to him for the rest of your lives. No matter what you do, where you go, who you choose to spend your life with, a thread will run between you."

Marigold hadn't considered that, but so be it. A thread wasn't such a noticeable thing. *"Live and let live, freely take and freely give."* She whispered the lines of an old poem in answer.

Alice's smile returned. "True enough for us. But he may feel differently. He wasn't born into this life. That changes things."

With that, she went back to the table and picked up a collection of things, then moved past Marigold to lay the items at the compass points. A black feather tipped in silver at north, a dagger of rock crystal at east, a bundle of cat's whiskers tied with red silk at south, and a thick beeswax candle at west.

In her hand remained a bundle of herbs.

Corette and Charisma completed their circles and returned the pouches of salt and ash to the table.

"Now we take our places." Alice walked to the fireplace. It flared to life as she approached. She tossed the bundle of herbs in. Soft curls of fragrant smoke wafted out. She went to the cat's whiskers, then pointed at Pandora. "You take north."

Pandora nodded and went to stand behind the black feather.

Next, Alice gestured to their mother. "West for you, Corette. And for Charisma, east."

The women got into position. Marigold stood outside the circle, waiting.

Alice nodded at her. "Once you step into this circle, any turning back will have dangerous consequences. Do you understand?"

"I do."

"Then enter and kneel at his left side."

Marigold walked forward, carefully stepping over the lines of salt and ash to take her place by Wyatt's side. He hadn't so much as grunted since she'd thought she'd heard him whisper something in the van. She hoped they weren't too late to save him.

Alice raised her hands. The beeswax candle flickered to life. Corette, Charisma, and Pandora lifted their hands as well as Alice spoke. "Bind this circle. Protect our sister in her sacrifice. Contain the dark spell already cast."

Corette, Charisma, and Pandora repeated the words. The candle flame sparked brightly, then settled down.

Alice dropped her hands to her sides. "The circle is sealed. Marigold, you may unbind him now. Once he is freed and at my command, your mother and sisters will hold him in place so the power of the jaundiced eye does not harm either of you further." She glanced at the other women. "Understood?"

All three nodded.

Alice returned her attention to Marigold. "Release him."

Marigold called up her magic, most likely, she realized, for the last time, and pushed it into the ivy. The leaves quivered at the touch of her magic. She urged them to unwind themselves from Wyatt.

They did as she asked, snaking away until he lay on a bed of ivy vines, completely free.

He shook himself and started to sit up. "You're going to pay for that, witch."

"Now, sisters," Alice commanded.

In unison, the three women thrust their hands toward him and spoke. "*Stagnacio!*"

Wyatt went as still as a statue. Then he jerked and a snarl bent his mouth. A deep, guttural growl came out of him.

Marigold looked at her mother. "I thought you had him."

"It's the pendant," Alice said.

"Yes," Corette agreed. "The pendant's magic is fighting us. The magic is very strong."

Alice snapped her fingers. "Put your hands on him, Marigold. We must do this now."

Marigold flattened her palms on his chest, one on either side of the jaundiced eye. The pendant seemed like it was staring at her, and the dark magic chewed at her skin the moment she made contact. She grimaced.

"You can feel the power of it, too, can't you?" Alice asked.

"Yes," Marigold hissed through clenched teeth. "I felt it earlier when we were bringing him here, but it's already gotten stronger."

"Then we have no time to lose." Alice crouched down and dug her fingers under the pendant's chain where it lay on the back of Wyatt's neck. She hissed as she touched the metal, and Marigold felt a slight lessening in the pain in her hands.

Alice gripped the chain so hard her knuckles went white. "There will only be a moment when the eye loses its hold on him. And only if you are successful in transferring your magic to him. When I feel that moment come, I will strip the pendant from him."

"But how do I transfer my magic into him? I've never attempted this before."

"The circle will make it possible. He is as open and receptive as he will ever be. You'll see. Feel for what's inside him. Find the part of him that's the most vulnerable. Everyone has a place like that, but some are hidden better than others. Let the magic be your guide. Once you find that part of him, you'll know where to direct your magic."

Marigold closed her eyes and did as Alice had told her. She called up every ounce of power within her and pushed forward into Wyatt.

A picture formed in her head. Wyatt. With a dark gaping hole in the center of him. Below his heart. The space wasn't really empty, though. A host of emotions filled it. Pain, longing, fear, loneliness, loss, hope, desire.

She summoned her magic with all the courage and love she could muster and directed it to fill that spot in him, to shove all those dark emotions out and replace them with her power.

The pain in her hands turned to fire. She winced and let out a soft cry.

"Hold strong, child," Alice urged. "I feel it too. We must fight the darkness."

Marigold nodded and pushed harder. The darkness pushed back. The pain burrowed into her palms and dug into the bones of her hands and wrists. She breathed openmouthed, trying not to pass out.

Self-doubt filled her. She wasn't strong enough to do this. Her magic wasn't capable of defeating such a powerful force. The pain in her hands was almost unbearable. Why had she even attempted this? She couldn't even hold on to the father of her child, how could she expect to make this—*no*. She shut the negative voice down.

That was the pendant talking. The jaundiced eye thrived on the weakness of others. She refused to let it intimidate her.

She was absolutely powerful. She could do this. She *would* do this. She was a green witch, bursting with earth magic. The insignificant influence of blood and ash was no match for what lay within her.

Magic poured out of her and into Wyatt. The emptiness inside him was no longer dark, but glowed green. Her power shoved out every last shadow the pendant had cast on him.

The jangle of metal registered distantly.

Then suddenly, there was nothing left in her to give. The pain disappeared from her hands. She opened her eyes.

Wyatt sat up and gasped like a man surfacing after being under a long time. He stared at her. "Marigold? What's going on?"

She opened her mouth to answer him and passed out.

Wyatt caught Marigold in his arms. He had no idea what had happened to her, where they were, no clue why he was sitting on the floor of a strange room on a bed of...ivy? No awareness of the time of day or why there was a circle of women around him, two of whom he recognized as Marigold's mother and sister.

What he *did* know was that he hadn't drowned in the darkness threatening to suffocate him. And that he felt changed in a way he couldn't fully pinpoint. It was as if all the rough edges of his past had been sanded down so that his memories didn't snag on them anymore.

A lightness filled him. A lightness he'd never felt before. It was a little unnerving, but nice.

But beyond that, he wasn't really sure of anything else. He blinked to clear the fog remaining in his head. What he mostly remembered was that Marigold had told him she was a witch.

And things sure looked very witchy up in here. He glanced around the room. There was a circle of stuff around him. Lines of what looked like salt and ashes. A candle. A little bundle of...whiskers? A crystal dagger. He raised his brows. "Am I being sacrificed? What happened to Marigold? She looks passed out."

Pandora snorted. "No, you're not being sacrificed. And Marigold's fine, just tired, I imagine." Then she looked at someone behind him. "Did it work?"

"I don't know."

He was about to turn to see who had spoken when he realized the voice had come from his left side. And he'd heard it. Loud and clear. "What happened to me? I can hear."

He held on to Marigold with one hand so he could reach up with the other to touch his ear. Nothing felt different, but then, he wasn't sure what he'd expected. Except that he could *hear* his fingers brushing the shell of his ear. "How is that possible? I'm completely deaf in this ear."

He looked over his shoulder as the older woman behind him answered. "It's the magic in you. You're still deaf in that ear. But the magic is compensating." She looked at Pandora. "It worked."

Corette sighed in obvious relief. "What about the pendant?"

The pendant. *Now* he remembered what happened. Well, some of it anyway. "Can we rewind? What magic in me? What's going on?"

Marigold shifted in his arms as she came around. She put her hand to her head. "Did we do it? Please tell me we did, because I'd hate to feel like this for nothing."

"We did it," the as-yet-unknown woman said. "*You* did it, Mari."

Marigold smiled, but there was sadness in her eyes. "Good. I'm glad. And very tired." She leaned against him, and it was as if he could sense her exhaustion. Whatever she'd done had left her drained.

He held on to her, still feeling lost. And getting a little angry. "I'm glad you did whatever you did, but I want some answers. *Now*."

The lights flickered.

The women looked up and laughed softly. Then Pandora shook her head. "Be careful. That's my sister's magic you're dealing with. And she's a very—that is, she *was* a very powerful witch. So take it easy."

He peered at her. "Are you saying I somehow did that? I caused the lights to flicker? But it's Marigold's magic?"

"Yes," Corette said.

But that answer told him nothing. "How is that possible? What does it even mean? I need some explanations here."

Corette nodded. "Of course. You see, you put the jaundiced eye pendant on and the dark magic within it took possession of you. The only way to save you was to force that magic out with different magic. Marigold sacrificed hers to save your life."

He stared at Corette. Maybe it was the lingering fog, but this seemed so farfetched. "Are you saying...what are you saying?"

Corette smiled patiently. "Marigold gave up her magic to save your life. And you are now in possession of it. You are technically no longer human. You're a wizard. Granted, you are a newborn in the scheme of things, but that's why Pandora advised you to take it easy."

There was nuts and there was nuts. This was next-level nuts. He scooped Marigold into his arms and got to his feet. For a woman with such a big personality and strong spirit, he'd thought she'd have weighed more. "I'm taking her home."

"Wyatt," Pandora called out to him. "There's a lot you need to learn. We'll teach you. We're not going to leave you hanging."

"Yeah, great. Thanks." He started for the doors.

"Also," Corette added. "We drove, so you don't have a ride unless you come with us."

He shifted Marigold so he could check his back pocket. His phone was still there. "I'll call a Ryde."

The unnamed younger woman stepped into his path. "You're not going anywhere with my sister."

Another sister? What had Marigold said her name was? Charity? "Whatever's happened, she's exhausted."

"And you've just been through a major life change. You both have, really. We'll take her home. And you back to your car."

"Yeah," Pandora said. "Then maybe we can all chill out before the rehearsal dinner."

Corette sucked in a gasp. "The rehearsal dinner!"

Pandora nodded. "I'd almost forgotten too."

A soft, insistent buzz interrupted them. Wyatt glanced down at Marigold, as it seemed to be coming from her. "I think that's Marigold's phone."

The other sister dug it out of Marigold's pocket and answered. "Hello, this is Charisma, Marigold's sister. She can't come to the—who are you?" She frowned. "What are you talking about?"

Then she went very pale. "I see." A second later, she hung up and stared at the group. "That was a man named Newton Mathers, and he said if we don't bring him the jaundiced eye, he's going to turn Leah into stone. We can exchange the pendant for her, but it has to be soon. As in he's going to text directions for the drop in an hour. Does anyone know who he is?"

"I do," Wyatt said. "That slimy little creep is the man who hired Marigold to attend the auction where the bookends containing the pendant were sold."

"He's also a lesser wizard," the older woman said. "He's one of many who have been trying to buy a jaundiced eye for many, many years. I had no idea he was around again."

Wyatt looked at her. "A lesser wizard?"

She nodded. "More of a practitioner than someone naturally gifted. The eye would give him the kind of power he could never obtain otherwise."

Corette wrung her hands. "What are we going to do? We can't give him the eye. But we can't let him hurt Leah either."

"We do what should have been done already," Wyatt said. "We call the police."

Corette nodded, surprising him. "I agree."

He shot her a look. "You're not afraid the sheriff will think all of this witchcraft stuff is crazy?"

Pandora laughed. "Considering he's a werewolf, no."

"He's a werewolf? I thought just that Birdie woman was." Wyatt realized he had a lot to learn about this town.

Marigold let out a soft little snore.

Charisma shook her head. "Birdie is his aunt." Then she looked past him. "Alice, do you have a place where Marigold can rest while we handle this Leah business?"

The older woman walked past them. "Follow me."

Wyatt went after her. She led him into a sitting room. He put the still sleeping Marigold on the couch, then moved a strand of hair out of the way to kiss her forehead. He and the older woman left and she shut the door.

"Who are you, by the way?" he asked her as they walked back.

"I'm Alice Bishop."

"And you're a witch too?"

She didn't offer much in the way of a smile, but she didn't seem bothered by the question either. "Yes. I'm sure you'll hear quite a few stories about me."

The set of her mouth made her seem defiant. He understood that look. "But they're not all true, are they?"

She narrowed her eyes. "You're perceptive for a human."

"I was a cop. Part of the job. And I thought I wasn't human anymore."

"You've been a wizard for ten minutes. Close enough." She walked back into the big room. "I would prefer not to involve myself further in this matter. I still have to prepare the ritual to destroy the pendant, and my attention is best focused there."

Corette nodded. "I understand. We'll be heading back to the flower shop to speak to the sheriff anyway."

"Hold up," Wyatt said. "I'm not leaving Marigold here."

Charisma put her hands on her hips. "I don't think we should be leaving the pendant here, either. We might need it to deal with this Newton person. After all, he expects us to give it to him tonight to get Leah back."

"No," Alice said. "Marigold can go, but the pendant is not leaving my possession. It must be destroyed. You'll have to figure out another way."

"We're not waiting until tonight to get Leah back, so we don't need the pendant," Wyatt said. "But we do need Marigold." At least he did. There was something in him now, something beyond his feelings for her that made the thought of being without her seem like the worst thing in the world.

Marigold woke up in the passenger's seat of her mother's car. The seat had been reclined all the way, which meant Marigold's first sight was of the headliner. She blinked up at it while she got her bearings. The car wasn't moving, and she was alone.

It was bright out, so still daylight. But why was she in her mother's car? She sat up. The car was parked behind her shop. Which was where she ought to be. She pulled on the door handle, but the car was locked. "Open."

Nothing happened. Her magic wasn't workin—oh, yes. It came back to her now. She wasn't a witch anymore.

She sat there for a moment, staring at the lock and having a pity party for herself. But being a mother had taught her pity parties were far too indulgent a thing to allow for more than a few moments.

Besides, there was a lot of good to focus on. She'd saved Wyatt's life, hadn't she? And the jaundiced eye was in safe hands. A lot of good.

She gave herself a mental pat on the back, unlocked the door manually, and headed inside through the rear entrance. The workroom was empty, except for Frank, who was sleeping on a stack of boxes.

Everyone else was in the front of the shop. The sheriff was there, along with Deputy Blythe, Corette, Charisma, Pandora, and Wyatt. They were all deeply engaged in conversation.

She walked to the workroom door and glanced around. "Hey, where's Leah?"

That stopped the talking. They all turned to look at her. Wyatt came toward her immediately, taking her hands as he reached her. "Newt took her. Kidnapped her. He wants to exchange her for the pendant."

Marigold's heart clenched. "Oh no. Newt?"

Everyone nodded.

"I can't believe he's behind this." She held on tight to Wyatt. "You know, he told me I was in danger from an outside source. Tried to make me think you were a bad guy. But now it makes sense. He was throwing up smoke screens."

"I guess he knows that didn't work." Then Wyatt lowered his voice. "I know what you did for me. That you saved my life. And gave up so much of yours to do it." He shook his head like he was struggling to find words. Then he kissed her forehead. "Thank you. That's insufficient. But for now, thank you."

"You're welcome. I'm sorry everything went down without us talking to you about it first, but you were sort of under the spell of evil, so..." She shrugged.

"Yeah, I get it. And it's weird." He let her hands go with a little smile. "But I'm alive, so weird is fine."

"I'm very glad you're alive too." She rubbed her jaw. "But we have to get Leah back. How are we going to do that?"

Wyatt glanced at the sheriff. "Brute force."

"What does that mean?"

Wyatt took her hand and tugged her toward the group. "Come on, we'll tell you."

She went with him to join the conversation.

Her mother's eyes held a great deal of concern. "How are you? You weren't asleep for more than fifteen minutes."

"I'm fine. There's too much to be done to sleep anyway." Marigold couldn't even think about all the wedding flowers yet to be finished, but there would be time for that after Leah was safe and Newt was in a holding cell. That creepy little weasel. She stood between Wyatt and her mother. "All right, what's the plan?"

Across from her, the sheriff took a deep breath. "Your boyfriend wants to storm the castle." Before Marigold could say anything, he continued. "And I have to agree. It's the way to go."

"It is?" What she'd expected, she wasn't sure, but it wasn't that.

Hank nodded. "Mathers won't be expecting it, for one thing. For another, he's a lesser wizard. We're not exactly going up against a big gun here." Hank tipped his head at Wyatt. "Plus, your boyfriend was on the force. That makes him an asset, not a liability."

"Then you and Wyatt are doing this?"

"It'll be me, Wyatt, and Deputy Blythe. We're going in fast and strong. A little Nocturne Falls shock and awe."

Men. She frowned at him. "But none of you has magic. And lesser wizard or not, Newt could cast a spell that would stop all of you in your tracks."

Wyatt cleared his throat.

She slanted her eyes at him. "You might have magic, but you don't know what to do with it yet."

"True." He shrugged one shoulder. "But I've had some training when it comes to extricating a hostage."

Hank clapped him on the shoulder. "That's all the magic we need."

Marigold crossed her arms. "You seem awfully sure about this. What if he throws an enchantment at you? You need at least one witch with you."

Pandora raised her hand. "I can go."

"No, you can't," Marigold said. "You have a wedding rehearsal and a dinner in…" She looked at her watch. "Three hours. Wow." Time was slipping away. "Charisma, you go."

Charisma put a hand to her sternum. "I've never been part of something like this, but why not? I'll do it."

Pandora snorted. "Do you own jeans? Because you might want something a little less Neiman Marcus for this."

Charisma made a face as she touched the lapel of her linen jacket. "I'll have you know this is from Saks." Then she sniffed a little. "And I own jeans."

"From Neiman Marcus," Pandora muttered.

"Girls," Corette snapped. "This is not the time.

Charisma will go and help the sheriff, Deputy Blythe, and Wyatt while they rescue Leah. She's certainly powerful enough to hold off whatever a lesser wizard might throw at them."

Marigold kind of liked it when their mother got all motherly. It wasn't often she raised her voice and let the steel magnolia out. "Good. That way we can get to the rehearsal."

"No we," Pandora said. "You need to rest. You don't need to practice walking down an aisle."

"Agreed," Corette said. "I think you should be resting, too. I can pick Saffie up and take her to rehearsal."

Marigold shook her head. "No more resting. I couldn't anyway knowing Leah is in danger. But if you're okay with me staying here instead of being at rehearsal, I could use the time to work on wedding flowers. I have a lot left to do. Then I can meet you at the restaurant for dinner."

"I'm fine with that," Pandora said.

Wyatt nodded. "I like that idea too. We'll both be there."

"Then that's the plan," Marigold said. It would be good to occupy herself, which the rehearsal would do, but going to that wasn't going to help these flowers get done. And being busy would help her pass the time until Leah was safe.

And maybe stop thinking about how powerless she was to help.

25

Mathers rented a house in one of the starter-home neighborhoods in town, which meant it was mostly single-story homes. But in Nocturne Falls, it was also the kind of place with white picket fences, cats lounging on the porch, dogs playing in the yard, and kids riding bikes in the street. There was a sense of pride in the neighborhood, and with the tree-lined streets and manicured lawns, it looked straight off a Hollywood studio lot to Wyatt.

Hard to believe a place like this really existed. And that it was filled with supernaturals. A group that inexplicably now included him.

"Let's go over this one more time," Wyatt said to the sheriff. The plan had changed a little since the addition of Charisma. He, Sheriff Merrow, and Deputy Blythe were two blocks away in his patrol car, looking at Mathers's backyard.

Charisma was in her car two blocks in the other direction. And still not in jeans. But then, she was playing the part of the neighbor in search of her missing dog.

"Once Charisma has him distracted at the front door, we'll go in the back." The sheriff nodded toward the house. "Blythe and I will take him down. You get the girl out."

"What if he runs?"

The sheriff turned to Wyatt, his eyes lighting with the feral glow Wyatt had seen in Birdie's once before. He now understood it was the beast in them. The sheriff grunted in amusement. "No one outruns a shifter."

Wyatt thought that over for a second. "Do you actually turn into a wolf?"

He rumbled what sounded like a yes. "So does my wife and my kids. Well, not my daughter yet. She's too young. But she will."

A whole family of werewolves. Wyatt tried to wrap his head around that. He wasn't even prepared to dig into Deputy Blythe being a valkyrie, which he'd always assumed to be a mythical creature. But then, nothing was off-limits anymore, was it? "This is all going to take some getting used to."

"Felt the same way when I had to go through boot camp with humans." He nodded ahead. "Charisma's on her way."

The pretty brunette was on the street, walking toward Mathers. Suddenly, a leash appeared in her hand, the air around it rippling with what Wyatt suddenly understood was the presence of magic.

Amazing. Not only could he hear out of his left ear, but he could *see* magic.

Deputy Blythe leaned forward from the backseat. "You sure she can handle this? I know she's a witch, but she's also a life coach. That doesn't exactly strike fear in the heart."

The sheriff grunted. "She doesn't need to strike fear in him. She just needs to keep him busy." He put his hand on the door. "She'll be getting close. Let's go."

The three of them exited the car and jogged toward Mathers's backyard. Adrenaline kicked up in Wyatt's system, the kind of charge he hadn't felt since leaving the force. It was a good feeling, but at odds with the cause. Leah being held hostage wasn't anything to be excited about. Still, he was revved and ready.

They jumped the small fence, crept up the back porch steps, then stopped on either side of the door, Blythe and the sheriff on one side, Wyatt on the other.

Neither the sheriff nor the deputy had their guns out. Apparently, you didn't need weapons when you were one. Suited Wyatt just fine. Less chance he'd get killed before he could kiss Marigold some more. He hoped. About the kissing. He really wanted that to happen. Then they could talk, because they had a *lot* to talk about.

The house was small, and the sound of Charisma ringing the doorbell carried.

Merrow held up his hand.

More sounds followed. The front door opening. Then Mathers's voice, distant as it was, could be heard. Charisma started talking immediately after, her frantic tones perfect for selling her lost-dog story.

Merrow sliced his hand through the air, giving them the go sign. He grabbed the door knob and ripped the door open, shattering the wood around the lock. He and Blythe disappeared into the house.

Literally disappeared. Then Wyatt realized they'd just moved so fast he'd been unable to track them.

He followed, seeing no signs of Leah. A second later, Mathers yelled. A loud thud came next, followed by a little scuffling and a lot of snarling.

Wyatt hustled through the kitchen to see a very wolfy-looking sheriff crouched on top of a struggling and defiant Mathers.

"Get off me!" The wizard tried to bring his hands up, but the sheriff was twice the guy's size. He started to mutter something in a language Wyatt didn't know.

Charisma immediately brought her hands up. *"Conquiesco!"*

The air rippled around her hands. More magic.

Mathers went still and silent.

Despite that, Deputy Blythe reached over her shoulder and unsheathed a sword, which she pointed at the wizard.

Wyatt had definitely not seen a sword strapped to her, but he had seen the air waver around her when she'd reached for the weapon.

The whole scene was the most unreal thing, and possibly one of the coolest, Wyatt had ever seen. He felt like a freaking Avenger. Although in that scenario he was more like the Avenger's mascot, seeing as how he had no clue how to do anything with whatever magic he supposedly had. "Looks like you've got this handled."

The sheriff nodded, but it was Blythe who spoke. "Get Leah."

"On it." Wyatt went room to room, which didn't take long in the small house, and found her in the second bedroom, tied to a desk chair. "You okay?"

She nodded. A strip of duct tape covered her mouth.

"You're safe now." He removed it gently. "Are you hurt?"

"I'm okay. Shaken up," Leah said. "He mostly just threatened me a lot, but I don't think he's got the stones to actually hurt anyone. Frankly, he's about as scary as an angry Pomeranian. You didn't give him the pendant, did you?"

Wyatt worked on the knots at her wrists first. The knots were intricate and precise, making him wonder if Mathers had used magic to create them. "No. This guy might be a wizard, but he was severely outclassed. The sheriff is currently sitting on him in the foyer."

Leah snorted. "Did he go full wolf?"

"Uh, judging by the looks of him, maybe half wolf? If that's a thing." He bent to work on the rest of the knots.

"It is." She rubbed her wrists as he freed them. "I hope Sheriff Merrow bites him a little too."

Wyatt loosened the last knot on her right ankle, almost getting it undone. "How did Mathers grab you? Magic?"

"Yes. He came in to get the bookends from Marigold, and when I said she wasn't there, he got really agitated. Then he cast some kind of truth spell on me and made me spill everything. As soon as I told him about the pendant, he went ballistic. He was ranting about how it was his and how much he'd paid for it and then he just freaked. Cast another spell on me that knocked me out. I woke up here."

"I'm really sorry this happened to you, but he won't bother you, or anyone, again." He pulled the last bit of rope off her.

She stood up and hugged him. "Thanks for rescuing me."

"You're welcome."

She pulled back. "Hey. You're not all evil zombie anymore. So I guess someone rescued you, too."

"They did. Marigold, her mom, and her sisters got that pendant off me. Oh, and a woman named Alice Bishop helped too. She's going to destroy the jaundiced eye completely."

Leah's eyes went big. "You met Alice Bishop?"

"Yes, why?" He waited to see what Leah would say. And if, as Alice had indicated, the words would be unkind.

"Dude, she's the boss witch in town. There's no one as powerful as she is. Was she nice? Or..." Leah's brows lifted in question. "I hear she's a little scary. I've seen her, but never talked to her."

"She was nice. But I can see how people would find her intimidating. Now we should go let the others know you're okay. C'mon." He walked her out to where he'd last seen everyone.

They were all still there except Deputy Blythe.

"She went to get the car," Charisma said, somehow knowing what Wyatt was thinking. "Hey, Leah. You okay?"

"I am, thanks." Leah peered at Mathers. "What are you holding him with?"

"*Conquiesco* spell. Keeps him still and quiet, but enables him to move or speak if needed. And only as needed."

Wyatt raised his brows. "Could you teach me to do that spell?"

Charisma smiled. "Sure. It's not beginner stuff, but it's not super advanced either. You should be able to handle it. Marigold could."

The sheriff shook himself, not in a doggy kind of way, but like he was waking himself up. As he did it, he returned to looking fully human. "Leah, we'll need to get a statement from you."

"Sure." She put her hand to the back of her head. "My head is killing me. I guess I must have whacked it on something when he knocked me out."

"Let me see." Wyatt looked at the spot she was touching, but her thick hair made it hard to see anything. "Mind if I touch?"

"Nope." She pulled her hand away.

He eased his fingers over her skull and found an enormous goose egg, but thankfully no blood. "I'll say you hit something. You'd better get that checked out."

The sheriff stood as Deputy Blythe pulled the patrol car up to the front of the house. "If Mathers did that to you, we're adding assault to his charges."

Leah shrugged. "I can't remember. But he did use magic to knock me out, so he's the reason it happened."

The sheriff nodded. "Deputy Blythe can take you to the emergency room after we get your statement. I'll deal with Mathers."

Wyatt looked at him. "You need me for anything else?"

"No. You did great. Thanks."

"Mind if I split?"

"Marigold?" the sheriff asked.

Wyatt nodded. "She's all I can think about."

An understanding look filled the sheriff's gaze. "See you at the wedding."

Charisma pointed toward the street. "I'll drive you to the shop if you want."

"Don't you need to keep Mathers under that spell?"

"No. By the time it wears off, Sheriff Merrow will have him in a cell."

"I'd love the ride, then. And not to belabor the point, but won't he be able to still do magic inside that cell? I mean, he could still cause problems."

Deputy Blythe gave Wyatt a sly look. "We have special cells for supernaturals."

Of course they did. "Then I'm ready to roll."

He followed Charisma to her car, a pretty little Lexus that was out of his price range. "So you're a life coach?"

"I am." She unlocked the vehicle and they got in. Once the doors were shut, she turned to him. "You have a long road ahead of you and a lot to learn. Which we're going to teach you. But I still have to ask, what are your feelings toward Marigold?"

Somehow, he'd known this was coming. "I like her very much." He actually thought he was falling for her, but he thought saying that might freak Charisma out. He and Marigold had known each other only a few days.

She was looking at him in an odd way. Almost like she was studying the air around him, which made no sense. "You love her. But that scares you."

The little hairs on the back of his neck stood up. "Are you trying to psychoanalyze me or something?"

"I can see and read auras. And yours has all the colors of love and fear. I see it a lot in my clients who are afraid of commitment."

"I'm not afraid of commitment. I haven't had much experience with it, outside of the police force, but I'm not afraid of it. Anymore."

She started the car, seemingly pleased with that answer. "What is it, then?"

"Marigold and I haven't known each other very long." He frowned. "I don't want to scare her off."

Charisma's mouth bent in a sharp smile. "She gave up her magic for you. I don't think she'd be scared off by finding out you want more from her than a couple of dates."

"What do you mean that she gave up her magic?"

She cut her eyes at him. "We told you. That's how she saved you."

"But she still has her magic, right? You can't lose a thing like that, can you?"

"You can when it's required to save someone's life. All the power she had went into you."

His throat went tight. "You mean she's not a witch anymore because of me?"

"She'll always be an honorary witch, but no, her powers are completely gone. Like I said, all of what she had, she gave to you."

He sat back and stared blindly ahead for a moment. "I somehow didn't get that." He swallowed as the magnitude of what she'd done for him sank in. It was too much. Too big of a gift. He'd taken her identity in a way. He didn't deserve that. Didn't want to do that to her, either. "I have to give it back."

"What?"

"I can't take her power from her. It's who she is. And I...I don't deserve it."

Charisma shook her head slowly. "This isn't a sweater that you can return." She cast an appraising glance at him. "It's a lot to live up to, hmm?"

"I'll say." He shoved a hand through his hair while he let out a long, ragged exhale. He and Marigold had a lot of talking to do.

26

The back door of the shop opened, and Wyatt walked in, making Marigold pause her work. "Is Leah safe? Tell me Leah's safe."

"She is. Little bump on the head but probably fine. Deputy Blythe is taking her to the ER for a checkup all the same." He closed the door behind him. "Mathers is probably already in a holding cell."

"Do you think that's the end of it then?"

He sighed. "I'm not going to lie to you. No, I don't think it is. Whoever hired those parking lot guys, whether it was Suzanne or Mathers, they could still have bad intentions. And someone undoubtedly still wants to get their hands on that pendant. But I'm not going to leave you alone. I will do my best to protect you."

"I appreciate that."

"And I will get to the bottom of this. I've already texted Suzanne that we need to talk."

"Good."

Wyatt strode toward her with unmistakable purpose.

"What's going—"

His hands threaded through her hair, and his mouth covered hers with a boldness that almost knocked her off her chair. The rose in her hand fell to the table.

She stood, the bolt of surprise pushing her to her feet.

He kissed her long and hard and made her joints melt and her spine tingle, and every single worry that had been buzzing around her flew away. His kiss became the focus of her world. Pleasure blossomed inside her as tendrils of heat and joy curled around her bones, strengthening the weak spots.

She sighed, and his arms wrapped around her. She leaned into him, loving the warmth of his body against her, the strength of it, the thrum of living, breathing male that pulsed into her from that simple connection.

Wyatt held on to her with a kind of possessive determination she'd never felt before. As if having her in his arms was something worth fighting for.

She almost wept with the overwhelming emotion of it all. Happy tears, of course, but then she reminded herself that she was probably extra sensitive because of the crazy, exhausting day she'd had.

She put her hands on his chest and gently pressed away from him enough that she could see his eyes. "That was some kiss."

"I owe you my life, Marigold. That's why I'm about to say what I'm about to say." He cleared his throat. "I'm a little nervous. That's not something I'm used to feeling. I'm feeling a lot of things I'm not used to feeling."

He laughed awkwardly. "Okay, so apparently I'm not the least bit suave when I'm about to lay my heart on the line."

She blinked extra hard. What on earth was he going to say? But she felt for him. She knew some men weren't great at expressing themselves. She imagined it was nearly impossibly hard for a man who'd grown up in foster care with no one to model that behavior for him. She took his hand. "Don't be nervous. Just tell me what you want to tell me."

He held on to her hand and used it as a focus point. "I didn't really understand what you've done for me. That by giving me your magic, you were also giving it up. I thought you were just sharing it with me. Or something."

He licked his lips. "I know better now. I know what you sacrificed for me. I don't feel worthy of it."

She shook her head. "But you saved my life at the auction house. You don't know what those men might have done to me."

"They weren't going to kill you. All they wanted were the candlesticks. I just ran them off. What you did for me is in a whole different arena. I want you to know that the debt I feel…it's going to take me a long time to repay you. If I even can."

"I didn't do it because I wanted you to owe me anything."

"I know that. You did it because you are an amazing, kind, generous, wonderful woman who is as beautiful on the inside as you are on the outside." He took a breath. "I am falling in love with you, Marigold."

Her lips parted, but no sound came out.

"I know it's early days for me to say a thing like that, but I had a real epiphany today. About…life. And what I want out of it. And what I want is not to *try* a long-distance relationship."

"It's not?" She wasn't sure if this was about to get better or worse.

"No." He blew out a breath this time and started looking a little flushed. "I'm going to move to Nocturne Falls. I want an up-close relationship. I want to be the person in your life you count on. The person you call when you need something. The person who, maybe someday, you might consider your other half."

Once again, she was left speechless.

"I know I have your magic. I don't feel like I should have it. I sure don't know what to do with it. And I know it was a very important part of who you are and how you made this business." He suddenly took on a very resolute expression. "If you'll teach me, I want to work here with you and use the magic you gave me to keep your business going the way it was."

There was so much to unpack. She just stared at him, trying to figure out what to respond to first.

"That's pretty much it," he said. "That's all I wanted to say."

"That was…a lot." She smiled. "I liked all of it. I'm just…processing."

He started looking a little determined. "Are you okay with me moving here?"

"Yes, totally yes. And if you want to work here—wait. You can't really want to work here. You're, like, a total guy. You were a homicide detective. Now you want to arrange flowers?"

He picked up the rose she'd dropped from where it lay on the worktable. "I think I like flowers now."

She laughed. "That's my magic influencing you. And we should probably stop calling it my magic. It's yours now."

"No," he said, shaking his head. "I like calling it your magic." He twisted the rose by its stem, twirling it slowly, but his eyes were on her again. "I like thinking that there's a piece of you in me. That maybe that piece of you is enough to keep you around."

She blinked. "Wyatt. Look."

"What?"

"The rose. It bloomed while you were talking."

"It did?" He stared at it. "Did I do that?"

"Yes." She sucked in a breath, trying not to get overwhelmed by the feelings that were bubbling up inside her. "Do you really want to work here? Because I will teach you everything. I will turn you into the best green wizard who ever walked the streets of Nocturne Falls."

"I guess that means you're okay with me moving here? And going headfirst into this relationship?"

She gave it one more second of thought. "Yes."

He grinned, an enormous smile that had its own magic. "What do we do next?"

She glanced at the wall clock. "We get ready for the rehearsal dinner, because it's in an hour."

"I should take my clothes and head to the hotel, then. Can you text me the directions?"

"Sure. I'll see you there, then?"

"Yes." He smiled. "You'll see me there. Is your daughter going to be there?"

"She will be. She's one of the junior bridesmaids."

"I hope she likes me."

"I think she will." How could Saffie not like him? He was amazing.

"I'll do my best to be likable. Afterward, we'll come back here and finish everything that still needs doing."

She laughed. "You have no idea what you're getting yourself into."

His brows lifted. "Probably not. But I like a challenge. See you in an hour."

Fifty-three minutes later, she was walking into Guillermo's, the best Italian restaurant in Nocturne Falls, and suffering from the kind of jitters that were more appropriate for a first date. She knew Wyatt. There was no reason to feel like they were meeting for the first time.

But this was different, and she knew it.

This was the first time he'd be meeting Saffron. And the first time they were going public as a couple. And all at her sister's rehearsal dinner. She bit the inside of her cheek and peered out the front window of the restaurant. Most of the guests, including Saffie, who'd come from the wedding rehearsal with Corette, were already in the private dining room.

"You okay?"

At the sound of her mother's voice, Marigold turned to see Corette and Saffie behind her. "I'm fine." She reached out a hand to her daughter. "Hey, baby. I heard you did great at rehearsal."

Saffron took Marigold's hand. "I'm like a natural bridesmaid."

"I bet you are." She looked out the window. "Mimi said you're waiting on your boyfriend."

"Oh, is that what Mimi said?" Marigold shot her mother a look.

Corette pursed her mouth. "Saffron's about to meet him. She should know who he is to you."

"Right, but—"

"It's okay, Mom. I like that you have a boyfriend."

Marigold raised her brows. "You do?"

Saffie nodded. "And if he makes you happy, then maybe you can get married someday too, like Aunt Pandy. And I can be your bridesmaid."

"Oh, honey, you sure can." Marigold hugged her daughter, her heart full with how good this kid was.

Her mother put a hand on Saffie's arm. "We should go back to the dining room."

Marigold straightened. "No, Saffie can stay with me."

Corette nodded. "Then I'll see you two inside."

She left, and Marigold peered out the window again.

"He'll be here, Mom."

"I know." Marigold smiled as best she could. "I'm just nervous. Do you like my dress?"

"You look like a movie star. Don't tell Aunt Pandy, but your new dress is prettier. Not prettier than her wedding dress, but the one she has on now."

Marigold laughed. "Now you're just saying that. You know this dress isn't new." She'd actually bought the little red-flowered sundress at a thrift shop for this very occasion, so it was new to her. It was a good brand. Probably a discard from one of the many wealthy women in town. And the strappy cork wedges she'd had for ages.

"Mom." Saffie rolled her eyes. "Stop doubting yourself. If this guy really likes you, he won't care if you're wearing a garbage bag. Right?"

"Right. How'd you get so smart?"

"I watch a lot of YouTube."

Marigold snorted as Saffie's gaze shifted beyond Marigold to something outside, and she pointed. "Is that him?"

Marigold turned. Wyatt was coming across the street. She smiled. "Yes, it is. And he looks really good in a sport coat."

"Yeah, he's not bad for an old guy."

Wyatt walked through the front door, took a look at Marigold, then went one step back. "You look fantastic."

She had to be blushing. "You like?"

"I was actually talking to the cutie beside you." He winked at Marigold.

She laughed softly. "This is my daughter, Saffron. Saffron, this is Mr. West."

Saffron stuck her hand out. "Nice to meet you, Mr. West."

"Nice to meet you too. You can call me Wyatt, if that's okay with your mom." Wyatt shook her hand, as he looked at Marigold.

She nodded. "It's okay."

"Wyatt it is then." He pulled a wrapped box from under his arm. "This is for you."

Saffie took the box. "A gift for me?"

"Let's be straight," Wyatt said. "It's a bribe, plain and simple."

Saffie looked at her mom. "You can keep him."

"Saffie!"

She giggled. "Thank you, Mr. West. Wyatt." With a huge smile, she ran off to the dining room.

Wyatt watched her go. "Cute kid. I like her."

"I'd say she already likes you. The gift was a nice touch, though."

"I like to hedge my bets." He took another look at her, then blew out a breath. "Man. You really do look fantastic."

"Likewise."

He stretched out his arms. "You think so? I'm not great at this dressing-up stuff."

"You look very handsome." She gave him a slow up and down. "You clean up really well."

"I have Dexter Guildman to thank for it. All I did was shower." He glanced toward the back of the restaurant. "Should we go in? This is your gig. Tell me what to do."

She nodded. "We should go in."

"Can I hold your hand? Or no PDA in front of family?"

She held her hand out.

He took it and smiled. "Good. I'll do my level best not to embarrass you."

"Wyatt, you're not going to embarrass me. Why would you think that?"

He sighed. "I don't have a lot of experience with family functions. I got invited to stuff when I was on the force, but this is…different."

"I don't think it's that different. A family gathering is a family gathering."

His brows pulled together, and he laughed nervously as he moved closer to her. "I wasn't hoping any of those families liked me because I was crazy about one of them in particular and wanted to keep seeing her with an eye on the future."

"Oh." She bit her bottom lip. "The future, huh?"

He nodded. "I'm nuts about you, Marigold. Scared of putting so much of myself out there, but being scared is a part of life, right? I'm sure you were scared of being without your powers."

His eyes suddenly filled with concern. "I'm sure you still are." He took hold of her arms. "Hey, are you okay? I've been so caught up in everything going on I haven't really asked how you're doing."

She smiled. He was such a good man. Maybe a little bit of a work in progress, but he was making all the right efforts. "I am scared. But I'm hopeful and optimistic. Especially since you've offered to stay in Nocturne Falls and help me. If nothing else, it'll give me some time to ease into life without my gifts."

She hooked her arm through his. "Now, come on. It's time to face the firing squad."

"Well, since you put it that way." He rolled his eyes and laughed.

"I should tell you before we go in that everyone in there is a supernatural. It would be a little odd to introduce them with their name and type, but I'll let you know who's what when we have some alone time."

"Maybe I'll be able to guess."

"Maybe. But let's not play twenty questions within earshot."

He snorted. "Wouldn't dream of it."

Together, they walked into Guillermo's private dining room, and she introduced him to the crowd gathered there. Corette, Pandora, and Charisma he already knew. But their partners were new to him. "Wyatt, this is Bartholomew Stanhill, my mother's fiancé. And you know my sister Pandora, the bride to be. This is her groom, Cole Van Zant."

Wyatt shook both their hands. "Nice to meet you."

"This is Cole's dad, Jack. You've met his date, Birdie Caruthers."

"Yes, we have." And now he knew she was a werewolf. It was impossible not to wonder what she looked like with pointy ears and a tail. Which was not a thought he'd ever had about anyone before, but especially not about a woman with faintly blue hair and a handbag the size of Texas.

By the end of the rehearsal dinner, Wyatt just about had everyone's names down. He'd made small talk, had some laughs, eaten way too much pasta, and had become completely enamored of Saffie. And really, with the whole lot of Marigold's friends and family.

They were more like one big family in truth. Maybe it was the supernatural element that bound them together, but they all seemed so comfortable with one another. And they'd welcomed him like he was one of their own.

Which maybe he was, sort of. He didn't feel that way yet, it was all too new.

He and Marigold walked hand in hand out of the restaurant. Behind them, Saffron was doing the same with a boy named Charlie, who was the sheriff's son, and whom, apparently, Saffron had decided some time ago she would be marrying. Ivy, the sheriff's wife, seemed pretty cool with that decision, so Wyatt had just rolled with it. Charlie seemed like a nice kid. He was carrying Saffie's new paint-by-numbers set.

The gift had gone over pretty well, so he was doubly glad he'd brought it.

Marigold smiled at him. "Was that completely overwhelming for you?"

"No, I loved it. They're all great." Family was fun. A little crazy, too. In the best possible way. "But then, you're great, so how could they not be?"

Her smile broadened as they stopped by her car. "Good. I'm glad."

"Thanks for inviting me." He glanced at Saffron. She seemed completely enthralled with Charlie, so Wyatt leaned in and gave Marigold a peck on the mouth. He would have loved to do more than that, but there were still a lot of the rehearsal dinner attendees coming out. He also didn't want to go overboard in front of the kids.

Her cheeks went a little pink, and her lashes fluttered in the most adorable way. "Thanks for coming with me."

"I wouldn't have missed it."

"Sadly, I now have to go back to the shop and work. Well, after I see Saffron off to my mom's, and then I go home and change."

"I know. And I'm coming with you. To work, I mean."

"You still haven't given that up, huh?"

He shook his head. "No way. With Leah on bed rest until tomorrow, you need me. I would have come even if Leah was fine, but you really need the help now."

"I do. I still feel bad about Leah, but at least she was able to text us to let us know what was going on. Hey, you don't want to work in your nice clothes, do you?"

"No, which is why I brought jeans and a T-shirt to change into." Actually, he'd brought everything.

His whole bag. Because he'd never helped with wedding flowers before, and he had no idea how late of a night this was going to be.

Or how early of a morning. Marigold would also need help getting everything to Pandora and Cole's house and carrying it all in and setting it all up. Wyatt wasn't leaving her on her own to do all of that, either.

She put her hands on his cheeks and kissed him hard and fast. "You're awesome. Come on. We'll change at my house. Let me just say goodbye to Saffie."

He leaned against the car while Marigold gave her daughter a hug and a kiss and sent her off with Corette, but not before Saffie waved at him and he waved back. Then he got into his rental and followed Marigold to her place.

She unlocked the door and opened it, then pointed toward the left. "You can change in the guest room. It's on that side of the house, next to Saffie's room."

Her bedroom must be on the other side. He hoisted his bag over his shoulder. "I'll find it. Meet you back out here."

They went in opposite directions, confirming what he'd guessed about the location of her room. The guest room was small, just a daybed, a single nightstand, and a bookshelf that was mostly kids' books and a couple stacks of games and puzzles.

But there was a picture of Marigold and Saffron on one of the shelves. Saffie must have been three or four, and Marigold was pushing her on a swing.

There was so much joy and happiness in the picture that the longing to experience that kind of emotion welled up in him again. Despite everything that had happened, he was in a good place.

That wasn't something he'd ever thought about such change and upheaval, but there was a lightness in him that he'd never really experienced before. And it had all started when Marigold had given him her magic.

Could this really be what being a supernatural felt like?

And if he had all this magic inside him, what was he capable of? He'd made that rose bloom without trying, so obviously he had some skills. He put his bag on the bed, then stared at it, focusing hard. "Levitate."

Nothing happened, but then, he didn't really know the right words. He tried a different approach, going back to concentrating.

He pictured the bag lifting off the bed, rising into the air just enough to see space under—the bag moved.

He jerked back. Had that really just happened?

He shucked his clothes, threw on a T-shirt and jeans, and ran out to see if Marigold was ready. "Marigold?"

"In the kitchen." She was filling a sports bottle with water and lemon slices. "What's up?"

"I think I just used magic."

She snorted. "Sorry, but you're adorable right now. What did you do?"

"I levitated my duffel bag." He glanced back at the bedroom. "At least I think I did. Or maybe I was imagining things."

"And maybe you weren't. Let's see if you can do it again." She took a wooden spoon out of a drawer and set it on the counter in front of him. "Levitate that."

He nodded. "All right." He focused like he had before, imagining the spoon lifting into the air. Imagining the air pushing the spoon up.

And it rose. He did his best not to react so that he could hold focus. It went a little higher. He shook his head. "How is that—"

The spoon fell.

He sighed. "I'm not very good at this, am I?"

She gaped at him. "Are you kidding me? You've had zero training. And you can levitate stuff with your mind? That's crazy good."

"It is?"

"Yes." She studied him, then raised a finger. "You know, it makes me wonder if you don't have a little something in your bloodline."

"A little something like what?"

"A little supernatural something."

"It could be, I guess. I don't know that much about my biological family. Could I do a DNA test?"

She shook her head. "No, supernatural abilities don't show up on those. Which is good. Think about when you were on the force."

"Yeah, I see what you're saying. Supernaturals wouldn't stay secret for long if there were markers for werewolves and witches."

"Nope." She smiled at him. "This should be fun."

"What?"

"Tonight. There are a lot of arrangements left to do, and they'll all need a little magic touch." She patted his chest. "I can't wait to see what a dash of Wyatt does."

He couldn't either. "Then let's go."

They settled into work at the shop pretty quickly. Marigold gave him a quick lesson in swag design, and he set about building the basic greenery background that would anchor the flowers she'd add to it later.

"That's the main piece that's going on the arch they're getting married underneath. After that, the side pieces have to be built. I'll put it all together on site in the morning."

"How do you do that?"

"A lot of wiring."

He attached two pieces of ivy the way she'd shown him. "I can help with that."

"Wyatt, you're already doing a lot. I can't ask—"

"Yes, you can. I want to be partners in this. I mean, it's your business. I'm not trying to take over. Not in the slightest. But I want to help. And I don't want your shop to suffer because you don't have your magic anymore. So just let me."

She laughed. "Okay, I will try to remember that."

"It's hard, though, isn't it? You've been on your own for so long that you're just used to doing everything by yourself. Right?"

She nodded. "Yes. That's a lot of it. My mom and sisters are always there, but they have their own lives and their own businesses. And when you're a single mom, you don't have a choice. If you don't do something, it doesn't get done."

"Being a foster kid has some elements like that too. No one really pushes you to do better in school, or to try out for sports, or clubs. At least, they didn't for me. You get used to being on your own for a lot of things. And you learn pretty fast that the only truly dependable person in your life is you."

She held his gaze for a long moment, the emotion in her eyes bright. "I don't want that for either of us anymore."

"Neither do I."

"Partners, then." She took a breath. "But I swear if you break my heart, I will call up every favor I have in this town and...do bad things to you."

"I'm making a big mental note of that right now. And I swear, breaking your heart is not my intention. At all." What he wanted to do was keep her heart happy and safe. For as long as she would have him.

"Good. Now we should probably get cranking."

"You got it, boss."

It took him nearly an hour and a half to get all three pieces of the arch done, but at last he stepped back. "What do you think?"

Marigold lifted her head to see. A sprig of greenery stuck out of her curls near the top of her head, giving her an impish look. "That's really good."

"But you can see a few places that need adjustment, can't you?"

She smiled like she was trying not to. "That obvious, huh?"

"Yes, but it's okay. I can take it. Just tell me."

"The top needs to be fuller in a way that tapers more at the ends, and the side pieces both need to be about a foot longer."

"I can do that." He went back to work. Another half an hour and he felt like he'd accomplished what she'd asked for. "Better?"

She looked up. A second piece of greenery had joined the first in her hair, but on the opposite side and farther down. "That's perfect. Nicely done, Wyatt. Better than I'd expected."

"Good." He grinned. "Maybe there's hope for me after all, hmm?"

"For sure." She stood up and brushed bits and pieces of leaves, stems, and petals off of herself. "But now we move on to phase two."

"Which is?"

She rubbed her hands together. "Applying your magic to everything we just built."

The look on Wyatt's face was a mix of excitement and worry.

That pleased Marigold. He should be eager, but not overconfident. Magic might come easy to him, or it might not. Levitating a spoon was cool, but it did not a great wizard make. Perfecting the power now within him could take years. And probably would.

But to her, that was just another good way to ensure he'd be around awhile.

She smiled. "Breathe. This will probably be a slow process. It could also be frustrating. But I'm going to walk you through it as best I know how, all right? We're going to do this together."

He nodded. "Yep."

"Let's start with the greenery swags you built. If they go wrong or get completely overgrown, they're easier to fix now than after I add the flowers."

He stood in front of the three swags where they were laid out on one of the worktables. "What do I do first?"

"The goal is to push some magic into the plants so that they grow and mature in a way that gives the arrangement a sort of wild, natural look. Not unkempt. Just…you want to take what you've made and give it the beauty that only nature can. So if you want to picture something like that, then go for it."

He hesitated. "I don't think my mental images and your mental images are the same. I'm not sure using the pictures my brain comes up with is the best route."

She nodded in understanding. "That's okay. Try opening yourself to the plants. Give them some of the power within you and just let them do their thing. But not too much. You're not looking to spend an hour pruning and reshaping, either."

"Got it. Open myself to the plants. Give them some power, but don't go nuts." He grimaced. "I don't have a clue what that means."

"Whatever you think it means is fine. Just go with it. Magic is a little different for everyone. It adapts to you, you don't have to adapt to it."

"Okay, cool." He shook his hands out and bounced back and forth on the balls of his feet.

She snorted. "You're not getting ready to fight the plants, you know."

He stopped rolling his shoulders to look at her. "Just loosening up, coach."

She gave him a pass. Didn't hurt that he was being pretty adorable right now. "Whenever you're ready."

He blew out a breath, extended his hands toward the swags, then closed his eyes.

A few seconds passed without anything happening, then the leaves trembled a bit.

He dropped his hands and opened his eyes. "Did I do it?"

"Not quite. I think you were close, though. So whatever you did, do it a little more."

Disappointment bent his mouth.

"Hey, you'll get it. Don't be so hard on yourself."

He cut his eyes at her. "I'm a man. It's what we do."

She grinned. She was very aware that he was a man. Very. Aware. "Go on then with your manly self."

Smiling a little, he resumed the stance. Again, seconds passed with nothing, then the leaves shivered. This time, they grew a little too, reaching out and unfurling in all directions.

He dropped his hands and opened his eyes, inspecting the greenery. "Hey, they look a little different."

"They were growing."

"But?" He looked at her. "I stopped too soon, didn't I?"

She shrugged. "It's okay. This takes practice. Maybe we should call it a night and—"

"No. You need these for the wedding, and that's tomorrow. I have to get this right."

"That's a lot of pressure you're putting on yourself."

"So what? I can handle it. Give me another shot."

She crossed her arms. "Take all the time you need."

He repeated his actions, causing the leaves to move and grow once again. Then suddenly, they shot up wildly on spindly stems.

"Whoa!"

He opened his eyes, saw what he'd done, and sighed. "So much for that. Are they ruined?"

"No, not even a little bit." She grabbed some shears and started trimming away the wonky bits.

He looked thoroughly frustrated. "Any suggestions on how to do this better?"

She thought for a moment as she reshaped the swags. "How about if I help you? I don't have any magic, but I think I could guide you maybe."

"I'm all in. What do you want me to do?"

"Just stand there." She finished with the shears, then moved in front of him so that they were touching, his front to her back. Then she laid her arms over top of his.

He looked over her shoulder, smiling. "This is much better already."

"Focus." But she smiled too. It was *very* nice. He was strong and solid and warm. She took a moment just to absorb how good it felt to be so close to him. The scent of him surrounded her. It was clean like soap and something woodsy. She liked it a lot. "Just, uh, focus."

"Oh, I'm focusing," he said, his warm breath tickling her ear. "Not on the plants, though, I can tell you that."

She snickered, almost surprised by the sound that came out of her. Then she remembered the task at hand and straightened up. "Wyatt. You're distracting me."

He glanced over her shoulder again. "I'm distracting *you*? You're the one who backed yourself into me. Nothing in my head has anything to do with plants right now, I promise."

She cleared her throat to keep from snickering a second time and made a little space between them. Not much. She wasn't an idiot. "Better?"

"Not really. But probably for what I'm trying to do, yes."

She grinned and inhaled the scent of him again. "Just let me guide you."

"So when you see the magic coming off me, are you going to give me a signal?"

"When I *see* the magic coming off you?"

"You know, those little wavy lines in the air."

She pulled to one side a bit to make eye contact. "You can see magic?"

"I can since I got yours. Can't you? Or did you lose that in the transfer too?"

"Huh." She thought about that a second. "That's interesting. I can't see magic, never could, but magic affects everyone differently. I guess that's just part of your supernatural makeup now. Pretty cool."

"You're right, that is interesting. But if you can't see when the magic's happening, how are you going to guide me?"

"When the plants start to do their thing, which I'll easily be able to see, I'll press against you. Use the pressure I apply as a guide and don't let up until I do. Got it?"

"Got it." He leaned into her. "Let's do this."

"Ready when you are." She settled in against his wonderfully firm chest, her arms up and overtop his, and forgot all about leaving a little space. He didn't seem to mind, somehow getting closer. Sweet fancy flowerpots, he was basically wrapped around her like a winter coat.

And she was loving it.

Was she...in love with him? The thought frightened her. It meant putting herself on the line, but then, hadn't she sort of done that for him already? And she'd been rewarded for it, too, in a sense. He'd bared himself to her emotionally. Something her ex had never, ever done. He wouldn't have even considered it.

She stiffened suddenly, realizing she'd completely forgotten about the plants and the magic. Now she was the one who needed to focus.

The leaves were just beginning to quiver. She pressed lightly on his arms. "Good," she whispered.

He kept going. So did the plants. Little tendrils shot out of the vines, and the ferns unfolded a little more, growing more feathery as the magic filled them. Buds appeared and new leaves sprouted.

She kept the pressure up until the swags were wild and perfect, then she lifted her arms, breaking that contact. "Done. And so good." She glanced up at him. "Look."

He opened his eyes as he dropped his arms and let out a breath. His chest was rising and falling with the effort. "I did that, huh? They look like they grew that way."

"Because they did. And yes, that's your handiwork."

He slipped his hands around her waist and pulled her tight against him. "That's *our* handiwork. No matter what you say about it being mine, the magic that's in me will always carry your signature."

How could she not fall for a guy like this? She smiled. "That's very sweet of you."

"You know what else is sweet?" He took her hand and spun her around to face him, then he kissed her with a slow, leisurely effort that made her mind go blank in the best possible way.

When he finally pulled back, he was smiling. "I could do that all night, but we have more work to do, don't we?"

She glanced at the table filled with arrangements and the cold storage that held many, many more. "More work is an understatement."

He rubbed his hands together. "Then let's get to it."

"You're sure? It's okay if you want to rest for a little bit. I know magic can be draining until you get used to it. It's like endurance. You have to work up to it."

He shook his head. He was a little drained, but she needed these flowers finished. For Marigold, he would suck it up. "I'm ready to go."

"You're sure?" She was studying him with a skeptical gaze. "If you get tired, you can lose control of the magic and it can go haywire. Or not work at all. Or you could exhaust yourself and we still have the wedding tomorrow."

"I'm fine."

Her skepticism hung on. "Put your hands out."

He did as she asked. They were solid and still, not trembling with exertion as she'd probably expected.

"All right. On to the rest, but we are going to take breaks. Blooming flowers is much more delicate work than growing the greenery out."

"You're the boss."

Marigold proved to be right. Not that he'd doubted her. Flowers were a lot harder. Two centerpieces later, he was shaking with fatigue. It took him nearly twenty minutes to recover enough to start again. With that pace, time slumped by, and it was almost two in the morning when everything was finally done.

He stretched, absolutely beat. "I can't believe how much work magic is."

"It gets easier with time and practice, I promise. You did great. I owe you. My sister owes you."

He shook his head. "No one owes me anything."

"Well, I feel like we do."

"How about we call it even? Although you saving my life and me helping with flowers doesn't seem like an exact swap."

"I'm good with it." She smiled. "You look completely wiped out. You can't drive back to Millersville. Why don't you stay at my house?"

He wasn't too tired to raise his eyebrows. "You trust me being alone in the house with you?"

She laughed. "Like you have the energy left to try anything."

He snorted. "You got me there."

"C'mon." She grabbed her purse and dug out her keys. "Let's get out of here and get some sleep. You know, so we can do this all over again in the morning."

Morning came way too early, but the excitement of the day was all the stimulant Marigold needed to wake up and get moving. Okay, maybe a little coffee wouldn't hurt, but the bottom line was...

Pandora was getting married today.

And because of that glorious, wonderful, overwhelming news, Marigold thrummed with nervous energy. Sure, she should have been dragging because of the late night and intense workload. But Wyatt had done the heavy lifting.

Wyatt.

She stopped halfway to the kitchen. She'd almost forgotten he was here. In her house. How could that have slipped her mind? Maybe because she'd been so tired she barely remembered getting home last night. But it all came back to her now. They'd stumbled in with the singular goal of getting to bed.

Separate beds, obviously. He was in the guest room.

She should probably wake him, even though she hated to do it. They'd worked so hard, and she knew using all that magic had worn him out. He hadn't complained once. Hadn't said word one about how taxing it was to focus that much power, but she knew better. After all, she'd been in his place once upon a time, and while she might not be a witch anymore, she remembered how demanding the learning process had been.

Poor Wyatt. He'd skipped the basics and gone right to practical application.

She glanced toward the guest room. Maybe she'd let him sleep until after she'd taken her shower. He'd earned it. And men didn't need as much time getting ready anyway.

With that in mind, she got a pot of coffee brewing, then went back to shower. The hot water was amazing and helped wake her up even more. She spent a few extra minutes under the spray thinking about all the work that still had to be done. The flowers had to be transported to Cole and Pandora's, everything had to be put in place, the swags had to go on the arbor, then everything had to be given a final magical touch to perfect it all.

She'd probably have to shower again. There was no way she could do all that work outside in August in Georgia and not get a little...damp.

Thankfully, Cole and Pandora had some really good shade trees in their backyard and plenty of tents for the reception. They were even setting up some big breezy fans to keep the air moving. It would be warm for sure, but not unbearable, and as the evening wore on and the sun went down, it would be beautiful. Especially with all the fairy lights and strings of Edison bulbs set in the trees and the candles that would be everywhere.

The whole event would be absolutely magical, in every way possible.

Marigold turned the water off and got out, squeezing her hair with a towel. Her plan was to get everything done, then get herself and Saffron ready for bridesmaid duties. After that, she could take care of getting the boutonnieres on the men, the corsages on the women, and the bouquets in the right hands.

It was going to be a lot of work, but it would get done, and the end result would be beautiful. Having Wyatt there to help was a huge bonus.

She threw on her big terrycloth robe and went to check on him. She hated to wake him, but they didn't have a lot of time to spare this morning. She opened her bedroom door and was greeted with the delicious aroma of breakfast.

How was that possible?

She padded into the kitchen and found the table set for two and Wyatt at the stove making eggs.

That wasn't something she'd ever seen in her house. A man preparing food. She shook her head in amazement. "And he cooks, too."

He looked over his shoulder as the toaster popped out two slices of browned bread. "Morning. I hope you like scrambled. My skills in the kitchen are decent but limited."

"Scrambled is great." She hadn't expected to eat breakfast this morning. She hadn't planned on taking the time, really. "I don't mean to rush you, but—"

He turned with plates in his hands. "Breakfast is served." He gave her a little smile. "I'm sure there are a thousand things on your to-do list today, but you have to eat or you will run out of energy."

He wasn't wrong. She took the plate. "This was really kind of you."

He grabbed a mug from near the stove. "You made coffee."

She went to the table. "But breakfast is a little more work."

"Not that much. Eggs and toast is about as basic as it gets."

They sat and ate. It was good. Simple, like he'd said, but it would get them through the morning.

He spread jam on his toast. "What needs to be done first?"

"We need to go to the shop and load the van with the big pieces, then get everything over to

Cole and Pandora's and start setup. I'll do a second run for the smaller things. Boutonnieres, corsages, bouquets, all of that. They need to stay refrigerated for as long as possible anyway."

He squinted at her. "Aren't you also a bridesmaid? And Saffie is a junior bridesmaid?"

"Yes to both of those."

"Well, I'm just a guest. B list, at best. I can make the second run. You'll have enough to do with all that wedding party stuff."

She thought about his very generous offer for three seconds before a small wave of panic hit her. "But you don't know what to bring."

"You can show me this morning. And how am I going to learn if you don't let me help?"

"True, but—"

He took her hand. "I know it's your sister's wedding. I promise I won't screw up. Not only do I want her day to be perfect, but I don't want to add to your stress by getting something wrong."

She nodded as she chewed, still thoughtful. "It's hard to give up control."

"Now you're preaching to the choir." He winked at her, and somehow that small gesture smoothed out a little of the panic. "I'm not asking you to give up anything. Just delegate."

"I know. I get that. Still hard to do. But I'll try." She sighed and picked up her toast. "Without Leah, what choice do I have?"

"True. And I'd like to add you should also be able to enjoy today, not spend it working yourself ragged."

"Stop making so much sense." She scooped the last bite of eggs onto her fork.

He shrugged, using the remaining triangle of his toast to punctuate his words. "It's a blessing and a curse."

She glanced at the time on the microwave. "We should really get moving. How much time do you need to be out the door?"

"I'm assuming we're starting this early so we have time to change and get ready for the wedding after all the grunt work is done?"

"Exactly."

"Then I can be ready to leave in five."

"Wow, okay, I better get moving. I need a few more minutes than that." She pushed back from the table. "Just leave the dishes, I'll clean up tonight."

"Go," he said. "I've got this."

"Thanks." She hustled back to her bedroom. Was Wyatt always this helpful? Or was this just what having a good partner was like? Either way, it was incredibly nice. She got herself together, and they were out the door in less than fifteen minutes.

Wyatt drove, which gave her a chance to text her mom and check in on Saffie. All was well. Saffie hadn't accidentally cast any spells that needed undoing, so that was good. Marigold had been a little afraid Saffie would want to show off her budding skills in front of her mimi.

"Everything okay?" Wyatt asked.

"Yep." Marigold finished texting her reply to Corette. "Saffie's been up since six, which isn't that big of a deal since my mom is an early riser, but apparently she's had her bridesmaid dress on since then too."

Wyatt laughed. "That's kind of adorable."

Marigold glanced at him. "It is, isn't it? Man, that kid loves weddings. I'm almost afraid of how much actually being in one is going to affect her. She's been planning the day she and Charlie Merrow walk down the aisle since about five seconds after she met him. I mean, that's crazy, right?"

"Not so much." He gave her a quick, sly look. "When you know, you know."

Her insides went all fluttery. Was he implying what it seemed like he was implying? She couldn't think about that right now, or she'd melt down into a happy but weirded-out puddle of goo.

Creeping myrtle, she liked him a lot.

Fortunately, they were pulling into the shop's parking lot, giving her a valid reason not to respond to his statement. She was almost out of the SUV before it stopped. "I'll get the shop unlocked."

He got out of the vehicle a couple seconds later. "I didn't mean to scare you."

She cranked the key and pushed the door open. "I know. You didn't. Just...there's no space in my head to think about more than the wedding right now."

"Totally get it. Let's get to work. What can I do?"

"Back the van up to this door? Then we can get loading." And she could take a second to process what he'd said.

He took the keys off the hook inside. "On it."

While he did that, she flipped the lights on and took care of Frank's food and water, then got her checklist out. She stared at the sheet in front of her, not really seeing it. Did Wyatt really mean he thought she was the one? The thought that he might be ready to commit to a future with her made her head spin. In a good way. Her heart beat a little faster. Then she shook herself. She couldn't think about that right now or nothing was going to get done.

She put that unbelievable thought from her head and focused on the checklist again. As long as he had this for the second trip, everything should be fine. He was a very capable guy. And he was right. If she didn't delegate, she'd never get to enjoy today.

He strolled back in, stooping to give Frank a scratch on the head. "Van's moved, doors are open, and I'm ready to work."

"Good." She could do a future with him. Also, so much for not thinking about what he'd said. She blinked, trying to clear her head of all the giddiness going on up there. "Because we have a lot of it to do."

Nearly forty-five minutes later, the van was loaded and they were ready to head to Cole and Pandora's. Marigold drove the van with Wyatt following behind in his rental. All of their wedding clothes were in his car, along with her toiletries and makeup bag.

The drive to her sister's took a little longer than usual, but then, she'd never driven to Pandora's house with a van full of flowers before. She backed into the drive while Wyatt parked on the street.

Cole walked out onto the front porch as they were getting out of the vehicles. "Pandora sent me out to help."

"Perfect." Marigold gestured toward the van. "You and Wyatt can start carrying the swags to the backyard while I take our wedding clothes into the house."

"Yes, ma'am." He headed for the van, giving Wyatt a nod.

The clothes could have waited, but she really wanted to see Pandora. She took both garment bags, the toiletries, and her makeup bag and headed in.

She found her sister at the kitchen table, leisurely sipping a cup of coffee and scrolling through her phone.

Marigold stared at her in shock. "What are you doing?"

Pandora put her phone down. "Having coffee and dealing with email. You know, like civilized people do."

"You should be upstairs, squirreled away where Cole can't see you. It's tradition, you know."

Pandora shook her head. "You sound like Gertrude."

"Well, for a ghost, she's very astute. Isn't Mom here yet? She can't be, or she'd have you locked upstairs too."

Pandora gave her sister a slightly patronizing look. "He won't see me in my dress until I walk down the aisle, I promise. And that's like eight hours away, so..."

"Still." Marigold sighed, overwhelmed suddenly by the day in front of them. "I can't believe you're getting married."

"I know." Pandora grinned. "It's been a long time coming, huh?" She got to her feet. "You want to hang that stuff in one of the guest rooms? Then you can have your own space to get ready in when all the flowers are taken care of."

"That would be great."

"Come on, I'll show you." Pandora picked up her coffee and headed for the second story.

Marigold followed her up the steps. Not a creak from any of them. The house, an old Victorian and one of the largest on the block, had been completely renovated and now looked like a showplace. "Are you nervous?"

"No. Just excited and ready and literally so happy that I almost can't stand it." She opened one of the doors and led Marigold into the guest room. "Speaking of happy, how're things with the detective?"

Marigold smiled, unable to do anything else. "He's...amazing."

"So you'll be next, then?"

"Pandy, stop that. You'll jinx things." Marigold hung the garment bags in the closet.

Pandora shrugged. "He's got your magic. You *should* marry him. You know, just to keep it in the family."

"Today is not the day for that conversation." She gave her sister a quick hug. "I'm so happy for you. I love you."

"I love you too."

"Now I better get downstairs and make sure the flowers are perfect."

Pandora squinted. "You're freaking out a little."

"Just a little. But everything's going to be fine, you'll see." Marigold meant it, too. There was no way anything was going to ruin her sister's day.

Wedding flower setup was a surprisingly sweaty job. How that, or anything, could surprise Wyatt after the week he'd already had, he wasn't sure. But it did. Good thing he liked the work. Plus, there was pride in a job well done, no matter what that job was.

And, if he really got truthful, he was starting to like flowers a lot, too. As in he'd never given them a second thought his entire life and now he was noticing how different all the petal shapes were, and how much the colors varied, and the way the scents all seemed to match each flower.

Sometimes it almost felt like he could…hear the flowers. Not that they were speaking to him with audible words. It was more like music. Or a soft hum.

Regardless of the sound, it shouldn't be possible.

Except he was filled with Marigold's green-witch magic, and that meant anything was possible. He understood that.

The same way that he understood he could not be without her. Maybe it was how tuned in to her magic he was becoming, or maybe it was the plain truth that he was fast falling in love with her, but she was unmistakably the woman for him.

He hoped she had similar feelings for him, but he had his doubts. She'd shut him down pretty quickly at the shop.

He was chalking that up to the craziness of the day, because he couldn't spend the whole day thinking there was any other reason. Not while he was going to be at her side during a wedding.

That would be torturous. He had to put it out of his head until all of this was behind them and they could talk some more. He was probably worrying for nothing. After all, she'd agreed to him helping at the shop and seemed amenable to him moving to Nocturne Falls. That meant she was okay with him being around, didn't it?

"Mr. Wyatt!"

He turned to see Saffie running barefoot toward him in a fancy flowered dress. "Hey, Saff. Don't you look pretty?"

She did a twirl, holding her dress out at the sides. "I'm a junior bridesmaid."

"Are you sure? Because for a second there I thought you might be the bride."

She giggled and batted her lashes at him. "Not yet. But soon."

Hoo boy, little Charlie Merrow was in trouble with this one. Wyatt changed the subject. "What do you think of the flowers?" He'd been working on the arbor for almost an hour already, getting the swags wired and zip-tied into place.

"They're very pretty. Did you help my mom with them?"

"I did. She put all the roses on before I strung them up, but I put the green part together."

She took a second look. "Did you use your magic?"

"Yes. Lots to learn there."

Her expression went deeply serious. "I know. It's hard. I'm getting a mentor. They do that for all the witches when they come into their powers. Maybe they can give you one too."

He wasn't sure who *they* were. "You mean your mom?"

"No, the coven."

"Oh." This was new territory for him. "I suppose I'd have to join that first."

She nodded solemnly. "There aren't any boys in it that I know about."

"No? That might be a problem, then, seeing as how I'm a boy."

She shrugged. "I'll help you with your magic."

Her offer caught him off guard, and unexpected emotion nearly closed his throat. "You will?"

She took his hand. "Yes. So will my mom."

Her hand was so small and delicate in his, her gaze so earnest. A fiercely protective urge rose up in him, the kind that made him realize why fathers met their daughters' dates at the door with a shotgun in hand. Wyatt had never thought he'd wanted kids. How foolish that line of thinking had been. How in the world had this child's biological father walked away from her? "You're something special, Saffron. Thank you."

She smiled. "I like you too. Are you in love with my mom?"

"Yeah, I think I am. You okay with that?"

Her smile got bigger, and she pulled her hand back like she'd suddenly gone shy. "I've never had a dad."

He scrubbed his hand across his face, trying not to lose his cool. "I had one, but I lost him when I was very young, so I don't really remember him."

"Did you get another one after him? Sheriff Merrow adopted Charlie."

"I never had Charlie's luck."

She cocked her head. "No other dad?"

"Nope."

She stared at him. Maybe sizing him up with that new information.

"Saffron," a female voice rang out. "Saffie. Where are you?"

Wyatt and Saffie both peeked around the arbor to see Marigold standing on the back porch, calling her name.

"I better go." Saffron hitched up her dress and took off without waiting for Wyatt's response.

He laughed softly. The kid was amazing. He was falling for her just as hard as he was for Marigold. He just hoped Saffron still thought he'd be good father material now that she knew he hadn't had one for most of his life.

He went back to work, weaving in the lights that Marigold had directed him to add once the swags were secured into place. It was going to make a great backdrop for the ceremony and, he imagined, the pictures afterward. But then, the whole place was a real showstopper.

The house and the yard were huge. Both must require a lot of upkeep, especially given the shape of the old Victorian. Everything about it was perfect. Maybe there was some kind of historical society in town. A house like this should be on a tour.

Marigold walked around the side of the arbor to where he was working. "This looks very nice."

"Good to hear. But if you're not happy with something, say so and I'll fix it."

She shook her head, still looking the arbor over. "No, you did a great job."

"I'll be through as soon as I get the last of these lights added, then give them a test to make sure they're all in working order. Where do you want me next? Porch swags?"

"Yes." She glanced toward the tents. "I'm going to start getting the centerpieces on the tables. Actually, don't do the porch swags yet. The prop company has assured me the ceremony area will be set up next, so do me a favor and make sure they don't touch this arbor while they're setting all of that up? The last thing I need is them accidentally knocking this over while they're bringing in chairs and the aisle runner."

"You got it."

"Good. Once they're done with this area, we can add the pew markers. Then the porch can get its swags."

"When do want me to make the second shop run?"

She unstuck a curl from her damp forehead. "How about after the porch is done? Then I can distribute all of that, and we can both get ready for the wedding. I'm last on the list to get my hair and makeup done, but that also means I have to be dressed and ready to go by then because some of the pictures are happening before the ceremony."

"Take whatever time you need. I can handle anything else that needs doing. Speaking of the second run, the list of what I need to bring is on the worktable, right?"

"Right."

He took a long look at her. She didn't seem entirely herself, but that was understandable. "You doing okay?"

She nodded. "I am. It's all coming together."

"It is. And it looks great." He gave her a little wink. "Saffie told me so."

Marigold smiled. "Boy, does she like you. She told me I'd better be nice to you."

He plugged in the strand of lights he was working on. "Smart beyond her years."

"Maybe too much." Marigold laughed and shook her head, then was all business again as she patted her hip. "I've got my cell phone if you need me or have questions about anything."

"You got it, boss." He patted his front pocket. "And I have the keys to the shop and the van, so all good there."

"Excellent. Thank you for all your hard work. You've been a life saver today. Well, all week, really."

"Happy to do it. Hey, in case I don't see you before things get underway, is there anywhere special I should sit for the ceremony?"

"Bride's side. But otherwise, wherever you like. For the reception, you're next to me at table three."

"Perfect."

Still smiling, she headed for the tents. "See you later. And thanks!"

He gave her a thumbs-up, then went back to work, knocking out everything she'd asked him to do and even helping the prop company get set up so things moved a little faster. At last, he was back in the van and headed for the shop.

Once inside, he followed her list to the letter, checking and double-checking all the boxes to make sure each specific item was there. Frank sat on one of the worktables, supervising, which helped immensely.

Wyatt loaded the van and, after one final list check, drove back to the house.

The next few hours were a blur of activity, during which he found time to get a quick shower in one of the guest rooms and get himself dressed. He didn't see much of Marigold, so he was glad he'd asked her about seating earlier.

He saw a few familiar faces as he joined the crowd outside, finally deciding on a spot near the back. He wasn't family and only a recent friend, so he didn't want to take one of the better seats.

He scanned the house for any sign of Marigold, but the wedding party wasn't out yet. Wait. There was Saffron and Kaley looking antsy and eager. If the junior bridesmaids were ready, the rest of them couldn't be far behind.

A low, happy murmur came off the crowd around him. Sun dappled through the branches of the big trees shading most of the backyard and a warm, but pleasant breeze kept things comfortable. It was a perfect day for a wedding, really.

He glanced back at the tents. The centerpieces were in water, so they should be holding up well, but he wasn't as sure about the swag on the cake table. Marigold wasn't worried about it, though, so he probably shouldn't be either. She'd said the tents had air conditioning.

A woman stood inside the nearest tent, partially hidden by the white vinyl wall. She looked familiar, but he couldn't see enough of her to tell. Not a wedding guest based on the fact that she seemed to be dressed in the same uniform as the catering staff, complete with white chef coat and matching cap.

His gut wasn't satisfied that's who she was, however. It was knotted up and telling him something wasn't right.

Did Pandora and Cole have any enemies who might want to ruin their day? Maybe *enemies* was too strong of a word, but his cop instincts couldn't be denied. He didn't know Cole and Pandora well enough to quell any doubts about who the woman might be, but now wasn't the time to let a suspicion go unchecked.

He watched her a little more. If she was working for the caterers, she'd probably head back to work any second. She didn't budge, just stared at the porch. Wyatt's gut knotted a little more. The woman looked at least twelve years older than Cole, so not likely an ex of his.

Whoever she was, Wyatt figured it couldn't hurt to have a closer look.

As he got up, the bluegrass quartet started to play. Another glance at the porch confirmed the wedding was beginning. Saffron and Kaley were stepping down onto the path of white fabric and heading toward the arbor. Behind them, Charisma and her groomsman waited their turn.

He had to hurry. He wanted to be in place when Marigold went past. He eased out of his row and went behind one of the big trees where he could see both the tent and the processional path.

The woman still hadn't moved. In fact, she seemed to be watching the wedding party very intently now. He started around the back of the tent. No way was he going to let one of Marigold's family get hurt.

But then again, maybe she was just a curious member of the catering staff wanting to see the bride. And willing to shirk her duties to do so. He slipped in through the side of the tent. A crew of people were bustling about, putting the final touches on the tables.

The air was definitely on. It was at least ten degrees cooler in here.

The woman remained glued to her spot. Charisma and her groomsman were gliding past, and Marigold and her groomsman were coming up behind them.

His jaw dropped at the sight of Marigold. She looked like a princess in her lilac gown. Certainly more beautiful than any woman he'd ever been involved with. His heart swelled at how gorgeous she was.

Then the woman moved, and he remembered why he was in the tent. She lifted her arms, her fingers outstretched toward…Marigold?

The air around her rippled with nearly invisible waves. *Magic.*

Then the waves shot forward. At Marigold.

31

Marigold held on to the arm of Ivan Tsvetkov. She didn't know Van that well, but the dragon shifter and former MMA fighter was a good friend of Pandora's. He was also a great guy, she knew that much.

Gripping his arm was like holding on to a tree trunk. Where had they found a suit to fit him? Probably Guildman's had special-made it. Come to think of it, Van probably had all his clothes specially made.

They made the slow turn toward the center aisle.

Just in time to see Wyatt tackling a member of the catering staff in the big reception tent.

What the—

She stopped dead. "Wyatt!"

Her screech brought everything to a halt, but a split second later, a wave of magic hit her, knocking her flat on her back. She might not be capable of magic herself, but she knew when magic had been used on her. Fortunately, it seemed the spell had only grazed her.

Even so, she was immobile, unable to do anything but stare up at the cloudless blue sky through the branches of a nearby tree. She tried to cry out for help, but only a strangled sound left her throat. How much worse would she be if the spell had made direct contact?

Thick arms lifted her. Van. He cradled her against his chest like a baby. Her head lolled against his. "I have you. No worries."

She could at least see Wyatt now. He was struggling with the woman in the tent. Or rather, she was struggling with him. He had her arms pinned behind her in what seemed to be a pretty effective hold.

The crowd pushed to their feet.

The woman snarled and twisted, trying to get out of his clutches. "Let go of me or the witch will spend the rest of her life paralyzed."

"What are you talking about?" He looked at Marigold. "Are you hurt? Did her spell hit you?"

Marigold could only grunt in response. Wyatt seemed to understand her despite that rudimentary answer.

He jerked the woman upright by the lapels of her catering jacket. "Free her from whatever spell you put her under."

She tried again to get away, but only ended up knocking off the cap she was wearing. Her silver-streaked hair tumbled free. "Not until I get the pendant."

Wyatt's eyes went wide. "Suzanne Anderson?"

She glared at him. "If you had won the auction like you were supposed to, none of this would have happened."

He pinned her arms and pulled her closer to stop her struggling. The move put his mouth inches from her ear. "Release Marigold *now*."

"Or what?" She laughed. "You do anything to me, and I'll complete the spell."

"What does that mean?" Wyatt asked.

"It means I'll paralyze the rest of her. Her heart. Her lungs. Her brain."

Wyatt's face filled with rage. "You hurt her," he snarled, "and I will tear you apart with my bare hands."

Sheriff Merrow came out of the crowd, followed by Alice Bishop.

Hmm. Marigold hadn't even known she was invited, but not inviting her would have seemed like an insult, probably. Pandora was too smart to make a gaffe like that. Strange thoughts to be having while on the verge of death, sure, but Marigold had never been on the verge of death before. Or struck by a spell while technically human. So who knew what the right reaction was?

The sheriff and Alice stopped a few feet away. Alice shook her head. "Suzanne Anderson? Is that the name you're going by?"

Wyatt nodded. "I've never met her in person, but we did one video chat when she first hired me. That's the name she gave me."

Alice shook her head. "That's not her real name."

Suzanne, or whatever her name was, glowered at Alice. "Get away from me, you abomination."

Saffie ran up, hands raised. "You fix my mother or I will turn you into a stump."

Alice caught Saffie and held her close. "Now, now, witchling. She's not worth your time. And Aunt Alice is going to make all this right."

Marigold would have shed a tear, had she been able. She'd never have guessed Alice had a softer side.

Alice was unfazed by it all. She spoke to the crowd. "This is Faleena Smalls. A miserable excuse for a witch who's been seeking out dark magic trinkets for years in an effort to boost her lackluster skills. She was banished from the American Council of Witches ten years ago and stripped of her magic for seven years."

"The ACW can get bent," Faleena growled.

Alice frowned. "Clearly, seven years wasn't long enough."

Corette had come up to take Saffie's hand. Now she stared daggers at Faleena. "I'll say."

The sheriff, looking slightly uncomfortable in his suit, scratched his head. "I can put her in a holding cell until—"

"No need," Alice said. "I am a certified ACW dark magic recovery agent and I am licensed to deal with offenders." She snorted. "That alone should have been reason enough for you to stay out of my town, Faleena."

"Your town," Faleena spat the words out. "So full of yourself."

"You're about to be full of nothing." Alice gestured to Van. "Bring Marigold here."

Van carried her forward, moving closer and closer until Alice touched his arm lightly to position him at Wyatt's side just behind Faleena. "Hold right there."

Marigold wasn't sure what Alice was up to, but she seemed to have a plan.

Alice lifted Marigold's hands and put one on Wyatt's shoulder and one on Faleena's. "Stay like that."

Faleena shrugged it off. Alice put Marigold's hand back and gave Faleena a warning. "Do that again and I'll apply the same spell to you that you did to Marigold. And I won't just graze you with it, the way you did her. I'll hit you right between the eyes."

Faleena went very still. Marigold couldn't see her face, but she wondered if Alice's words had knocked the snarl off it.

Alice reached across Faleena on both sides to put her hands on Wyatt's and Marigold's forearms, then while touching all three, she began to chant softly, "*Imperiatum omni acciperé, imperiatum omni acciperé, imperiatum omni acciperé.*"

Her voice grew stronger as power filled it. Marigold understood what she was attempting to do. If she'd had a voice, she would have begged Alice to stop until they could prepare better. Wyatt wasn't in any kind of shape to go through this again.

Wyatt suddenly closed his eyes. His jaw tightened, and the muscles there and in his neck strained with intensity.

Then Faleena let out a muted cry and her head fell back. She wobbled like she might faint as her eyes rolled skyward.

Marigold's head went woozy as Faleena's spell lost its grip. Then the presence of new magic surrounded Marigold. And even after just a day without it, the manifestation of power made her faint. If not for Van's arms, she was sure she would have collapsed. She closed her eyes to find some equilibrium.

Magic surged through her like water overflowing a fountain. She was awash in it, floating in it, drenched head to toe. It filled her lungs and her heart and her soul.

She opened her eyes and sucked in a breath as the realization hit her that she had been made whole. And not just with random magic.

With her own magic.

She glanced at Wyatt in time to see his eyes start to roll back. "Van!" She jumped from his arms and grabbed hold of Wyatt.

Then Faleena slumped to the ground, out cold, and the crowd gasped. No one moved to help her. Instead, Alice stood over her like a guard.

Van took Wyatt's other arm and looped it over his shoulders for support. "I have you, my friend."

Wyatt blinked a few times and shook his head. "I'm okay. I think. Just a little knocked out."

Alice nodded. "You will be fine. Both of you. But you should not have done what you did, young man."

He met Alice's gaze. "It worked, didn't it?"

"Yes. But it was still a dangerous and foolish thing to do. I should have used Corette as my amplifier."

"Amplifier?" Marigold glanced from Wyatt to Alice, no longer sure of anything. "What did he do? What did you do?"

"I opened a gateway to strip Faleena's powers from her permanently and give them to you. Her ability is subpar to what you had, but I figured it would be better than none as you had. It's a powerful and draining spell and best done with the help of a secondary. I chose Wyatt because he was close and I knew the strength of the power within him."

Alice made a perturbed face at Wyatt. "He used the opening to return your power to you. As a result, Faleena's abilities went to him."

Wyatt was standing without Van's help now, and as he spoke, he took Marigold's hand. "So I still have magic?"

"You do," Alice answered. "Nothing like what you had before, but with training…" She shrugged. "You're deaf again, aren't you?"

He nodded. "I don't care."

Alice peered at him. "Faleena's magic isn't strong enough to compensate."

He shrugged. "Small price to pay."

Marigold stared at her for a moment. Then at Wyatt. "You did that for me?"

"It seemed like the right thing to do."

She put her hand to her mouth, her emotions already high on this special day. "Oh, Wyatt."

"Was that…okay?"

She nodded, a little choked on tears. "I love you," she whispered.

He pulled her into his arms. "I love you, too."

The crowd let out a happy sigh, then started clapping.

Cole walked out of the crowd and cleared his throat. "Speaking of love…"

Marigold laughed and tapped Wyatt's shoulder. "You'd better let me go. My sister needs to get married."

He released her and gave Cole a nod. "Sorry about that."

Cole smiled. "Nothing to apologize for. You've certainly made this a day none of us are ever going to forget."

Corette, still holding Saffie's hand, looked buoyant. "And what you did for Marigold is just…so good." She sighed, then went all business and addressed the crowd. "If everyone could take their places so that we can resume this ceremony? Except for you, Sheriff Merrow. Perhaps you can call one of your deputies to remove our intruder?"

The sheriff took out his cell phone. "On it."

The rest of the audience obeyed her request. Even the bluegrass quartet started up again. Only the sheriff remained in the tent with the still unconscious Faleena.

Van offered Marigold his arm. "Are you good to walk?"

"I am." She took it, but kept her eyes on Wyatt. "I'll see you in a few."

"I'll be here. I promise, I'm not going anywhere."

As his beautiful girl walked down the aisle, Wyatt brushed himself off. A soft moan from Faleena made him glance at the sheriff, who had just ended his call. "You probably don't have any cuffs on you in that suit, do you, Sheriff?"

The sheriff frowned. "No, I don't. And call me Hank."

Wyatt dug into the inside pocket of his suit jacket and pulled out a handful of zip ties he'd tucked away in case any of the swags went droopy. "These do?"

The sheriff smiled. "Like a charm."

Hank crouched and made quick work of restraining the comatose woman. When he straightened, he shot Wyatt a look. "You interested in a job? We don't have much in the way of homicides here in Nocturne Falls, but we could use a detective now and then."

"How did you know I was a homicide detective?"

A smirk bent his mouth. "My aunt likes to investigate people."

"I see. She works in the right place, then. You know I'm deaf in one ear."

"I do. Don't care."

"Then I'm interested in the job. Especially since I plan on staying." Wyatt went back to watching beautiful, in-love-with-him Marigold. "Let's talk later."

Wyatt held Marigold close as they swayed on the dance floor to the soulful strains of Etta James's "At Last." The words of the song made sense to him now. His lonely days were definitely over and the skies above him could not have been bluer.

Even though right now they were actually a dusky purple with the fall of twilight.

He inhaled the fragrance of her hair. Lilacs. He'd never smell that scent again and not think of her. He smiled and whispered into her ear, "You look beautiful, by the way. Not sure I said that."

She moved her head off his shoulder to look at him. "You did. At least twice."

"Three times is better."

She patted his chest. "I like how you matched your shirt to my dress, too. Don't think I missed that."

"Dexter Guildman is a force to be reckoned with."

"I'll say. And here I thought only Birdie had the lowdown on what happens in this town."

He tipped his chin toward a spot behind her. "Have you seen Saffie?"

"You mean since she caught the bouquet? I can only guess. Where is she?"

"Dancing with Charlie Merrow like this is their wedding. Hang on." He swanned Marigold around to change her line of sight.

Marigold laughed. "Oh, that child. Catching Pandie's bouquet has only convinced Saffron more that she and Charlie are meant to be. That poor boy."

Wyatt shrugged. "He seems to be okay with it."

"I guess." She was still smiling, though. "Maybe he likes the attention."

"Maybe the Williams women are just irresistible."

She smiled at him, one of those easy, knowing smiles that made her eyes sparkle like diamonds. Which was something he was seriously thinking about buying her. "Is that what I am? Irresistible?"

"You are to me." He kissed the tip of her perfect nose. "This has all happened pretty fast, hasn't it?"

She nodded. "It has, but then, going through stressful situations has a way of bonding people. Don't you think?"

"I do. Especially when those stressful situations involve things like one person saving the other person's life and giving up the essence of themselves to save that person."

"You're never going to let that go, are you?"

"You saving my life? No. Never."

"But you gave that magic back to me."

"You still saved my life." He laced his fingers together at the small of her back, pulling her closer. "So in stress years, how long have we actually been...a thing?"

"A thing?" Amusement danced in her eyes. "I'd say a couple months, easy. I mean, look. You already slept over."

He nodded with great thoughtfulness. "And made you breakfast."

Corette and her fiancé waltzed by at that exact moment. Her mother shot them both a questioning look.

They laughed, and Marigold shook her head. "I'm going to have to explain that one."

"You *are* a grown woman."

"I know, but that's what a close family is like. Especially a family of women. We're up in each other's business. You ready for that, Mr. West?"

He sighed contentedly. "Ready and looking forward to it, Ms. Williams. In fact, I'm ready for all of it. Love, marriage, kids—"

"Kids?" Her brows rose.

"I, uh, is that not—"

She kissed him, cutting him off. "I think you'd make a great dad."

"You do?"

"Yes. I've seen you with Saffie. She adores you."

An odd, nervous excitement swept through him. "I adore her right back. And maybe someday, if you're willing and she's willing, I could do for her what no one ever did for me."

Marigold stared at him for a long moment, her lips parted, her eyes suddenly liquid in the sparkling lights of the tent. "Are you saying that you'd consider adopting her?"

He swallowed, hoping he hadn't overstepped. "I am."

She sniffed once, then laughed joyfully. "Yes, that would be amazing. Saffron would be willing, I'm sure of it. She's always wanted a dad."

The song came to an end, and the DJ announced the next song was for all the single ladies.

She took Wyatt's hand and started to lead him back to their table.

He pointed at the dance floor. "You're a single lady."

She poked him in the ribs. "Oh no, I'm not. My days of living in Singletown are over."

He slipped his arm around her waist, grinning as they walked to the table. "Is that so?"

"For sure. I'm moving out. My bags are packed."

He was trying not to laugh, but he wasn't sure when he'd had more fun. "I can't wait to hear this. Where are you going then?"

The Detective Wins The Witch

"Isn't it obvious?" She leaned up, took hold of his lapels, and kissed him again soundly before smiling at him like he'd just won something. "I'm headed West."

Want to be up to date on new books, new audiobooks & other fun stuff from Kristen Painter? Sign-up for my newsletter at www.kristenpainter.com. No spam, just news (sales, freebies, and releases, you know, all that jazz).

If you loved the book and want to help the series grow, tell a friend about the book and take time to leave a review!

Other Books by Kristen Painter

PARANORMAL ROMANCE:

Nocturne Falls series:
The Vampire's Mail Order Bride
The Werewolf Meets His Match
The Gargoyle Gets His Girl
The Professor Woos The Witch
The Witch's Halloween Hero – short story
The Werewolf's Christmas Wish – short story
The Vampire's Fake Fiancée
The Vampire's Valentine Surprise – short story
The Shifter Romances The Writer
The Vampire's True Love Trials – short story
The Dragon Finds Forever
The Vampire's Accidental Wife
The Reaper Rescues The Genie
The Detective Wins The Witch

Can't get enough Nocturne Falls?
Try the NOCTURNE FALLS UNIVERSE books.
New stories, new authors, same Nocturne Falls world! www.http://kristenpainter.com/nocturne-falls-universe/

Sin City Collectors series:
Queen of Hearts
Dead Man's Hand
Double or Nothing
Box set

Standalone Paranormal Romance:
Dark Kiss of the Reaper
Heart of Fire
Recipe for Magic
Miss Bramble and the Leviathan

COZY PARANORMAL MYSTERY:

Jayne Frost series
Miss Frost Solves A Cold Case – A Nocturne Falls Mystery
Miss Frost Ices The Imp – A Nocturne Falls Mystery
Miss Frost Saves The Sandman – A Nocturne Falls Mystery
Miss Frost Cracks a Caper – A Nocturne Falls Mystery
When Birdie Babysat Spider – A Jayne Frost short
Miss Frost Braves the Blizzard – A Nocturne Falls Mystery

Happily Everlasting series
Witchful Thinking

URBAN FANTASY:

The House of Comarré series:
Forbidden Blood
Blood Rights
Flesh and Blood
Bad Blood
Out For Blood
Last Blood

The Crescent City series:
House of the Rising Sun
City of Eternal Night
Garden of Dreams and Desires

Nothing is completed without an amazing team.

Many thanks to:

Cover design: Janet Holmes
Interior formatting: Author E.M.S
Editor: Joyce Lamb
Copyedits/proofs: Marlene Engel/Lisa Bateman

About the Author

USA Today Best Selling Author Kristen Painter is a little obsessed with cats, books, chocolate, and shoes. It's a healthy mix. She loves to entertain her readers with interesting twists and unforgettable characters. She currently writes the best-selling paranormal romance series, Nocturne Falls, and the cozy mystery spin off series, Jayne Frost. The former college English teacher can often be found all over social media where she loves to interact with readers. Learn more at her website:

www.kristenpainter.com

Made in the USA
Middletown, DE
19 April 2023